M. E. Saltykov-Shchedrin

FOOLSBURG:
The History of a Town

Mikhail Saltykov-Shchedrin (1826–1889), known during his life by his pen name, Nikolai Shchedrin, was a major Russian writer and satirist. Born to a noble family, he worked as a civil servant while writing for and editing radical journals, which led to a banishment of seven years. His most famous novels are the family saga *The Golovlyov Family* (1880) and the political satire *Foolsburg: The History of a Town* (1870).

About the Translators

Richard Pevear and Larissa Volokhonsky have translated works by Tolstoy, Dostoevsky, Chekhov, Gogol, Bulgakov, Leskov, and Pasternak. They were twice awarded the PEN/Book-of-the-Month Club Translation Prize (for Dostoevsky's *The Brothers Karamazov* and Tolstoy's *Anna Karenina*), and their translation of Dostoevsky's *Demons* was one of three nominees for the same prize. They are married and live in France.

FOOLSBURG:

The History of a Town

FOOLSBURG

The History of a Town

M. E. Saltykov-Shchedrin

*Translated from the Russian by Richard Pevear
and Larissa Volokhonsky*

VINTAGE BOOKS
A DIVISION OF PENGUIN RANDOM HOUSE LLC
NEW YORK

FIRST VINTAGE CLASSICS EDITION, AUGUST 2024

Library of Congress Cataloging-in-Publication Data
Names: Saltykov, Mikhail Evgrafovich, 1826–1889, author. |
Pevear, Richard, [date] translator. | Volokhonsky, Larissa, translator.
Title: Foolsburg : the history of a town / M. E. Saltykov-Shchedrin ;
translated from the Russian by Richard Pevear and Larissa Volokhonsky.
Other titles: Istoriia odnogo goroda. English (Pevear and Volokhonsky)
Description: New York : Vintage Books, 2024.
Identifiers: LCCN 2024013832 (print) | LCCN 2024013833 (ebook) |
ISBN 9780593687314 (trade paperback) |
ISBN 9780593687321 (ebook)
Subjects: LCGFT: Satirical literature.
Classification: LCC PG3361.S3 I713 2024 (print) |
LCC PG3361.S3 (ebook) | DDC 891.73/3—dc23/eng/20240412
LC record available at https://lccn.loc.gov/2024013832
LC ebook record available at https://lccn.loc.gov/2024013833

Vintage Books Trade Paperback ISBN: 978-0-593-68731-4
eBook ISBN: 978-0-593-68732-1

Book design by Nicholas Alguire

www.vintagebooks.com

Printed in the United States of America
1st Printing

Contents

Introduction

The History of a Town, by Mikhail Evgrafovich Saltykov-Shchedrin (1826–1889), was first published serially in the liberal journal *Notes of the Fatherland* and then as a book in 1869–70. The title is rather flat—deliberately so, we may assume, since Saltykov's readers knew very well what to expect from their most famous and scathing satirist. The flatness itself is satirical. However, since most readers of our translation will not know what to expect, we have added to the title the name of the town itself—Foolsburg, from the Russian Glupov—as a hint at what will follow.

In response to the first apearance of the book, Ivan Turgenev, in exile and writing in English for the London journal *The Academy* on 1 March 1871, asserted that Saltykov "knows his own country better than any man living," and noted that "the funnier his satire, the more aggressive it is and the greater its capacity to strike its targets," concluding that he "offers a picture of Russian history which is, alas! too true."

Saltykov had firsthand experience of Russia in all its aspects. He was born into the landowning gentry on his father's side and wealthy merchants on his mother's side, and spent his early years on a large estate near Moscow. There he acquired a knowledge of "serfdom at its worst," as he put it. He was educated at home at first and by the age of six had learned French and German. Four years later he entered the Dvoryansky Institute, a school for boys from the nobility, and in 1838, at the age of twelve, he went on to the imperial lyceum in Tsarskoye Selo near Petersburg, founded by the emperor Alexander I in 1811, where Pushkin had been in the first graduating class. Later he was rather critical of the education he received there, but he had also found time to write poetry and to translate works from English and German.

On his graduation from the lyceum in 1844 he was immediately taken into the chancellery of the Ministry of Defense, and he remained in government service until 1868—but not without difficulties, because he was also drawn to the ideas of French socialist thinkers like Charles Fourier and Saint-Simon. The second French revolution took place in 1848; a year earlier, Saltykov had published a first short novel entitled *Contradictions*, which touched on radical ideas and led to his arrest and deportation to the city of Vyatka, some 560 miles northeast of Moscow, on an order signed by the repressive emperor Nicholas I himself.

In Vyatka, Saltykov continued his work in the government, which brought him into contact with rural and small-town life all over the region. A few years later he married the vice governor's daughter, Elizaveta Boltina. Meanwhile he also went on writing, publishing short pieces in the liberal journal *The Russian Messenger* under the pen name of Nikolai Shchedrin. Collected in a much-praised book entitled *Provincial Sketches*, they were sharply critical of serfdom and of the provincial bureaucracy.

In 1855 Nicholas I died and his eldest son took the throne as the emperor Alexander II. In spirit he was the opposite of his father, a change that made itself felt at once. Saltykov was allowed to return to Petersburg, and in 1856 *Provincial Sketches* was published. In 1857 his play *Pazukhin's Death* appeared in the journal *The Russian Messenger,* edited by Mikhail Katkov, who had also published the *Sketches.* And at the same time he remained a government official, now in the Ministry of the Interior, strongly supporting the abolition of serfdom enacted by the "tsar-liberator" Alexander II in 1861. He also went on writing short works, collected in the volumes *Satires in Prose* and *Innocent Stories,* which came out in 1862–63.

Despite his devotion to government service, Saltykov decided to retire and moved to Moscow in 1862 with the intention of starting a magazine of his own. The necessary official permission was not forthcoming, however, and instead he returned to Petersburg, where he joined the staff of *The Contemporary,* a journal then edited by the poet and liberal critic Nikolai Nekrasov. In need of money, he went back into the civil service in 1864, but four years later he retired permanently and joined the staff of the monthly *Notes of the Fatherland* as head of the journalism section, a position he held until 1884, when the journal was officially closed down. That was one small result of the fact that in 1881, after several previous attempts, the tsar-liberator had been assassinated by radicals and had been replaced by his arch-reactionary second son, Alexander III, who reversed the spirit and the policies of his father's reign.

Most of Saltykov's books were collections of satirical sketches, stories, fairy tales, fictional letters, though he did occasionally try his hand at novels as well. His two most important longer works are *Foolsburg: The History of a Town,* published in 1870, and the novel *The Golovlyovs*, a dark portrayal of the degeneration of a noble family over three generations, published in 1880.

Foolsburg is not a novel. It is a purely satirical narrative like *Gulliver's Travels*. Where Swift used travel writing to give form to his satire, Saltykov modeled his satire on the form of the historical chronicle, of which there was an actual example known as *The Primary Chronicle*, covering the period of Kyivan Rus' from 852 to the early twelfth century. Saltykov presents himself as a publisher who has happened upon "a voluminous bundle of documents under the title of *The Foolsburg Chronicler*," written by four chroniclers in succession from 1731 to 1825. But the chronicles constantly jump from that period into Saltykov's own time and social conditions, just as Gulliver's travels to exotic countries sail into the life of eighteenth-century England. In the notes appended to our translation we give a detailed commentary on this play between fantasy and fact.

Swift once said that his aim in writing *Gulliver's Travels* was "to vex the world rather than divert it." Saltykov certainly wanted to vex the Russia of his own time in writing his *History of a Town*—taking aim not only at the ongoing tyranny of the official world but also at the passivity of the oppressed peasants even after their liberation by Alexander II. But as it turns out the "jump" is not only into his own time but also into ours. Today's reader cannot miss the relevance of Saltykov's satire to the behavior of our own world's absurd leaders and their passive followers. What we also should not miss is his liberating laughter, which combines the mockery of others with mockery of ourselves. The play between fantasy and fact in *Foolsburg* is play in the most serious sense.

FOOLSBURG:

The History of a Town

Based on Original Documents
Published by M. E. Saltykov (Shchedrin)

FROM THE PUBLISHER

For a long time now I have been intending to write the history of some town (or region) at a given period of time, but various circumstances have hindered me in this undertaking. I have been prevented chiefly by a lack of material at least to some extent reliable and plausible. Recently, rummaging through the Foolsburg town archive, I accidentally came across a voluminous bundle of notebooks under the title of *The Foolsburg Chronicler*. Having examined them, I found that they could contribute considerably to the realizing of my intention. The contents of *The Chronicler* are quite uniform, consisting almost entirely of biographies of the town's mayors, who in the course of almost a whole century ruled over the destinies of Foolsburg, and of descriptions of their most notable deeds, such as: the speedy driving of post-horses, the energetic exaction of tax arrears, military campaigns against the inhabitants, the making and unmaking of roads, the laying of tributes on tax farmers,[1] and so on. Nevertheless, even these scanty facts allow us to form an idea of the town's character and to track the various changes that took place in its history and, simultaneously, in higher spheres. Thus, for instance, the mayors of the time of Biron are distinguished by recklessness, the mayors of Potemkin's time by administrative prowess, and the mayors of Razumovsky's time by their obscure origin and chivalric valor.[2] They all flog the inhabitants,[3] but the first flog absolutely, the second explain the reasons for it by the requirements of civilization, the third wish the inhabitants to rely on their courage in everything. Such a variety of measures could not fail to affect the inner cast of their life: in the first case the inhabitants trembled unconsciously, in the second with a consciousness of their own benefit, in the third they rose to the trembling filled with trust.[4] Even the energetic driving of post-horses—even that had inevitably to have its measure of influence, fortifying people's spirit with the examples of the horses' vigor and endurance.

The chronicle was kept by four town archivists in turn and covers the period from 1731 to 1825. After that, apparently, literary activity ceased to be admissible even for archivists.[5] *The Chronicler* looks perfectly authentic; that is, there cannot be a moment's doubt of its genuineness: its pages are as yellow and covered with scribbling, as nibbled by mice and befouled by flies as the pages of any document of Pogodin's depository.[6] One can just see some Pimen poring over this archive under the quivering light of a tallow candle, guarding it from the inevitable inquisitiveness of Messrs. Shubinsky, Mordovtsev, and Melnikov.[7] The chronicle is prefaced by a special list or "register" composed evidently by the last chronicler; to it, besides, are attached, by way of supporting documents, several school notebooks that contain specific studies on various topics related to the theory of administration. Such, for instance, are the following reflections: "On the

Administrative Like-Mindedness of All Mayors," "On the Pleasing Appearance of Mayors," "On the Salutary Effect of Punitive Measures (with pictures)," "Reflections on the Collecting of Tax Arrears," "The Inconstant Current of Time," and, finally, a rather voluminous dissertation "On Strictness." One can positively assert that these exercises owe their existence to the pens of various mayors (many are even signed) and are valuable in that, first, they give a perfectly faithful notion of Russian orthography of the time, and second, they portray their authors more fully, convincingly, and vividly than even the stories of *The Chronicler*.

As for the inner content of *The Chronicler*, it is mostly fantastic and in places even almost incredible in our enlightened time. Such, for example, is the totally incongruous story of the music-box mayor. Elsewhere *The Chronicler* tells about a mayor who flew in the air; in yet another story there was a mayor whose feet were turned backwards and he almost ran away from the boundaries of the mayorship. The publisher, however, did not feel it his right to conceal these details; on the contrary, he thinks that the possibility of such facts in the past will show the reader what an abyss separates us from that past. Moreover, the publisher was guided by the thought that the fantastic character of the stories in no way deprives them of their administratively educative significance, and that even now the reckless self-assurance of the flying mayor may serve as a salutary warning to those present-day administrators who wish to avoid a premature dismissal from their post.

Be that as it may, to forestall malicious commentary the publisher feels obliged to mention that all he did in the present case was to correct the heavy and old-fashioned style of *The Chronicler* and to keep a necessary control over the orthography, without any interference in the content. From the first to the last moment, the publisher had before him the terrible image of Mikhail Petrovich Pogodin, and this alone may guarantee the respectful awe with which he treated his task.

Address to the Reader

from the Last Chronicler*

If the ancient Hellenes and Romans were allowed to sing praises to their godless rulers and transmit their abominable deeds to posterity for edification, will we Christians, who have received the light from Byzantium,[1] turn out in this respect to be less worthy and grateful than they? Can it be that in any country Neros of great glory and Caligulas of shining valor will be found,[2] and only among us their like do not exist?[†]

It is ridiculous and preposterous even to think of such absurdity, still less to proclaim it aloud, as do those freethinkers who fancy their thoughts to be free because they fly freely

---

* This address is given verbatim in the words of the last chronicler. The Publisher has only taken care that the rules of orthography were not too unceremoniously violated.—*Publisher*

† Obviously in defining the qualities of these historical figures, the chronicler had no idea even of what is written in school textbooks. Strangest of all is that he was not familiar even with the verses by Derzhavin:

Caligula! your steed in the Senate
Could not shine as gold shines:
It is good deeds that shine!

— *Publisher*

back and forth in their heads like flies without ever settling down.

Not only any country, but any town, and even any small village, must needs have, cannot but have, their own Achilleses of shining valor set up by the authorities. Look at any puddle—in it you will find a reptile who excels and outshines all the rest with its heroism. Look at a tree—in it you will find one branch that is bigger and stronger, and, consequently, more valorous than the rest. Look finally at your own person—in it, too, you will first encounter the head, and only then notice the belly and other parts. What, in your opinion, is more valorous: your head, even if filled with light stuff, but still striving upwards, or your down-striving belly, good only for producing . . . Oh, how truly light is your free-thinking!

These were the thoughts that prompted me, a humble town archivist (on a salary of two rubles a month, yet singing praises all the same), together with my three predecessors, to sing praises with my incorruptible lips of those glorious Neros,* who have wondrously adorned our most glorious town of Foolsburg not with godlessness and false Hellenic wisdom, but with their firmness and administrative boldness. Having no gift for versification, we dared not resort to meters, and, trusting in the will of God, expounded worthy deeds in a language unworthy yet proper to us, only avoiding low words. I think, however, that this bold undertaking of ours will be forgiven us in view of the particular intention we had as we embarked on it.

This intention was to portray the succession of mayors appointed to the town of Foolsburg at various times by the Russian government. But in undertaking such an important

---

* Again the same deplorable error.—*Publisher*

matter I have asked myself more than once: will I be able
to carry out this task? In my life I have seen many of these
amazing heroes; so, too, had my predecessors seen many of
them. The total number of them was twenty-two, following one another without a break in majestic order, except
for seven days of calamitous anarchy that almost threw the
whole town into desolation. Some of them like a violent
flame flew from end to end, purifying and renewing everything; others, on the contrary, like a burbling brook, irrigated
meadows and pastures, leaving violence and destruction to
the lot of the chief clerks. But all of them, the violent as
well as the meek, left a grateful memory in the hearts of the
townsfolk, for they were all mayors. This touching compliance is in itself so astonishing that it causes no small worry
to the chronicler. You do not know what to praise more: authority with its measure of boldness, or this vineyard with its
proper measure of gratitude.[3]

On the other hand, this same compliance provides no
small relief for the chronicler. For what, in fact, is his task? To
criticize and condemn? No, not that. To reason? No, not that,
either. What, then? It is, O light-minded freethinker, merely
to depict the abovementioned compliance and to transmit it
to posterity for proper edification.

Taken this way the task becomes feasible even for the
humblest of the humble, because he becomes only the
earthen vessel which contains the praise poured out everywhere in abundance. And the more earthen the vessel, the
better and more delicious will seem the sweet, glorifying
liquid it contains. And the earthen vessel will say to himself:
"So I, too, am good for something, even though my salary is
two copper rubles a month!"

Having thus voiced some excuse for myself, I cannot but
add that our native town of Foolsburg trades extensively in

kvass, liver, and boiled eggs. It has three rivers and, like ancient Rome, is built on seven hills, on which, in icy times, a great many carriages get broken and as many horses get crippled. The only difference is that in Rome ungodliness blossomed, and with us—godliness; Rome was afflicted with violence, and with us it was all meekness; in Rome it was the mobs that rioted, and we have the authorities.

And I will also say: this chronicle was put together in succession by four archivists: Mishka Triapichkin, and another Mishka Triapichkin,[4] and Mitka Smirnomordov, and I, humble Pavlushka Masloboinikov. In this we had only one fear, lest our notebooks wind up in the hands of Mr. Bartenev and he publishes them in his *Archives*.[5] And so, glory be to God and my speechifying is over.

On the Roots of the Foolsburgers' Origins

"I have no wish, like Kostomarov, to roam as a gray wolf over the earth, nor, like Solovyov, to spread a blue-gray eagle's wings soaring under the clouds, nor to let my thoughts, like Pypin's, wander here and there, but I wish to sing of my most gentle Foolsburgers, and to show the whole world their glorious deeds and the good root from which their illustrious tree grew and covered the whole earth with its branches."[1]*

Thus the chronicler begins his story, and then, having spoken a few words in praise of his own modesty, he goes on:

In ancient times, he says, there was a people called the Headwhackers, and they lived far in the north, in those parts where Greek and Roman historians and geographers posited the existence of the Hyperborean Sea. These people were called Headwhackers because they had a habit of "whacking"

---

* Here the chronicler obviously imitates *The Song of Igor's Campaign*: "Boyan the seer, when he wanted to make a song about someone, had his thoughts wander here and there, like a gray wolf over the earth, like an eagle under the clouds." And farther on: "O Boyan! the nightingale of old / If you had sung these hosts" and so on. —*Publisher*[2]

their heads against whatever came their way. If it was a wall, they whacked against the wall; if they started praying, they whacked against the floor. Next door to the Headwhackers lived a great many independent tribes,[3] but only the most notable ones are listed by the chronicler, namely, the Walrus-eaters, the Onion-eaters, the Dregs-eaters, the Cranberrians, the Pranksters, the Whirlibeans, the Froggies, the Bump-kins, the Sooty-huts, the Peckers, the Crackskulls, the Born-blinds, the Mushmouths, the Lop-ears, the Skewbellies, the Whitefish-eaters, the Corner-snoopers, the Hashers, and the Gropers. Having no religion or government, these tribes re-placed it all by constantly feuding with one another. They concluded alliances, declared wars, made peace, swore friend-ship and fidelity, and when they lied they added "shame on me," knowing beforehand that "shame doesn't sting the eyes." In this way they mutually devastated their lands, mutually violated their women and maidens, all the while priding themselves on being cordial and hospitable. But when in the end they tore the bark off the last pine tree for flatcakes, and when there were no women or maidens left and no means of continuing "to make the human race," the Headwhack-ers were the first to come to their senses. They realized that someone had to have the upper hand, and they sent a mes-sage to all their neighbors: "Let's whack heads with one an-other until someone outwhacks all the rest." "That was clever of them," says the chronicler. "They knew they had strong heads growing on their shoulders, and so they suggested it." And, indeed, as soon as the simplehearted neighbors ac-cepted this perfidious suggestion, the Headwhackers, with God's help, immediately outwhacked them all. The first ones to surrender were the Born-blinds and the Gropers; the ones to hold out longer were the Dregs-eaters, Whitefish-eaters, and Skewbellies.[4] To defeat these last ones they were even forced to resort to a ruse. Namely: on the day of the battle, when the two sides stood facing each other, the Headwhackers, uncertain of their success, resorted to sorcery: they sent the sun at the Skewbellies. The position of the sun was such that it was shining in the eyes of the Skewbellies anyway, but the Headwhackers, to make it seem like sorcery, began to wave their hats at the Skewbellies: "See how we are, even the sun is on our side." The Skewbellies, however, were not frightened at first, but had their own idea: they emptied sacks of oatmeal and tried to catch the sun in the sacks. Try as they might, they failed, and only then, seeing that truth was on the side of the Headwhackers, gave themselves up.[5]

Having united the Pranksters, the Dregs-eaters, and other tribes around themselves, the Headwhackers began to organize, obviously intending to achieve some sort of order. The chronicler does not give a detailed history of this organizing, but cites only some episodes.[6] They started by pouring oatmeal into the Volga River to make batter, then dragged a calf to the bathhouse, then cooked kasha in a moneybag, then drowned a billy goat in malted batter, then bought a pig instead of a beaver, and killed a dog instead of a wolf, then went looking everywhere for six lost bast shoes and found seven, then greeted a crayfish with bell ringing, then drove a pike off its eggs, then went five miles to catch a gnat that sat on a passerby's nose, then traded a priest for a hound dog, then caulked the jail walls with pancakes, then fettered a flea, then sent the devil to army service, then poled up the sky, then finally got tired and began to wait and see what would come of it all.

But nothing came of it. The pike went back to its eggs; the pancakes used to caulk the jail walls were eaten by the inmates; the moneybags in which they cooked kasha burned and the kasha with them. And discord and racket set in greater than before: again they mutually devastated their lands, took women into captivity, violated maidens. There was no order, and that was it. They made another attempt at headwhacking, but this, too, came to nothing. At this point they got the notion to look for a prince.

"He'll provide us with everything in a trice," the wise old Goodthink said. "He'll fabricate some soldiers for us, and build a jail good and proper. Come on, lads!"

They searched and searched for a prince, and almost lost themselves among three pine trees, but luckily they ran into a Born-blind passerby who knew these three pine trees like the five fingers of his hand. He led them out to the right path and straight to a prince's courtyard.

"Who are you? And why have you come to me?" the prince asked.

"We are Headwhackers! No people on earth are wiser and braver! We threw hats at the Skewbellies and defeated them!" boasted the Headwhackers.

"What else have you done?"

"We went five miles to catch a gnat," the Headwhackers began, and it suddenly seemed so funny, so funny . . . They looked at one another and burst out laughing.

"It was you, Pyotr, who went to catch a gnat!" Ivashka jeered.

"No, you!"

"No, not me! It was your nose it sat on!"

Then the prince, seeing that even here, before his face, they would not end their discord, was infuriated and began to instruct them with his rod.

"You're fools, fools!" he said. "You shouldn't be called

Headwhackers from your deeds, but fools! I don't want to rule over fools! Go search for a prince who is the greatest fool on earth—he will rule over you."

Having said this, he gave them a bit more instruction with his rod and dismissed them honorably.

The Headwhackers pondered the prince's words; they went on their way and went on pondering.

"Why did he berate us like that?" some said. "We came to him with heart and soul, and he sent us to look for a foolish prince!"

But at the same time some were found who saw nothing offensive in the prince's words.

"So what!" they countered. "A foolish prince may be even better! We'll hand him a gingerbread: 'Munch and don't punch!'"

"True enough," the others agreed.

The fine lads went home, and first tried again to organize among themselves. They tied a rooster with a cord so he wouldn't escape, they ate a dog . . . Still it was all no use. They pondered and pondered and went looking for a foolish prince.

They went over a flat land for three years and three days, and still did not arrive anywhere. However, they finally came to a swamp. At the edge of it they saw a Groper from Chukhloma.[7] His mittens were tucked behind his belt, while he was looking all around for them.

"Do you happen to know, our gentle Groper, where we can find a prince who is the greatest fool on earth?" begged the Headwhackers.

"I do, there's one over that way," said the Groper. "Just go straight across the swamp and he'll be there."

They all rushed into the swamp and half of them drowned right then ("Many of them showed zeal for their native land," says the chronicler); finally they got out of the mire and saw at the other end of the swamp, right before them, a prince—foolish as could be! He sits and eats fancy gingerbreads. The Headwhackers rejoiced: "That's a prince for us! Couldn't be better!"

"Who are you, and why have you come to me?" asked the prince, munching on gingerbreads.

"We are Headwhackers! No people are wiser or braver! We defeated even the Dregs-eaters!" boasted the Head-whackers.

"What else have you done?"

"We drove a pike off its eggs, we poured oatmeal into the Volga to make batter . . ." the Headwhackers began to enumerate, but the prince refused even to listen.

"Fool though I be," he said, "you're still bigger fools than I am! Does a pike sit on its eggs? Can you make oatmeal batter in a free river? No, you should be called Foolsfolk, not Headwhackers! I don't want to rule over you—go find your-selves a prince who is the greatest fool on earth—he will rule over you!"

And, having punished them with his rod, he dismissed them honorably.

The Headwhackers pondered: "That son-of-a-gun Groper hoodwinked us! He said this prince was the most stupid—but he's smart!" However, they went home and again tried to organize themselves. They dried their footcloths under rain, climbed a pine tree to see Moscow. But there was no order and that was it. Then Pyotr Gnat had an idea.

"I have a friend," he said, "he's called the stealer-dealer.[8] If a rascal like him can't find a prince, judge me mercifully, cut off my luckless head!"

He spoke with such conviction that the Headwhackers listened to him and summoned the stealer-dealer. He haggled for a long time, asking three-and-a-half kopecks, the Headwhackers offering him two kopecks plus whatever else they had. They finally came to terms somehow and went to look for a prince.

"You should find a none-too-smart one for us!" the Head-whackers said to the stealer-dealer. "We've got no use for smart ones, devil take them!"

The stealer-dealer first led them through a woods of firs and birches, then through a thick forest, then through a copse, and brought them to a clearing, and in the middle of this clearing sits a prince.

The Headwhackers looked at the prince and almost fainted. There is this prince sitting before them, and he is smart as can be; he fires his gun and he brandishes his sword. His every bullet pierces a heart, he swings his sword and a head rolls. And the stealer-dealer, having done this nasty deed, stands there patting his belly and grinning into his beard.

"You must be out of your mind! He won't come to us. The others were a hundred times more foolish, and they refused!" The Headwhackers fell upon the stealer-dealer.

"Never mind! I'll take care of it!" said the stealer-dealer. "You just wait, I'll say a couple of words to him."

The Headwhackers saw that the stealer-dealer had gotten the better of them, but they did not dare back out of it.

"Well, brothers, that's not the same as whacking heads with the Skewbellies; here you've got to answer: what sort of man are you? what's your rank and title?" they murmured among themselves.

The stealer-dealer meanwhile went up to the prince, doffed his sable-fur hat, and began whispering in his ear. They exchanged whispers for a long time, but it was impossible to hear what it was about. All the Headwhackers did catch was the stealer-dealer's words "And as for thrashing them, Your Princely Highness, there's no limit to that."

Finally their turn came to stand in the presence of His Princely Highness.

"What sort of people are you, and why have you come to me?" the prince asked them.

"We are Headwhackers! There are no braver people . . ." the Headwhackers began and suddenly became embarrassed.

"I've heard, gentlemen Headwhackers!" smiled the prince ("and this smile of his was so warm, as if the sun shone forth!" observes the chronicler). "I've heard all about you! And I know how you greeted a crayfish with church bells—I know well enough! One thing I do not know is why you have come to me."

"We've come to Your Princely Highness to tell you this: we have committed many killings among ourselves, we have caused devastation and outrage to each other, and still we don't know right from wrong. Come and rule over us!"

"And to whom among my brother princes, may I ask, have you gone with such a petition?"

"We went to one foolish prince, and to another prince, also foolish—and they had no wish to rule over us!"

"Very well. I wish to rule over you," said the prince, "but go and live with you I will not. Because you live like beasts: you skim profit from unassayed gold, you debauch your own daughters-in-law! I am now sending to you, instead of myself, this same stealer-dealer: he will rule over you at home, and I will order both him and you around from here!"

The Headwhackers hung their heads and said:

"Yes, sir!"

"And you will pay me many tributes," the prince went on. "If anyone has a sheep with a lamb, let him write the sheep off to me and keep the lamb; if anyone happens to have a penny, let him break it into four parts: give one part to me, another one also to me, and the third one as well, and leave the fourth part for yourselves. And if I go to war—you go, too! The rest is none of your business!"

"Yes, sir!" said the Headwhackers.

"And on those who mind their own business I will have mercy; but all the rest I will punish."

"Yes, sir!" answered the Headwhackers.

"And since you have been unable to live by your own will and have yourselves wished to be in bondage, henceforth you will be called not Headwhackers but Foolsfolk."

"Yes, sir!" answered the Headwhackers.

Then the prince ordered the ambassadors to be served vodka and each to be given a pie and a crimson neckerchief, and having imposed many tributes on them, he dismissed them with honor.

On the way home the Headwhackers sighed. "They sighed unceasingly, they wept hard," witnesses the chronicler. "That's princely right and wrong for you!" they said. They also said: "We yessed and yessed, and yessed ourselves away!" One of them, taking up the harp, sang:

> Rustle not, dear mother green grove!
> Do not keep me, fine fellow, from thinking my
>   thoughts,
> For tomorrow I, fine fellow, will go to be questioned
> Before the terrible judge, the tsar himself . . . [9]

As the song went on, the Headwhackers hung their heads more and more. "There were among them," says the chronicler, "gray-haired old men who wept bitterly, having forfeited their sweet freedom; there were also young ones, who had barely had a taste of that freedom, but they too wept. Only

now did they understand how beautiful freedom was." And
when the concluding words of the song rang out—

And for that, fine lad, I will grant to you
A lofty mansion in the wide field
Two posts and a crossbar.

—they all fell on their faces and sobbed.

But the drama had been accomplished irreversibly. On
reaching home, the Headwhackers immediately chose a
swampy place and founded on it a town called Foolsburg,
themselves thereby becoming Foolsburgers. "Thus did this
ancient stock blossom forth," adds the chronicler.

But this submissiveness did not please the stealer-dealer.
He was in need of rebellions, for by suppressing them he
hoped to find favor with the prince and also to extort bribes
from the rebels. He began to pester the Foolsburgers with
all sorts of injustice, and, indeed, before long he stirred up
rebellions. The first to rebel were the Corner-snoopers, then
the Haggis-eaters. The stealer-dealer went against them with
a cannon, fired nonstop, and, having destroyed them all, concluded a peace—that is, went to the Corner-snoopers and
ate halibut, then went to the Haggis-eaters and ate haggis.
For this the prince praised him greatly. However, he stole
so much that the rumor of his unquenchable stealing even
reached the prince. The prince was greatly inflamed and sent
the unfaithful servant a noose. But the dealer, being a veritable stealer, wheedled his way out of it: without waiting for
the noose, he forestalled the punishment by doing himself in
with a cucumber.

After the stealer-dealer, a man from Odoevo came "instead
of the prince," the one who "bought a pennyworth of Lenten
eggs." But he, too, figured that he would not survive without

rebellions, and also took to pestering them. The Skewbellies, the Fancy-breaders, the Porridgers all rose up, defending
the old times and their rights. The man from Odoevo went
against the rebels, and also fired at them relentlessly, but it
was all in vain, because not only did the rebels not submit, but
they drew in the Sooty-huts and the Loose-lips. The prince
heard the mindless shooting of the mindless fellow and suffered it for a long time, but in the end could not stand it, went
personally against the rebels, and, having destroyed them all
to a man, went back to his place.

"I sent a real stealer, and he stole," the prince lamented.
"I sent another nicknamed 'sell-a-pennyworth-of-Lenten-
eggs,' and he, too, stole. Who shall I send now?"

He spent a long time deciding which candidate to prefer:
a man from Orel, on the basis of the saying "Orel and Kromy
are the foremost thieves," or the Shuy man who "went to
Petersburg, slept on the floor, and didn't fall down," but he
finally gave preference to the Orel man, because he belonged
to the ancient family of the "Cracked-heads." But as soon
as the Orel man arrived, the Staritsa people rebelled, and,
to mock their chief, greeted a rooster with bread and salt.[10]
The Orel man went to them, hoping to be regaled on sturgeon, but all he found there was "a whole lot of mud." Then
he burned down Staritsa and gave the Staritsa women and
maidens over to himself to be violated. "On hearing about it,
the prince cut out his tongue."

Then the prince attempted once again to send "a thief of a
simpler sort" and, with that in mind, selected a Kaliazin man,
who "bought a pig instead of a beaver."[11] But he turned out
to be a still greater thief than the stealer-dealer and the man
from Orel. Having driven everyone to rebellion, he "killed
and burned them."

The prince rolled his eyes and exclaimed:
"No foolishness is more grievous than foolishness!"
And, coming to Foolsburg in person, he shouted:
"Flog 'em all!"
With these words historical time began.

The Register of Mayors

Appointed to the Town of Foolsburg by

the Higher Authorities at Various Times

(1731–1826)[1]

1. *Klementy, Amadei Manuilovich.* Brought from Italy
   by Biron, the Duke of Courland,[2] for his skill in
   cooking macaroni; being suddenly promoted to an
   appropriate rank, he was made mayor. On arriving
   in Foolsburg, he not only did not abandon cooking
   macaroni, but even strove to force many to do the
   same, which was his claim to glory. Beaten with a
   knout for treason in 1734, he had his nostrils torn
   out and was exiled to Berezov.

2. *Ferapontov, Foty Petrovich,* brigadier.[3] Former barber for the same Duke of Courland. Conducted
   multiple campaigns against the tax defaulters, and
   was such a lover of spectacles that he did not allow
   any floggings unless he himself was present. In 1738
   torn to pieces by dogs in the forest.

3. *Gigantov, Ivan Matveevich.* Taxed townsfolk three
   kopecks per head in his own account, preliminarily
   drowning the Director of Economic Affairs in the

river. Gave bloody beatings to many police officers. In 1740, during the reign of the meek Elizabeth, was caught having a love affair with Avdotia Lopukhina,[4] beaten with a knout, and, after having his tongue cut out, exiled and imprisoned in Cherdyn.

4. *Urus-Kugush-Kildibaev, Manyl Samylovich*, lieutenant-captain from the Leib Company.[5] Distinguished himself by mad courage and once even took the town of Foolsburg by storm. When this became known, he was not praised, and in 1745 was dismissed with public disclosure.

5. *Lamvrokakis*, a runaway Greek with no name or patronymic, and even without rank, caught by Count Kirill Razumovsky at the market in Nezhin. He traded in Greek soap, sponges, and walnuts; besides that was a proponent of classical education. In 1756 was found in his bed bitten to death by bedbugs.

6. *Blockheadov, Ivan Matveevich*, brigadier. Was seven feet tall and prided himself on being a direct descendant of Ivan the Great (a famous bell tower in Moscow). Broken in half during a storm that raged in 1761.

7. *Pfeifer, Bogdan Bogdanovich*, sergeant of the guards, a native of Holstein. Having accomplished nothing, replaced in 1762 for ignorance.[6]

8. *Shagmug, Dementy Varlamovich*. Was appointed hastily and had in his head a special device, for which he was called "Music Box." This, however, did

not prevent him from putting in order the arrears, neglected by his predecessor. During his administration disastrous anarchy took place, lasting for seven days, which will be recounted further on.

9. *Epikurov, Semyon Konstantinovich*, state councillor and chevalier. Paved Grand and Gentry Streets, started beer and mead brewing, introduced the use of mustard and bay leaf, collected arrears, was a patron of learning and solicited for setting up an academy in Foolsburg. Authored the work *Lives of Remarkable Apes*. Being of sturdy build, he had eight consecutive mistresses. His wife, Lukerya Terentievna, was also very indulgent, thereby contributing greatly to the splendor of her husband's rule. He died a natural death in 1770.

10. *Marquis de Sanglotte, Anton Protasyevich*, of French origin and a friend of Diderot. Was distinguished by his frivolity and liked to sing bawdy songs. Flew in the air in the town garden and almost flew away, except that he caught the skirts of his frock coat on the spire and it took some effort to take him down. This caused his dismissal in 1772, but he did not lose heart and the very next year performed in Isler's garden at the mineral waters.[7]*

11. *Ferdyshchenko, Pyotr Petrovich*, brigadier. Former orderly of Prince Potemkin.[9] Was none too bright and also tongue-tied. Neglected tax collecting; liked to

---

* This is certainly a mistake.—*Publisher*[8]

eat baked ham and goose with cabbage. During his mayorship the town suffered from hunger and fire. Died in 1779 of overeating.

12. *Wartbeardin, Basilisk Semyonovich.*[10] His term of rule was the longest and the most brilliant. He led a military campaign against the defaulters of tax payments and burned thirty-three villages. By this means he collected two rubles fifty kopecks of arrears. Introduced the card game *la mouche* and olive oil; paved the marketplace and planted birch trees along the street leading to the public offices. Resumed petitioning to create an academy in Foolsburg but, his petition denied, built a jailhouse instead. Died in 1798 supervising a flogging and with a police captain by his side.

13. *Blaggardov, Onufry Ivanovich,* former stoker in the Gatchina Palace.[11] Unpaved the streets paved by his predecessors and built monuments out of the obtained stone. Replaced in 1802 for disagreements with Novosiltsev, Czartorysky, and Stroganov (a famous triumvirate at the time) on the subject of a constitution, in which controversy he was later proved correct.[12]

14. *Mikaladze, Prince Xavery Georgievich,* a Circassian, descendant of the sensuous Princess Tamara.[13] Possessed of seductive appearance, he was so fond of the female sex that he increased the Foolsburg population twice. Left a useful handbook on the subject. Died in 1814 from exhaustion.

15. *Benevolensky, Feofilakt Irinarkhovich*, state councillor, a friend of Speransky at the seminary.[14] Was wise and had a penchant for lawmaking. Predicted open courts and the zemstvo.[15] Was in amorous relations with Raspopova, a merchant's widow, who fed him savory pies on Saturdays. In leisure time wrote sermons for the town priests and translated the writings of Thomas à Kempis from the Latin. Reintroduced mustard, bay leaf, and olive oil for reason of being good for people's health. Was the first to impose a levy on tax farmers, and profited three thousand rubles a year from that. In 1811 was called to account for condoning Bonaparte and sent to prison.

16. *Pustule, Ivan Panteleich*, major. Turned out to have a meat-stuffed head, for which he was exposed by the local marshal of nobility.[16]

17. *Ivanov, Nikodim Osipovich*, state councillor. Was so small that he was unable to contain the extensive laws. Died in 1819 from strain, trying to comprehend a certain senate decree.

18. *Du Chariot, Viscount Angel Dorofeevich*, of French origin. Liked to dress in woman's clothes and feast on frogs. On closer inspection turned out to be a girl. Exiled abroad in 1821.

19. *Melancholin, Erast Andreevich*, state councillor. Karamzin's friend.[17] Was distinguished by tenderness of heart and sensitivity, liked to drink tea in the town park, and was unable to see the heath-cock

mating dance without tears. Left several treatises of idyllic content and died of melancholy in 1825. Raised the levy on tax farming to five thousand rubles a year.

20. *Sullen-Grumble*, scoundrel, former army latrine cleaner, also responsible for floggings. A downright stinker. Destroyed the old town and built a new one in another place.

21. *Hijack-Swashbucklin, Archistratig Stratilatovich*, major.[18] Will pass over this one in silence. He rode into Foolsburg on a white steed, burned down the school, and abolished learning.

MUSIC BOX*

In August 1762 there was an unusual flurry in Foolsburg on the occasion of the arrival of a new mayor, Dementy Varlamovich Shagmug. The inhabitants exulted; not having seen the newly appointed superior yet with their own eyes, they were already telling anecdotes about him, calling him "a good-looker" and "a smarty." They congratulated each other with joy, kissed, shed tears, went into the taverns, came out of the taverns, went back in again. Transported with ecstasy, they recalled the former Foolsburgian liberties. The town notables gathered in front of the cathedral bell tower, formed a people's assembly, and the air shook with their exclaiming: "Our father! Our good-looker! Our smarty!"

Dangerous dreamers even turned up. Guided not so much by reason as by the stirrings of their grateful hearts, they maintained that under the new mayor trade would

---

* No. 8 in the Register of Mayors. The Publisher found it possible not to keep strictly to chronological order as he presented to the public the contents of *The Chronicler*. Besides, he considered it best to present only the most remarkable mayors, since the less remarkable are sufficiently represented by the preceeding Register. —*Publisher*

flourish and that under police surveillance science and art would spring up. People could not keep from making comparisons. Recalling the previous mayor, who had just left the city, they found that while he, too, had been a good-looker and a smarty, even so the preference should now be given to the new ruler, if only for the fact of his being new. In short, on this occasion, as on other similar ones, both the usual Foolsburgian rapturousness and the usual Foolsburgian frivolity were fully manifest.

Meanwhile, the new mayor turned out to be taciturn and sullen. He came galloping to Foolsburg at full speed (the times were such that there was not a single moment to lose), and having barely burst into the town common, immediately, at the very edge, gave a flogging to a whole lot of cabbies. But even that did not cool the raptures of the Foolsburgers, because their minds were still filled with memories of the recent victories over the Turks, and everyone hoped that the new mayor would take the Khotyn Fortress by storm once again.[1]

Soon, however, the townsfolk realized that their exultation and their hopes were, to say the least, premature and exaggerated. There was the usual reception, and here, for the first time in their lives, the Foolsburgers had to learn in practice the bitter ordeals that the most tenacious love of the authorities can be subjected to. Everything at this reception was somehow mysterious. The mayor silently walked along the ranks of the official dignitaries, flashed his eyes, uttered "Insufferable!" and disappeared into his study. The officials were dumbfounded; following them, the townsfolk were also dumbfounded.

Despite their insuperable firmness, the Foolsburgers are a pampered and in some ways a spoiled people. They like it that an amiable smile plays on a superior's face, that affable catchphrases come from his lips, and they get perplexed when those lips only grunt or produce mysterious sounds. A superior may accomplish various undertakings, or may accomplish none at all, but if with all that he does not blabber, his name will never become popular. There were truly wise mayors, to whom even the thought of setting up an academy in Foolsburg was not alien (such, for instance, was State Councillor Epikurov, who figures under No. 9 on our Register), but since they did not grace the Foolsburgers either with "Hey, brothers" or with "Hey, lads," their names remained in oblivion. There were, on the contrary, those who were not really foolish—there were none such—but whose deeds were of the middling sort, that is, they did flog and did exact arrears, but since they always added something amiable, their names were not only written down in stone, but even served as the object of a multitude of oral legends.

Here is what happened in the present case. However ardent the hearts of the townspeople became on the occasion of the new mayor's arrival, his reception cooled them off significantly.

"What's that, really! He just grunted and showed us his back! As if we haven't seen backs before! You should have a heartfelt talk with us! Gentleness, probe us with gentleness! First threaten us, threaten us, and then show mercy!" Thus spoke the Foolsburgers, tearfully recalling the previous superiors, all of them cordial, and kind, and good-lookers—and all of them in uniforms! They even recalled the runaway Greek, Lamvrokakis (No. 5 on the Register), remembered Brigadier Blockheadov (No. 6 on the Register), and what a fine fellow he showed himself to be at the very first reception.

"Onslaught," he said, "and with that speed, indulgence, and with that strictness. And with that reasonable firmness.

This, my dear sirs, is the goal, or, to be precise, the five goals, that I, with God's help, hope to achieve by means of certain administrative acts, which constitute the essence or, better say, the nucleus, of the plan of campaign I have conceived!"

And how then, having deftly turned on one heel, he addressed the town headman and added:

"And on feast days we'll come to you to eat savory pies!"

"That's how real superiors used to receive, sir!" sighed the Foolsburgers. "Not like this one! Grunted something incoherent, and that was it!"

Alas! subsequent events not only confirmed the public opinion of the townsfolk, but even exceeded their boldest apprehensions. The new mayor locked himself in his office, did not eat, did not drink, and kept scribbling something with his pen. From time to time he ran out to the hall, threw a pile of handwritten pages to the chief clerk, pronounced "Insufferable!" and disappeared into his office again. Unprecedented activity suddenly boiled up in all ends of the town: police sergeants went galloping; police captains went galloping; assessors went galloping; the policemen on duty forgot what it meant to have a normal meal and acquired the pernicious habit of snatching pickings on the run.[2] They snatch and catch, flog and thrash, seize and sell . . . And the mayor goes on sitting and scribbling fiat after fiat . . . Noise and thunder roll from one end of town to the other, and over all this turmoil, all this hubbub, like the cry of a predatory bird, reigns the ominous "Insufferable!"

The Foolsburgers were horrified. They recalled the general flogging of the cabbies, and it suddenly dawned on them all: What if he flogs the whole town the same way! Then they began to wonder what meaning was attached to the word "Insufferable!" Finally, they resorted to the history of Foolsburg, started looking into it for examples of salutary mayoral strictness, found an extraordinary diversity, and still did not come up with anything appropriate.

"He could simply say how much he wants to get for each head!" the confused townsfolk talked among themselves. "But he just snorts, and that's it!"

Foolsburg, the carefree, good-natured, and cheerful Foolsburg, was downcast. There were no more animated gatherings outside the gates of the houses, the cracking of sunflower seeds ceased, there was no playing knucklebones! The streets were empty, predatory beasts appeared on the squares. People left their houses only for necessity and, having shown their frightened and exhausted faces for a moment, hid themselves at once. The old-timers said that something similar had happened in the time of the Tushino "little tsar," and also of Biron,[3] when the streetwalker Tanka the Pockmarked almost brought punishment to the whole town. But even then it was better; then people understood at least something, but now all they felt was fear, a sinister and unaccountable fear.

It was especially painful to look at the town late at night. By then Foolsburg, usually little animated, became totally still. Hungry dogs reigned in the streets, and even they did not bark, but gave themselves in great order to self-indulgence and decadence. Heavy darkness enveloped the streets and buildings, and only in one room of the mayor's quarters deep at night did a sinister light still glimmer. An awakened town inhabitant could see the mayor sitting bent over his desk and scribbling something with his pen ... He would suddenly come up to the window, shout "Insufferable!"—and again sit down at the desk, and again start scribbling ...

Ugly rumors began to circulate. People said that the new mayor was not even a mayor, but a werewolf sent to Foolsburg out of carelessness; that during the night, in the guise of an insatiable vampire, he soars over the town and sucks the blood of the sleeping townsfolk. Of course, all this was told and transmitted in a whisper; but some brave hearts turned up who suggested that the whole lot of them, to a man, kneel and ask forgiveness, but even they wavered. What if this is just as it should be? What if it had been decided that Foolsburg, for its sins, must have precisely this kind of mayor, and not any other? This reasoning seemed to make so much sense that the brave ones not only renounced their suggestions, but immediately began to reproach each other for rabble-rousing and sedition.

And suddenly it became known to everyone that the clock and organ maker Baibakov secretly visits the mayor. Reliable witnesses said that once, between two and three past midnight, he walked out of the mayor's apartment, all pale and frightened, carefully carrying something wrapped in a napkin. And what was most remarkable of all, on that memorable night none of the townsfolk were awakened by the cry "Insufferable!"—but the mayor himself seemed to have ceased for a time to conduct the critical analysis of the list of arrears and to have fallen fast asleep.*

The question arose: What need did the mayor have of Baibakov, who, besides being a chronic drinker, was also an avowed adulterer?

Tricks and trip-ups began with the aim of discovering the secret, but Baibakov remained mute as a fish and, in response to all exhortations, only shook all over. They tried to get him

---

* An obvious anachronism. In 1762 there were no lists of arrears, the taxes were just exacted, a proper sum from each person. Consequently, there were no critical analyses thereof. Though this is not an anachronism but, rather, a foresight that the chronicler occasionally manifests to such a degree that it even makes the reader feel slightly awkward. Thus (and we will see this later) he foresaw the invention of the electric telegraph and even the setting-up of provincial management.—*Publisher*

drunk, but he, without rejecting the vodka, merely sweated and did not give anything away. The boys apprenticed to him could tell only that, indeed, a policeman once came during the night and led the master away, and he returned an hour later with a little bundle, locked himself in the workshop, and had been languishing ever since.

That was all they were able to find out. Meanwhile, the mysterious meetings of the mayor with Baibakov became more frequent. As time went on, Baibakov not only stopped languishing, but even became so bold as to promise the town headman to have him recruited as a soldier without the right of replacement, unless he provided him with a jigger of vodka every day. He had a new suit made for himself and boasted of his intention to open such a shop in Foolsburg that Winterhalter himself would have his nose put out of joint.*

Amidst all this talk and gossip, a summons suddenly fell as if from the sky, inviting the most notable citizens of the Foolsburg intelligentsia, on such-and-such day and hour, to come to the mayor for admonition. The notables were perplexed, but began to prepare.

It was a beautiful spring day. Nature exulted; sparrows chirped; dogs joyfully squealed and wagged their tails. The townsfolk, holding offerings under their arms, crowded in the courtyard of the mayor's quarters, and with trembling awaited the terrible judgment. Finally the awaited moment arrived.

He came out, and for the first time the Foolsburgers saw on his face the affable smile they had been longing for. It seemed as if the beneficent rays of the sun affected him, too (at least many townsfolk afterwards insisted that they

---

* Yet another example of foresight. There was no Winterhalter shop in 1762.—*Publisher*

saw with their own eyes the tails of his frock coat tremble).
He walked up to each person one by one and benevolently,
though silently, accepted from them everything there was to
accept. Having finished this business, he stepped back to the
porch and opened his mouth ... And suddenly something
inside him hissed and buzzed, and the longer this mysterious hissing went on, the more intensely his eyes rolled and
flashed. "Ss ... ss ... sfrble!" finally burst from his lips ...
With this sound he flashed his eyes for the last time and
rushed headlong through the open door of his quarters.

Reading the description of such an unprecedented event
in *The Chronicler*, we, the witnesses and participants of other
times and other events, are certainly quite capable of taking it with equanimity. But let us be carried in thought to a
hundred years ago, let us put ourselves in the place of our celebrated ancestors, and we will easily understand the horror
that had to come over them at the sight of those rolling eyes
and that mouth, open yet producing nothing but a hissing
and a meaningless sound unlike even the striking of a clock.
However, such precisely was the great merit of our ancestors that, no matter how shocked they were by the above-
described sight, they did not fall for the then-fashionable
revolutionary ideas or the temptations presented by anarchy,
but remained faithful to the love of the authorities, and allowed themselves only the slightest commiseration and reproach for their more-than-strange mayor.

"And where did they find us such a rogue!" the amazed
townsfolk asked one another, without giving any particular
meaning to the word "rogue."

"Look out, brother! What if by chance we ... sort of ...
have to answer for him—for this rogue!" added others.

And after that they calmly went to their homes and gave
themselves to their ordinary occupations.

Our Shagmug would have remained the shepherd of this vineyard for many years,[4] and would have gladdened the hearts of his superiors with his efficiency, and the townsfolk would not have sensed anything extraordinary in their existence, were it not that a perfectly accidental circumstance (a simple slip-up) stopped his activity in full swing.

Some time after the above-described reception, the mayor's chief clerk, having entered his study for the morning report, saw this sight: the mayor's body, dressed in uniform, was sitting at the desk, and before it, on top of a pile of lists of the arrears, in the guise of a fancy paperweight, sat the mayor's totally empty head . . . The clerk fled in such a panic that his teeth were chattering.

Messengers ran to fetch the deputy mayor and the police chief. The former began by reprimanding the latter, accusing him of negligence and pandering to brazen coercion, but the police chief succeeded in vindicating himself. He maintained, not without good reason, that the head could have been emptied only with the consent of the mayor himself, and that someone belonging to the Craftsmen's Guild must have taken part in it, because there were found on the table, counting as material evidence, a chisel, an awl, and a little file. The chief town doctor was summoned for a council and asked to answer three questions: (1) Could the mayor's head be separated from the mayor's body without a hemorrhage? (2) Was it possible to suggest that the mayor himself had taken his own head off his shoulders and emptied it? And (3) Was it possible to suppose that the mayor's head, once abrogated, could afterwards grow back again by way of some unknown process? The Aesculapius fell to thinking, muttered something about a certain "mayoral substance" supposedly exuding from a mayoral body, but then, seeing that he had tied himself in knots, declined to resolve the questions directly, excusing himself by referring to the mystery of the mayoral organism, which had not yet been sufficiently studied scientifically.*

Hearing such an evasive response, the deputy mayor faced a dilemma. He had either to report the incident at once to the authorities, and meanwhile start an underhand investigation, or to keep quiet for the time being, waiting to see what happened. In view of such difficulty, he chose a middle way—that is, he initiated an inquiry while ordering all and sundry to maintain the deepest secrecy about the subject, so as not to stir people up and arouse chimerical dreams in them.

No matter how strictly the policemen kept the secret entrusted to them, the unprecedented news about the abrogation of the mayor's head spread through the whole town in a matter of minutes. Many of the townsfolk wept, feeling themselves orphaned and, besides, fearing to be counted responsible for obeying a mayor who had an empty vessel on his shoulders instead of a head. Some others, though they also wept, on the contrary insisted that they should look forward to praise and not punishment for being obedient.

At the club that evening all the members presented themselves. They were excited, talked, recalled various circumstances, and found some facts that were quite suspicious. Thus, for instance, the assessor Talkovnikov recounted how, having once entered the mayor's study unexpectedly on urgent business, he had caught the mayor playing with his own head, which he, however, hastened to put back where it belonged. The assessor paid no proper attention to this fact, and even took it for a figment of his imagination, but it was

---

* It has been proven that the bodies of all superiors generally obey the same physiological laws as all other human bodies, but we should remember that in 1762 science was still in its infancy.—*Publisher*

now clear that the mayor, in view of temporary relief, occasionally took his head off, putting on a skullcap in its stead, just as a cathedral archpriest, when among his family, takes off his priest's hat and dons a casual one. Another assessor, Infantilov, recalled going past the clockmaker Baibakov's workshop once and seeing in one of the windows the mayor's head surrounded by various metal- and woodworking tools. But Infantilov was not allowed to finish, because at the first mention of Baibakov everyone remembered his strange behavior and his mysterious nightly escapades to the mayor's quarters . . .

Nevertheless, nothing clear followed from all these accounts. The public even began to incline towards the opinion that this whole story was nothing but an invention of idle people, but then, recalling the London agitators[5]* and passing from one syllogism to another, they concluded that treachery had made its nest in Foolsburg itself. Then all the members became excited and noisy, and, inviting the inspector of public schools, asked him a question: Have there been examples in history of people governing, conducting wars, and concluding treaties, with an empty vessel on their shoulders? The inspector thought for a moment and replied that many things in history are shrouded in darkness, but that there was, however, a certain Charles the Simple, who had on his shoulders a vessel not really empty, but *as if* empty, and even so conducted wars and concluded treaties.[6]

While all this talk was going on, the deputy mayor was not napping. He, too, remembered Baibakov and immediately called him to account. For some time Baibakov kept mum and said nothing except "Don't know, no idea," but when he was shown the material evidence found on his table, and on

---

* The chronicler anticipated even that!—*Publisher*

top of that was promised fifty kopecks for vodka, he became wiser and, being literate, gave the following evidence:

"My name is Vassily, son of Ivan, surname Baibakov. A Foolsburg craftsman; do not go to confession and communion, belonging to the sect of the Freemasons, and being a false priest of that sect. Was taken to court for cohabiting outside marriage with the wench Matrenka, and was legally recognized as an avowed adulterer, to which rank I still belong. Last year, in winter—I do not remember the month and the day—I was awakened during the night and, accompanied by a police officer, was taken to our mayor, Dementy Varlamovich. On arriving, I found him seated and rhythmically wagging his head from side to side. Beside myself with fear, and being burdened with alcoholic drinks, I stood speechless on the threshold, when suddenly Mr. Mayor beckoned to me with his hand and gave me a scrap of paper. On it I read: 'Don't be surprised, but fix what's broken.' After that Mr. Mayor took off his own head and handed it to me. On close inspection of the container before me, I discovered in one corner of it a small music box, capable of playing some simple pieces of music. Of pieces there were two: 'Smashitall!' and 'Insufferable!' During the trip the head got dampened and some cogs came loose, and others fell out. This caused Mr. Mayor's inability to speak clearly, or to speak missing letters or syllables. Being desirous to set this right, and having received permission to do so on the part of Mr. Mayor, I, with all due zealousness, wrapped the head in a napkin and went home. But here I discovered that I should not have counted on my zeal, for try as I might to fix the lost cogs, I succeeded so poorly in my endeavor that the least carelessness or fit of sneezing caused them to fall out again, and of late all Mr. Mayor had been able to say was 'Ss . . . sfrble!!' In this extremity, he was so furious that there was the danger of a great misfortune for me, but I prevented it by suggesting that Mr. Mayor turn to the clock and music-box master Winterhalter in Saint Petersburg for help, which was just what he did. Since then quite some time passed, during which I inspected the mayoral head daily, cleaning it out inside, which occupation I was engaged in this morning, when you, Your Honor, confiscated the tools of my trade. Why the new head ordered from Mr. Winterhalter has not yet arrived I do not know . . . I think, however, that, owing to the spring floods, this head is now sitting somewhere in idleness. To Your Honor's question whether, in case of its arrival, the new head, first, can be set up in its place, and, second, whether this set-up head will function properly, I humbly reply thus: I can set it up and it will function, but have real thoughts it cannot."

This testimony is signed by the avowed adulterer Vassily Ivanovich Baibakov in his own hand.

Having heard Baibakov's evidence, the deputy mayor reasoned that, since it was once allowed that the mayor of Foolsburg should have a simple kit instead of a head, this was how it should be. Therefore he decided to wait it out, and meanwhile sent Winterhalter an urgent telegram.[7]* Then, having locked up the mayor's body, he turned his activity to the pacifying of public opinion.

But by now all his contrivances were in vain. Two days went by; the long-expected Petersburg mail finally came; but there was no head in it.

In other words, anarchy set in. Government offices were in desolation. There were so many arrears that a local treasurer, having peeked into the cash box, opened his mouth and stayed with his mouth open for the rest of his life; po-

---

* Admirable!!—*Publisher*

licemen got out of hand and were brazenly idle; official holidays were no longer observed. Moreover, murders began, and right on the town common the headless corpse of an unknown man was found, which, by the skirts of the uniform, could be identified as belonging to a lifeguardsman, yet, no matter how the police chief or other members of the provisionary department tried, the head separated from the body could not be found.

At eight o'clock in the evening, the deputy mayor received a telegraphic message that the head had been sent long ago. The deputy mayor was totally bewildered.

Another day went by, the mayor's body was still sitting in his study and even beginning to go bad. The love of authority, temporarily shaken by Shagmug's odd behavior, came forth on timid but firm steps. The best people formed a procession and went to the deputy mayor, insisting that he give orders. The deputy mayor, seeing that the arrears were accumulating, drunkenness increasing, lawfulness in the courts disappearing, and decisions not being confirmed, addressed the staff-officer for help.[8] This latter, being a conscientious man, sent a telegram to his superiors about this occasion, and received a response, also by telegram, that he was being dismissed from service for absurd information.*

On hearing that, the deputy mayor came to the office and burst into tears. The assessors came and also wept; the solicitor came, and he, too, was unable to speak for tears.

Meanwhile, Winterhalter was telling the truth, and the head had indeed been fabricated and sent in due time. But he had acted rashly in entrusting the package to a young boy, inexperienced in matters of music boxes. Instead of supporting

---

* This worthy official vindicated himself and, as we will see below, actively participated in later events in Foolsburg.—*Publisher*

the package carefully, the inexperienced messenger dropped it on the floor of the post carriage and himself fell asleep. Thus he rode through several stations, when he suddenly felt that someone had bitten his calf. Taken unawares by the pain, he quickly untied the bast wrapping that contained the mysterious object, and his eyes beheld a strange spectacle. The head kept opening its mouth and rolling its eyes; moreover, it uttered loudly and quite distinctly: "Smashitall!"

The boy simply lost his mind from fear. His first impulse was to throw the speaking package out on the road; his second, to inconspicuously get out of the carriage and disappear in the bushes.

This strange incident might have ended with the head, having lain for a while on the road, being eventually crushed by passing carriages and finally taken into the field in the guise of fertilizer, were it not for the interference of something so utterly fantastic that the Foolsburgers themselves were at a loss. But let us not run ahead of events and first look at what was happening in Foolsburg.

Foolsburg was seething. The townsfolk, not seeing the mayor for several days in a row, were upset and, not inhibited in the least, accused the deputy mayor and the police chief of embezzling government property. Some sort of prophets and holy fools wandered about town without hindrance, predicting various calamities. A certain Mishka Snotnose declared that in his sleep he had had a vision of a fearsome man clothed in a bright cloud.

Finally the Foolsburgers could not stand it anymore; led by their chosen townsman Potbelliev, they formed a square in front of the state buildings and demanded that the deputy mayor be taken to the people's court, threatening otherwise to destroy both him and his house.

Antisocial elements surfaced with frightening speed. There was talk of impostors, of some Stepka, who, leading a band of outlaws, had abducted two merchants' wives just the day before and in front of everybody.

"What have you done with our dear father?" screamed the crowd, enraged to the point of frenzy, when the deputy mayor came before them.

"My fine lads! How can I present him for you, since he's locked up!" the trembling official, roused from administrative torpor by the events, tried to bring the crowd to reason. At the same time he secretly winked to Baibakov, who, seeing this sign, immediately vanished.

But the unrest would not be calmed.

"Lies, you flip-flopper!" the crowd answered. "You and the policemen ganged up on purpose to get rid of our dear father!"

God only knows how this general commotion would have been resolved, were it not that just then came the sound of a bell, and a carriage arrived in which sat the police chief and beside him . . . the vanished mayor!

He was wearing the uniform of a lifeguards regiment; his head was very dirty and bruised in several places. Despite that, he adroitly jumped out of the carriage and flashed his eyes on the crowd.

"Smashitall!" he roared in such a deafening voice that everybody instantly became hushed.

The uprising was suppressed at once; this crowd, recently so menacingly noisy, became so hushed that one could hear the buzzing of a gnat that flew from a neighboring swamp to marvel at "this absurd and ludicrous Foolsburg commotion."

"Rabble-rousers, step forward!" the mayor commanded in an ever louder voice.

They began to choose the instigators from among the defaulters on taxes, and had already counted out some dozen persons, when a new and totally outlandish circumstance gave the whole thing an entirely different turn.

While the Foolsburgers exchanged anxious whispers, trying to remember who had accumulated the most arrears, the mayor's droshky, so familiar to the townsfolk, approached the gathering unnoticed. They had no time to blink when—right in front of their eyes—Baibakov jumped out of the carriage, followed by the same mayor who, just a moment before, had been brought in a carriage by the police chief! The Foolsburgers were dumbfounded.

This second mayor's head was perfectly new and even varnished. Some perspicacious citizens found it strange that the big birthmark that a few days earlier had been on the mayor's right cheek was now on the left.

The impostors met and looked each other up and down. The crowd slowly and silently dispersed.*

---

* The Publisher considered it best to finish the story here, although the chronicler supplied various explanations . . . Thus, for instance, he says that the first mayor had on his shoulders the head thrown out of the carriage by Winterhalter's messenger, which was attached by the police captain to the body of an unknown lifeguards officer. The second mayor had the former head hastily fixed by Baibakov at the order of the deputy mayor but, instead of music, it had been packed full with various obsolete instructions . . . All these reflections are positively infantile, and one unquestionable thing is that both mayors were impostors.—*Publisher*

The Tale of the Six Mayoresses

A Picture of Foolsburg Internecine Strife

As one should have expected, the strange events that took place in Foolsburg were not without consequences.

The pernicious dual power had had no time to strike its malignant roots when a messenger arrived from the provincial capital, who took both impostors, put them in a special container filled with alcohol, and immediately carried them off for examination. But this apparently natural and lawful act of administrative firmness became all but a source of still more grievous difficulty than that produced by the incomprehensible appearance of two identical mayors.

As soon as the trail of the messenger who carried off the impostors went cold, as soon as the Foolsburgers found that they remained without any mayor at all, they, moved by the power of love for authorities, immediately fell into anarchy.

"And the town would have lain in this fatal abyss to this day," says the chronicler, "had it not been extracted from it by the resoluteness and self-denial of a certain dauntless staff-officer from among the local inhabitants."

Anarchy began with the Foolsburgers gathering by the belfry and throwing from the ramparts two citizens: Stepka and Ivashka. Then they went to the fashionable establishment of the Frenchwoman, Miss de Sans-Culotte (in Foolsburg she was known under the name of Ustinya Protasievna Chimneysweepova; later she turned out to be the sister of Marat and died of remorse).[1]* Having broken all the windows there, they proceeded to the river, drowned two more citizens, Porfishka and another Ivashka, and, having achieved nothing, went their separate ways.

Meanwhile, treason was not napping. Ambitious persons turned up who had the idea of using the disorganization of power to satisfy their egoistic purposes. And, strangest of all, on this occasion the representatives of the anarchist element were all women.

The first who decided to steal the reins of Foolsburg governance was Iraida Lukinishna Paleologova, a childless widow of unbending character, of masculine build, with a face of a dark brown hue reminiscent of old prints.[3] No one remembered when she had settled in Foolsburg, and some old-timers thought that this event coincided with the darkness of times out of mind. She lived alone, on scant food, lending money on interest, and cruelly torturing her four serf wenches. Obviously, she had thought over her bold enterprise maturely. First, she figured out that it was absolutely impossible for the town to remain without administration even for a moment. Second, she saw a mysterious sign in her name being Paleologova.[4] Third, no small encouragement for her was the circumstance that her late husband, a former wine clerk, had once occupied the post of mayor somewhere, for lack of anyone better.[5] "Having figured all that out," says the chronicler, "this malignant Iraidka went into action."

---

* Marat could not have been known at the time; this mistake can be explained by the fact that the chronicler described the events not immediately after, but several years later.—*Publisher*[2]

The Foolsburgers barely had time to recover from the events of the day before when Paleologova, seizing the moment when the deputy mayor lodged himself in a club over a game of whist, pulled her late wine clerk's sword out of its scabbard and, pouring some vodka into three veteran soldiers for courage, invaded the treasury. Having taken the treasurer and the accounting clerk prisoner, and shamelessly robbed the treasury, she went back home. On the way she threw copper money to people, and her drunken acolytes cried: "Here's our dear mother! Now, brothers, we'll have vodka aplenty!"

When the deputy mayor woke up the next morning, it was all over. He saw from his window the townsfolk congratulating and kissing one another, shedding tears. He did make an attempt to take back the reins of governance, but since his hands trembled, he dropped them right away. In despair and anguish he hastened to the town administration to find out how many policemen were still faithful, but was intercepted by the assessor Talkovnikov and brought before Iraidka. There he found the already-bound government attorney, who was also awaiting his fate.

"Do you recognize me as your mayoress?" shouted Iraidka.

"If you have a husband and can prove that he is the mayor here, I do!" the courageous deputy mayor responded firmly. The official attorney was shaking all over, as if confirming by his shaking his colleague's courage.

"You are not being asked whether I am a husband's wife or a widow, but whether you recognize me as your mayoress!" Iraidka grew still more furious.

"If you don't have clearer proofs, then I don't!" the deputy mayor responded, so firmly that the attorney clacked his teeth and tossed to all sides.

"Why talk to them! Take them to the ramparts!" Talkovnikov and his associates screamed.

There is no doubt that the fate of these officials who remained faithful to their duty would have been quite lamentable, were it not for an unforeseen circumstance that saved them. While carefree Iraidka triumphantly celebrated her victory, the dauntless staff-officer was not napping and, guided by the saying "Fight fire with fire," instructed the adventuress Klemantinka de Bourbon to claim her rights. Those rights consisted in Klemantinka's father, the chevalier de Bourbon, having once been a mayor somewhere, and having been dismissed from this post for cheating at cards. On top of that, this new pretendress was of tall stature, liked to drink vodka, and sat in a saddle like a man. Without much trouble she drew the four local veterans to her side, and, being secretly supported by the Polish intrigue, this worthless swindler won over people's minds almost instantly. The Foolsburgers again dashed to the belfry, threw Timoshka and yet another Ivashka from the ramparts, then went to Miss Chimneysweepova and razed her business to the ground, then dashed to the river again and drowned Proshka and a fourth Ivashka in it.

This was the state of affairs when the courageous sufferers were taken to the ramparts. On the way they were met by the crowd led by Klemantinka, in the middle of which the dauntless staff-officer's sleepless eye was ever on the alert. The prisoners were instantly released.

"So, you old codgers, do you recognize me as your mayoress?" asked the wayward Klemantinka.

"If you have a husband and can prove that he is our mayor, then we do!" the deputy mayor answered courageously.

"Well, God help you! Give them a spot of land for a kitchen garden! Let them grow cabbage and raise geese!" Klemantinka said meekly, and marched to the house that was Iraidka's stronghold.

A battle took place. Iraidka defended herself for a whole day and a whole night, skillfully making a human shield from the captured treasurer and accounting clerk.

"Surrender!" said Klemantinka.

"Submit, shameless wench! And calm down your curs!" Iraidka rejoined bravely. However, by the next morning Iraidka began to weaken, but only because the treasurer and the accounting clerk, filled with civic spirit, resolutely refused to defend the stronghold. The situation of the besieged became quite doubtful. Apart from the need to repulse the besiegers, Iraidka had to suppress treason in her own camp. Foreseeing eventual defeat, she decided to die a hero's death and, gathering the money she had filched from the treasury, she flew up into the air together with the treasurer and the accountant.

In the morning the deputy mayor, while planting cabbages, saw the townsfolk again congratulate one another, kiss one another, and shed tears. Some made so bold as to approach him, pat him on the shoulder, and facetiously call him a swineherd. Of course, the deputy mayor straightaway wrote all these daredevils down on a scrap of paper.

News of the "absurd and ludicrous commotion" in Foolsburg finally reached the authorities. They gave orders to locate and turn in this wayward Klemantinka, and if she had associates, they, too, were to be located and turned in. The Foolsburgers were to be very firmly ordered not to drown innocent townsfolk in the river for no reason, or to throw them off the ramparts in a beastly manner. But word of the appointment of a new mayor still had not come.

Meanwhile, things in Foolsburg became more and more embroiled. A third candidate presented herself, a Reval-born woman, Amalia Karlovna Stockfisch, whose claims were based solely on her having once been the favorite of some mayor.[6] Again the Foolsburgers dashed to the belfry, threw Semka off the rampart, and were about to send a fifth Ivashka after him, when they were stopped by the distinguished citizen Sila Terentyevich Potbelliev.

"Listen, my fine lads!" said Potbelliev, "if we go on like this, we'll kill off all the good folk and wind up nowhere!"

"Right!" agreed the fine lads, having come to their senses.

"Wait!" shouted others. "Why is Ivashka clamoring? Who told him to clamor?"

The fifth Ivashka stood on the rampart neither dead nor alive, mechanically bowing in all directions.[7]

Just then Miss Stockfisch arrived on the scene riding a white horse, in the company of six drunken soldiers leading the captured wayward Klemantinka. Miss Stockfisch was a stout blond German woman, with full breasts, ruddy cheeks, and plump cherry lips.[8] The crowd stirred.

"Look, what fat-flesh, what big ones she's got herself!" came from all sides.

But Miss Stockfisch had obviously weighed all the dangers of her position beforehand and hastened to fend them off coolheadedly.

"Listen, fine boys!" she barked, dashingly pointing at the vodka-crazed Klemantinka. "Here's this wayward Klemantinka, who's expected to be found and turned in! See her?"

"We do!" cried the crowd.

"You really see her? Do you recognize her as that same wayward Klemantinka for whom there was an order to find her and immediately turn her in?"

"We see her! We recognize her!"

"Then roll out three barrels of brew for them!" the dauntless German woman cried to the soldiers, and unhurriedly rode out of the crowd.

"That's her! That's her, our dear mother Amalia Karlovna! Now, brothers, we'll have enough drink!" the fine boys barked into the back of the departing woman.

That day the whole of Foolsburg was drunk, most of all the fifth Ivashka. The same wayward Klemantinka was put in a cage and taken to the central square; the fine boys came and teased her. Some, the more good-natured ones, treated her to vodka, but demanded that she cut some caper in return.

The ease with which the fat-fleshed German Stockfisch prevailed over the wayward Klemantinka is very easily explained.[9] As soon as Klemantinka annihilated Iraidka, she immediately locked herself up with her soldiers and gave herself to sybaritic morals. In vain did the Pans Kshepshizulski and Pshekshizulski, of whom she was a secret weapon, protest, admonish and threaten her—within five minutes Klemantinka was so drunk that she did not understand anything. The Polish gentlemen held out for a time, but seeing the uselessness of further persistence, retreated. And, indeed, that very night the oblivious Klemantinka was lifted from bed and dragged outside in her nightgown.

The dauntless staff-officer (one of the townsfolk) was in despair. All his ruses, tricks, and disguises came to precisely nothing. Total anarchy reigned in the town; there was no one in authority; the marshal of nobility fled to his country estate; the police chief and the inspector of schools together buried themselves in straw on the fire department premises and trembled. A search was announced for the staff-officer himself all over the town, with a reward of three kopecks. The townsfolk were excited, because anyone would be happy to pocket the three kopecks. He even thought maybe it would be better for him to make use of it for himself by coming to the fat German woman and pleading guilty, when suddenly an unexpected circumstance gave the situation a totally new turn.

It was easy for the German woman to manage the wayward Klemantinka, but it was far more difficult to disarm the Polish intrigue, the more so since it worked in the invisible underground way. After the crushing defeat of Klemantinka, Pans Kshepshizulski and Pshekshizulski were sadly returning home and loudly lamenting the ineptness of the Russian people, who even on such an occasion were unable to put forth a single talented person, when their attention was distracted by an apparently insignificant incident.

It was a fresh May morning with an abundance of dew coming from the sky. After the sleepless and riotous night, the Foolsburgers went to bed, and a deep silence reigned over the town. Two lads were bustling about next to a nondescript wooden house, smearing the gates with tar. Seeing the pans, they were obviously embarrassed and tried to flee, but were stopped.

"What are you doing here?" asked the pans.

"Smearing Nelka's gates with tar," confessed one of the lads. "She's been hussying around too much all over the place!"

The pans looked at each other and snorted meaningly. They went on, but a plan had already hatched in their heads. They remembered that the decrepit wooden house belonged to their compatriot Anelya Aloisievna Devilovskaya, who kept it as a boardinghouse, and although she had no right to be called a mayor's consort, she had once been summoned to a mayor. This last circumstance was perfectly sufficient for putting forth a new pretenderess and cooking up a new Polish intrigue.

For them to succeed in their intention was all the easier because just then the scope of the Foolsburgers' highhandedness had reached unprecedented dimensions. Not only did they throw off the ramparts and drown in the river dozens of the best townsfolk in one day, but they arbitrarily stopped an official at the town gates who was coming from the capital of the province on a government errand.

"Who are you? And why are you coming here?" the Foolsburgers asked the official.

"I'm the official So-and-So from the provincial capital, coming here to investigate the doings of the worthless Klemantinka!"

"He's lying! He's a spy sent by the vile Klemantinka! Drag him to the police!" shouted the fine boys.

In vain did the visitor protest and resist, in vain did he show some papers; the people did not believe anything and did not let him go.

"No, brother, we've seen whole piles of these papers, it's all empty business! And it's not right for us to deal with you, because anyone can see by your looks that you're the wayward Klemantinka's mole!" shouted some.

"Why all this trifling talk with him! Throw him into the river and there's an end to it!" shouted others.

The luckless official was taken to the police station and handed over to the officers.

Meanwhile, Amalia Stockfisch was ruling the roost. She laid a three-kopeck tax on tradesmen, and a pound of tea plus a big sugar loaf on the shopkeepers. Then she went to the barracks and offered each soldier a glass of vodka and a slice of pie with her own hands. On her way home she met the deputy mayor and the attorney, who were driving geese from a meadow with a switch.

"So, my old codgers? Have you thought better of it? Do you recognize me now?" she asked them benevolently.

"If you have a husband and can prove that he is our mayor, then we do!" the deputy mayor answered firmly.

"Well, God help you! Take care of your geese!" said the fat-fleshed German, and she walked on.

In the evening it rained so hard that for a few hours the streets of Foolsburg became impassable. Owing to that circumstance, the night went well for everyone except the wretched visiting official, who, for a reliable testing, was put in a small and dark closet, which from old had been called "the big flea farm," as opposed to a small farm, where less dangerous criminals were tested. The next morning was not favorable for the machinations of the Polish intrigue, either, because this intrigue always works in the darkness and does not bear sunlight. The fat-fleshed German woman, deceived by the quiet in the streets, decided she was well established and made so bold as to go out without an escort and began to flirt with the passersby. However, toward evening, for the sake of form, she summoned the most experienced town policemen and opened a conference. The policemen unanimously advised: first, to drown without delay that same wayward Klemantinka, to prevent her confusing and teasing people; second, to subject the deputy mayor and the attorney to torture; and third, to find and turn in the dauntless staff-officer. But so great was the blindness of this unfortunate woman that she would not hear of these strict measures and even ordered the transfer of the visiting official from the big flea farm to the small one.

Meanwhile, the Foolsburgers gradually began to come to their senses, and the forces of law and order, hiding up to then in backyards, sheepishly but with firm steps, came forth. The deputy mayor, with support from the attorney and the dauntless staff-officer, began to persuade the Foolsburgers to keep away from Klemantinka's and the German woman's perfidious charms, and return to their occupations. He sternly denounced the order owing to which the visiting official was placed in the flea farm, and predicted great woes to Foolsburg from that. At these words Sila Terentyevich Potbelliev wagged his head so anxiously that had the fine boys been a bit friskier, they would certainly have pulled the police station to pieces. On the other hand, the same wayward Klemantinka rendered no small service to the party of order . . .

The thing was that she went on sitting in the cage on the central square, and it was a sweet pleasure for the Foolsburgers to come and tease her in their time off, for this made her unspeakably ferocious, especially when they touched her body with the ends of scorching-hot iron rods.

"What, Klemantinka, isn't that sweet?" some guffawed, seeing the wayward one cringe with pain.

"And how much of our vodka the bitch guzzled up—terrible to think!" added others.

"As if it was yours I drank!" the wayward Klemantinka snarled back. "If it weren't for my unfortunate weakness, and my dear *pans* abandoning me, I'd show you what's what and how I really am!"

"The fat-fleshed one got ahead of you and showed how *she* is!"

"That's it, 'the fat-fleshed one'! I'm a mayor's daughter after all, and you've chosen a common German woman for yourselves!"

The Foolsburgers paused to think about these words of Klemantinka's. She gave them something to puzzle over.

"So, brothers, maybe this Klemantinka is wayward, but what she says is right!" said some.

"Let's go and deal with the fat-fleshed one!" clamored others.

And if the policemen had not arrived just then, it would have gone badly for the fat-fleshed one, she would have flown headfirst off the rampart! But since the policemen were stern folk, the cause of order was postponed, and the fine boys, after some more clamoring, went home.

Still, the triumph of the "free German woman" was coming to an end of itself. That night, as soon as she closed her eyes, she heard a suspicious noise outside, and at once understood that it was all over for her. In her nightgown, barefoot, she rushed to the window, to avoid at least the disgrace of being put in a cage like Klemantinka, but it was too late.

The strong arm of Pan Kshepshizulski held her firmly by the waist, while Nelka Devilovskaya, "in unprecedented fury," demanded an answer.

"Is it true, hussy Amalka, that you deceitfully usurped power and were pleased to falsely call yourself mayoress, thereby leading many simple people into temptation?" Miss Devilovskaya asked.

"True," Amalka replied, "only not deceitfully and not falsely, but I was and am a mayoress according to the most veritable truth."

"How did this ridiculous idea come into your bitchy head? And who taught you to do that, bitch that you are?" Miss Devilovskaya went on with her questioning, ignoring Amalka's response. Amalka was offended.

"Maybe there is a bitch here," she said, "only it's not me."

No matter how many questions they put to hussy Amalka after that, she was scornfully silent; no matter how they tried to get her to acknowledge her guilt, she refused to do it. A decision was taken to lock her in the cage with the wayward Klemantinka.

"Terrible was the sight," says the chronicler, "of these two wayward hussies given by a third hussy, a still more wayward one, to devour each other! Suffice it to say that by the next morning there was nothing left in the cage but their stinking bones!"

On waking up, the Foolsburgers were astonished to learn what had happened; but this did not trouble them. Again they all went out and started congratulating each other, kissing each other, and shedding tears. Some asked for the hair of the dog.

"Ah, deuce take them all!" said the dauntless staff-officer, gazing at this picture. "What are we going to do now?" he asked the deputy mayor in anguish.

"We must get to work," the deputy mayor replied. "Here's what! Why don't we spread a rumor among the people that this rogue Anelka ordered Polish churches to be put everywhere in place of our Russian ones?"

"Brilliant!"

But toward noon the rumors had grown still more alarming. Events followed one another incredibly swiftly. In a soldiers' suburb another pretenderess showed up, Dunka Fatheels, and in the streltsy's suburb the same claim was made by Matrenka Nostril. Both based their rights on having been at the mayor's more than once "for delicacies." Thus the need now was to repel not one but three mayoresses at the same time.

Both Dunka and Matrenka were unspeakably outrageous. They went into the street and knocked the heads off passersby with their fists. They went single-handedly against pothouses and demolished them. They caught young lads and hid them in the basements; they ate infants, cut women's breasts off and ate them, too. Letting their hair loose in the wind, in nothing but morning negligées, they ran around the streets of the town as if frenzied, spat, bit, and uttered unseemly words.

The Foolsburgers simply lost their minds with horror. Again they all ran to the belfry, and it is even impossible to figure out how many persons were killed and drowned there. A general trial began; everyone remembered all sorts of things about his neighbor, things that it was impossible to dream up, and since the trial procedures were brief, all the town could hear was: splash-splash-splash! By four in the afternoon the police station caught fire; the Foolsburgers ran there and were petrified, seeing that the visiting official had burned up without a trace. Again there was a trial, to investigate who had caused the crime, and it was decided that the fire was caused by that thief and wastrel the fifth Ivashka. They hoisted Ivashka on a rack, demanded a sincere admission of everything, but just at that moment the small cockroach farm caught fire in the cannoneers' suburb, and everyone dashed there, leaving the fifth Ivashka hanging on the rack. The alarm bell was sounded, but flames had already spread far and wide and burned up all the cockroaches. Then people caught Matrenka Nostril and began quite politely to drown her in the river, demanding that she tell who had prompted her, a veritable wastrel and thief, to undertake this thievery and assisted her in it. But Matrenka only produced bubbles in the water, and did not betray any associates and accomplices.

Amid all this general alarm the rogue Anelka was completely forgotten. Seeing that her enterprise did not work out, she stealthily moved back to her boardinghouse, as if she had nothing to do with anything, and Pans Kshepshizulski and Pshekshizulski set up a pastry shop and began to sell decorated gingerbreads. Only the fat-heeled Dunka remained, but there was no way of handling her at all.

"Brothers, you absolutely must get rid of her!" Sila Teren-tyevich Potbelliev admonished the fine boys.

"Sure! Just go try, deft as you are!" the fine boys responded. This was already day six of the uprising.

What took place then was moving and unprecedented. The Foolsburgers suddenly plucked up their courage and performed the modest feat of saving themselves. Having killed and drowned a whole lot of people, they had reasons to conclude that now there was not a whit of sedition left in Foolsburg. Only loyal citizens survived. Therefore they boldly looked one another in the eye, knowing that no one could be reproached for Klemantinka, or Iraidka, or Matrenka. They decided to act unanimously and to start by getting in touch with the suburbs. As might be expected, the first to step forward was the dauntless staff-officer.

"Compatriots!" he began in an emotional voice, but since his speech was a secret one, naturally no one heard it.

Nevertheless, the Foolsburgers waxed tearful and began urging him to take back the reins of government; but he firmly refused to do so before Dunka had been caught. There were sighs in the crowd, exclamations—"Ah! great are our sins!"—but the deputy mayor was unshakable.

"Fine boys! Those in whom there's any sedition left—come forth!" a voice in the crowd barked.

The crowd was silent.

"Everybody's clean?" the same voice inquired.

"Everybody! Everybody!" the crowd droned.

"Cross yourselves, brothers!"

They all crossed themselves, and a people's general campaign was announced against Dunka Fatheels.

Meanwhile, the suburbs, one after another, kept sending the most comforting messages to Foolsburg. They all unanimously agreed that sedition should be uprooted, and first of all each of them should purify his own self. The most touching message came from the suburb of Half-wits. "Therefore, brethren, test yourselves diligently," the local people wrote, "that sedition not make its nest in your hearts. Be sensible, not evil-minded before the face of the authorities, but be most diligent, most praiseworthy, and most obliging." As this message was being read, sobs were heard in the crowd, and a suburban woman, Mangy Aksinya, inflamed with great zeal, poured forty kopecks out of her purse right on the spot to make a foundation of capital for catching Dunka.

But Dunka refused to surrender. She fortified herself in the big bedbug farm, armed with a cannon, which she used like a rifle.

"What a sly dog! Such tricks with a cannon!" the Foolsburgers said, not daring to go near her.

"Ah, may the bedbugs eat you!" exclaimed others.

But the bedbugs also seemed to be on her side. She set whole hosts of them against the besiegers, who scattered in horror. They decided to defend themselves with pitch, and that seemed to work. Indeed, the bedbug sorties ceased, but it was still impossible to get near the house, because the bedbugs formed rank upon rank, and the cannon went on sowing death. They tried to set fire to the bedbug farm, but there was little unity in the actions of the besiegers, since no one wanted to take upon himself the duty of being the leader—and the attempt failed.

"Dunka, surrender! We won't lay a finger on you!" shouted the besiegers, hoping to win her over with wheedling words.

But Dunka responded with coarseness.

Thus it went on till evening. Night fell, and the sensible besiegers retreated, having left a line of patrols by the bedbug farm just in case.

It turned out, however, that the strategy with the pitch was not without consequence. Finding no food beyond the boundaries of the fortress, and roused by the smell of human flesh, the bedbugs turned inside, seeking to satisfy their bloodthirstiness. In the deep of the night Foolsburg was shaken by an unnatural scream: it was fat-heeled Dunka giving up the ghost, being eaten by the bedbugs. Her body, which was literally one wound all over, was found the next day lying in the cottage, and beside it the cannon and countless numbers of squashed bedbugs. The rest of them, as if ashamed of their deed, hid in the cracks.

This was day seven since the beginning of the uprising. The Foolsburgers exulted. But, despite the defeat of the internal enemies and the disgrace of the Polish intrigue, the fine boys were somehow uneasy, because there was neither sight nor sound of a new mayor. They loitered around town like poisoned flies, not daring to undertake anything, since they did not know how the new superior would like their recent endeavors.

At last, at two o'clock in the afternoon, he arrived. The newly appointed "veritable" mayor was the state councillor and chevalier Semyon Konstantinovich Epikurov.

He immediately came out to the rioters on the square and demanded to see the ringleaders. Stepka Loudmouth and Filka Luckless were handed over.

The new superior's wife, Lukeria Terentievna, graciously bowed on all sides.

Thus ended this worthless and ridiculous violence; it ended and has not been repeated since.

NEWS ABOUT EPIKUROV

Semyon Konstantinovich Epikurov was the mayor of Foolsburg from 1762 to 1770. A detailed description of his activity as mayor has not been found, but since it coincided with the initial and most brilliant years of Catherine's epoch, we should suppose that it was probably all but the best time of its history.

The Foolsburg Chronicler mentions the person of Epikurov three times: first in the Register of Mayors, then at the end of the report about the time of troubles, and finally when it narrates the history of Foolsburgian liberalism (see the description of Sullen-Grumble's term as mayor). These mentions all show that Epikurov was a progressive man and regarded his duties more than seriously. It must not be thought that the chronicler willingly made such a biographical omission in the history of his own town; rather, we should suppose that Epikurov's successors deliberately destroyed his biography as witnessing to much too obvious liberalism, which could serve the explorers of our history as a tempting pretext for looking for liberalism even where, in fact, there was nothing but the principle of liberal flogging.[1] This surmise is partly justified by the fact that to this day there exists in the Foolsburg archive a page evidently belonging to the full biography of Epikurov, marked up to such an extent that, despite his efforts, all the Publisher could figure out was the following: "... being of no small stature ... allowed for the firm hope that ... But overcome with horror ... was unable to fulfill ... remembering that, spent his whole life in sorrow ..." That is all. What do these mysterious words mean? Naturally, it is impossible to give a fully reliable answer to that, but if guesswork may be allowed in such an important matter, we could suppose one of two things: either that Epikurov, being of no small stature (about seven feet), was supposed to have some special talent (for instance, for pleasing women), but did not prove equal to expectations, or that he was entrusted with a certain charge which, being frightened, he did not fulfill. And then felt sad all his life.

Be that as it may, Epikurov's activity in Foolsburg was undoubtedly fruitful. The fact alone that he introduced mead and beer brewing and made mandatory the use of mustard and bay leaf proves that he was the ancestor in a direct line of those bold innovators who, seventy-five years later, fought wars in the name of potatoes.[2] But the most important undertaking of his mayorship was undoubtedly his memorandum on the necessity of establishing an academy in Foolsburg.

Luckily this memorandum has survived in its entirety and enables us to pronounce a perfectly fair and impartial judgment. The Publisher allows himself to conclude that the thoughts expounded in this document testify not only that in that distant past there were people with a right view of things, but that it could serve even now as a manual for realizing undertakings of this sort. Of course, our present-day academies have a somewhat different nature than the one Epikurov planned to give them, but since power is not in the name but in the essence implied in the project, which is none other than "the scrutiny of learning," it is obvious that as long as the need for "scrutiny" holds sway, Epikurov's project will retain all its significance as an educative document. That names are arbitrary and rarely change anything was very well proven by one of Epikurov's successors, Wartbeardin. He, too, petitioned to establish an academy and on receiving a refusal, without further reflection built a jailhouse instead. The name was different, but the proposed aim had been achieved—Wartbeardin could not wish for anything more. And who could tell whether an academy built by Wartbeardin would have existed for long and what fruit it would have borne? Maybe it would have turned out to be built on sand; maybe, instead of "scrutinizing" learning, it would have begun propagating it? All this is in the highest degree conjectural and uncertain. As for a jailhouse—that is a sure thing: it is sturdily built, and will not deviate anywhere from the line of "scrutiny."

This is the thought that Epikurov develops in his project with such indisputable clarity and consistency as, sadly, no one possesses nowadays. Of course, he was not as resolute as Wartbeardin—that is, he did not build a jailhouse instead of an academy—but resolution was not generally in his character. Should we blame him for this shortcoming? Or, on the contrary, should we see this circumstance as evidence of his inclination to constitutionalism? We leave the resolving of this question to the present-day examiners of our country's past, whom the Publisher hereby refers to the original document.

THE HUNGRY TOWN

The year 1776 arrived under the happiest auspices for Fools-burg.

For a whole six years there were no fires, no hunger, no mass epidemics, no cattle plagues, and the townsfolk—not without reason—ascribed this unprecedented well-being to the simplicity of their superior, the brigadier Pyotr Petrovich Ferdyshchenko. And indeed Ferdyshchenko was so simple that the chronicler finds it necessary to underline this quality repeatedly and with special insistence as the most natural explanation of the contentment Foolsburgers experienced during his term as mayor. He did not interfere in anything, was satisfied with moderate tributes, willingly went to the taverns to chat with the publicans, in the evening came out to the porch of his house in a greasy housecoat and played Slap-the-Nose with subordinates, ate heavy food, drank kvass, and liked to garnish his talk with the endearment "brother-buddy."

"So, brother-buddy, now you'll get it!" he would say to a townsman found at fault.

Or:

"You, brother-buddy, will have to sell your cow, since pay-ing arrears, brother-buddy, is a sacred thing!"

Naturally, after the whimsical behavior of the Marquis de Sanglotte, who flew about in the air in the town gar-den, the peaceful rule of the elderly brigadier had to seem "prosperous" and "worthy of wonder." For the first time the Foolsburgers breathed freely and realized that life "without oppression" was far better than life "with oppression."

"Never mind that he doesn't have parades and go at us with regiments," they said. "Instead, with him, the dear fel-low, we can see the light of day! You go out the gate and can stay where you are, or you can go wherever you like! And before—God help us!—all those rules we had!"

But in the seventh year of his governing, the devil got hold of Ferdyshchenko. This good-natured and somewhat lazy brigadier suddenly became active and extremely pushy: he threw off his greasy housecoat and walked around town in a uniform. He demanded that the townsfolk not gawk here and there, but keep both eyes open, and to crown it all he got into a mess that could have ended very badly for him if, in a moment of extreme vexation, it had not occurred to the Foolsburgers: "And what, dear brothers, if we get blamed for it!"

The thing was that at that time, by the exit from town, in the Dung suburb, there lived a tradesman's wife, Alena Osipovna, a woman of blossoming beauty. Apparently this woman represented the type of sweet Russian beauty which, at a glance, provokes in a man not the flame of passion, but the feeling that his whole being is slowly melting. Of me-dium height, she was full-bodied, white-skinned, and red-cheeked; her big, slightly prominent eyes were something between shameless and shy; she had plump cherry lips, thick, well-outlined eyebrows, a dark blond braid down to her heels, and had a lovely "gray-ducky" gait. Her husband, Dmitry Prokofiev, was a cabbie and a fitting match for her: young, strong, and handsome. He wore a velveteen coat and a felt hat with colorful peacock feathers. Dmitry adored his Alenka and Alenka adored her Mitka. They often went to the neighborhood tavern and happily sang songs there together. The Foolsburgers could not have enough of admiring their harmonious life.

So they lived—whether a long time or short—until, in the beginning of 1776, the tavern in which they so peacefully enjoyed their leisure time was visited by the brigadier. He came in, drank a glass of vodka, asked the tavern keeper how much the number of drunkards had increased, and happening to catch sight of Alenka, felt his tongue stick in his throat. However, he was embarrassed to announce it in public, but walked outside and beckoned to Alenka.

"Would you, good woman, come to live with me and love me?" asked the mayor.

"And what would I do with you . . . mangy one?" Alenka replied, looking at him insolently. "I have my own good husband!"

That was all they said then, but it did not go well. The next day the brigadier sent two veterans to stay in Dmitry Prokofiev's house, with orders to act "suppressively." He himself, having put on his uniform, went to the market and, to gradually accustom himself to strictness, shouted boldly at the shopkeepers:

"Who is your superior? Tell me! Maybe it's not me, but somebody else?"

Dmitry Prokofiev, for his part, instead of submitting and gently talking sense to his wife, talked uselessly, and Alenka, arming herself with an oven fork, drove the veterans out, shouting for the whole street to hear:

"Look at our mayor! Like a bedbug trying to crawl under a married woman's blanket!"

Clearly the brigadier was very upset when he learned about these words of praise. But since that was a liberal time and there was talk among the people of the advantages of the electoral principle, the old man was afraid to make personal use of his power. Gathering his favorite Foolsburgers, he gave them a brief account of the matter and demanded immediate punishment for the disobedient persons.

"You, my old buddies, who can help me if not you?" he added liberally. "As many strokes as you say, I accept it beforehand! Because ours is a time when each gets his own, as long as it's a flogging!"

The favorite ones took counsel, clamored a bit, and came up with the following answer:

"As many as there are stars in the sky, so many strokes should Your Honor appoint to instruct each of these rogues!"

The brigadier started counting the stars ("simpleton as he was," repeats the chronicler on this occasion), but having reached a hundred, he became confused and turned to his orderly for an explanation. The orderly replied that there was no end of stars in the sky.

It appears that the brigadier must have been pleased with this answer, because when Alenka and Mitka went home after the flogging they reeled as if drunk.

Still, Alenka did not calm down even now, or, as the chronicler puts it, "did not learn anything useful from the brigadier's treatment." On the contrary, she seemed to grow even more fierce, and proved it a week later, when the brigadier again came to the tavern and again beckoned to Alenka.

"So, stupid thing, have you thought better of it?" he asked.

"You've really got it bad, you old cur! Didn't you have enough just looking at my shame?" snarled Alenka.

"Very well!" said the brigadier.

However, the old man's persistence made Alenka stop and think.

Coming back home after this conversation, she was unable to do anything for a while and wandered about as if lost; then she clung to Mitka and wept bitterly.

"Looks as if, like it or not, I'm going to be the brigadier's lover!" she said, drenched in tears.

"Just go ahead! And I . . . I'll hurl your filthy scraps to the wind!" Mitka gasped, and in a rage went to the stovetop to fetch his reins, then suddenly changed his mind, shook all over, collapsed on the bench, and howled.

He shouted as loudly as he could, but what he was shouting about was impossible to tell. One could see only that the man was rebelling.

The brigadier learned that Mitka was of a mind to rebel and was twice as upset as before. The rebel was put in fetters and taken to jail. Alenka rushed like a madwoman to the brigadier's place, but could not say anything sensible, and only tore her sarafan and shouted indecently:

"Here, cur, gobble, gobble, gobble!"

Astonishingly, the brigadier not only was not offended by these words, but, on the contrary, before seeing anything, he made Alenka the present of a fancy gingerbread and a jar of pomade. Seeing these gifts, Alenka was taken aback; she did not shout, but only sniffled softly. Then the brigadier had his new uniform brought, put it on, and showed himself to Alenka in all his glory. Just then the old brigadier's housekeeper ran out and began to admonish Alenka.

"Well, what are you so sorry about, slattern, just think!"

the smooth-tongued old woman said. "The brigadier's going to bathe you in honey mead."

"Poor Mitka!" Alenka replied, but in such a hesitant voice that it was obvious she was already thinking of surrendering.

That very night a fire broke out in the brigadier's house, which, fortunately, they managed to extinguish at the very beginning. Only the archive burned, in which a pig had been placed temporarily to be fattened up for the feast. Naturally a suspicion of arson arose, and it fell upon none other than Mitka. It was learned that Mitka had gotten the jail guards drunk and had gone off during the night, no one knew where. The criminal was caught and subjected to enhanced interrogation, but, being an inveterate robber and villain, he denied everything.

"I know nothing about it," he said. "All I know is that you took my wife from me, you old cur, and I forgive you for it . . . Gobble away!"

Nevertheless they did not believe Mitka's words, and since the case was an urgent one, a simplified procedure was carried out. A month later Mitka was beaten with a knout on the square, branded, and sent to Siberia along with real thieves and robbers. The brigadier triumphed; Alenka quietly sobbed.

However, this business took its toll on the Foolsburgers. As it happens, the brigadier's sins affected them first of all.

Everything in Foolsburg now changed. The brigadier, in full uniform, ran around the shops every morning and kept snatching, snatching. Even Alenka began to snatch in passing, and suddenly, just like that, started demanding that she be considered not a cabbie's wife but a priest's daughter.

That was not all: nature itself ceased to be benevolent toward the Foolsburgers. "This new Jezebel," the chronicler says of Alenka, "brought drought upon our town." Since

the day of the spring Feast of Saint Nicholas, from the time
when the river's water level lowers, and up till Saint Elijah's
Day, not a drop of water fell.[1] The old-timers did not remember
anything like it, and, not without grounds, ascribed this
phenomenon to the brigadier's falling into sin. The sky was
torrid and poured scorching heat on everything alive; the air
was as if trembling and smelled of burning; the soil cracked
and became hard as stone, making it impossible to till it with
either plow or spade; herbs and sprouting vegetables faded;
the rye bloomed and went into ear unusually early, but was
so sparse and the grains were so small that there was no hope
of gathering enough even for seed; the spring crops did not
sprout at all, and the sown fields stood black as pitch, aggriev-
ing the eyes of the townsfolk with their hopeless nakedness;
even the goosefoot did not grow; the livestock rushed about,
lowing and mooing; finding no food in the fields, they ran to
the town and filled the streets. The people looked wretched,
as if pinched, and walked about downcast; only the potters
were glad of the good weather, but they soon changed their
minds, once they could see that there were many pots, but
nothing to cook in them.

However, unable to perceive the whole depth of the disaster before them, the Foolsburgers did not despair. As long
as the previous year's supplies lasted, many, out of light-
mindedness, ate, drank, and banqueted, as if there were no
end to the supplies. The brigadier walked about town in his
uniform, ordering very strictly that people who had "a dejected look" be taken to the police station and turned over
to him. To cheer people up, he charged the tax farmer with
organizing a picnic with fireworks in the suburban park.
The picnic took place, the fireworks were fired off, but that
"did not provide the populace with food." Then the brigadier
summoned "the favorite ones" and told them to go and cheer

the people up. The favorite ones went about the neighbor-hoods, not passing by a single dejected one without cheering him up.

"We're accustomed folk!" some said. "We're good at hold-ing out. If you put us all in a pile now and set fire to us—we won't say a word against it!"

"What's there to say!" others added. "We can hold out! Since we know we've got superiors over us!"

"What are you thinking?" still others encouraged. "You think our superiors are asleep? No, brother, maybe their one eye is sleeping, but the other one certainly sees everything!"

But when they stacked the hay, it turned out they did not have enough to feed the cattle; when they reaped the har-vest, it turned out that the people also did not have enough to eat. The Foolsburgers were frightened and started visiting the brigadier's premises.

"So then, Mister Brigadier, how about a bit of bread? Will you do it?" they asked him.

"I'm doing, dear brothers, I'm doing!" replied the briga-dier.

"That's it; give it your best!"

At the end of July useless rain poured down, and in Au-gust people started dying, because they had eaten all they had. They kept inventing food that would make them feel full; they mixed flour with chopped rye stems, but that did not make them full; they tried if it might be better mixed with ground pine bark, but they obtained no real satiety from it.

"This grub does make your stomach seem full, but it must be said, brothers: the food itself is empty!" the Foolsburgers said among themselves.

The markets were now empty; there was nothing to sell, and no one to sell it to, since the town was deserted. "Some died," says the chronicler, "some lost their minds and scattered in all directions." The brigadier, meanwhile, did not stop his lawlessness and bought Alenka a new broadcloth shawl. When the Foolsburgers learned of it, they were alarmed, and a whole crowd of them barged into the brigadier's yard.

"This isn't right, Brigadier, you living with a woman you took from her husband!" they said to him. "The authorities didn't send you here to make us suffer calamities for your folly!"

"Hold out, dear brothers! There'll be enough of everything!" the brigadier tried to dodge.

"So, then, we agree to hold out! We're accustomed folk! But you think about what we say, Brigadier, because who knows: hold out we will, but some foolish fellows may turn up amongst us! Anything can happen!"

The crowd dispersed peacefully, but the brigadier fell to thinking. He himself saw that Alenka was the source of all the evil, but he was unable to part with her. He sent for the priest, hoping to find consolation in talking with him, but the priest upset him still more by telling the story of Ahab and Jezebel.

"And until the dogs tore her to pieces, all the people kept dying!" the priest concluded his story.

"Come on, Father! I can't give Alenka to the dogs!" said the frightened brigadier.

"I don't mean that!" the priest explained, "though it won't hurt to think about the following: our flock are all indifferent people, earnings are small, food is expensive . . . where can a priest get anything, Mister Brigadier?"

"Oh! God has punished me for my sins!" the brigadier moaned and wept bitterly.

And so he sat down to write; he wrote a lot, he wrote everywhere.

He reported thus: if there is no bread, then at least send

soldiers. But he was not granted any response from anywhere to any of his letters.

And the Foolsburgers were getting more and more importunate from day to day.

"Well, Brigadier, have you received an answer?" they asked him with unheard-of insolence.

"I haven't, brothers dear!" answered the brigadier. The Foolsburgers looked him in the eye in their "absurd way" and wagged their heads.

"You're mangy, that's what!" they reproached him. "That's why they don't reply to you, vermin that you are! You're not worthy!"

In short, the questions of the Foolsburgers were becoming ticklish as could be. There comes a moment when the belly begins to speak, and all reasoning and subterfuge are powerless.

"True, I'll get nowhere with these folks by persuasion," the brigadier reflected. "I need one of two things: either bread or . . . soldiers, not persuasion!"

Like all good superiors, the brigadier allowed for this last idea only with regret; but it gradually sank in so much that he not only mixed soldiers with bread, but even began to wish for the first more than the last.

The brigadier would get up early in the morning, sit down by the window, and listen: wouldn't the sound come from somewhere: rooty-toot, rooty-toot?

> *Scatter, boys!*
> *Hide behind the stones, the bushes!*
> *Two in a row!*

No! No sound came!

"As if God has forgotten our parts!" the brigadier would say. And meanwhile, the Foolsburgers lived on and on.

The young ones all scattered. "They ran and ran," says the chronicler, "and many of them did not get anywhere and perished; many were caught and put in jail; those considered themselves lucky." Only old people and small children who had no legs for running stayed home. At first things eased up for those who remained, because the rations of those who had left slightly increased the rations of the rest. Thus they lived for another week, then again began to die. Women howled, churches were filled with coffins, the corpses of the lowborn lay about in the streets unburied. The infected air was hard to breathe; there was a fear that famine would combine with plague. To prevent this evil they formed a committee at once, wrote a project to set up a makeshift hospital for ten beds, plucked lint, and sent a report to all places. But, despite these visible signs of administrative care, the hearts of the townsfolk were already hardened. Not an hour went by without someone showing the brigadier a fig, calling him "mangy," "vermin," and so on.

To crown the calamity the Foolsburgers became reasonable. Following a seditious custom established from time immemorial, they gathered by the belfry, began to fuss and discuss, and in the end chose from among themselves a spokesman—the oldest man in town, Evseich. They spent a long time bowing down to each other, the people to Evseich and Evseich to the people: the people asked him to do them a service, and he asked them to spare him. Finally the people said:

"You, Evseich, have lived so many years, have seen so many superiors, and you're still living!"

That was more than Evseich could bear.

"I've lived many years!" he cried, suddenly flaring up. "I've seen many superiors! I'm alive!"

He said it and wept. "His old heart leaped in him, and

he prepared to serve," adds the chronicler. Evseich became a spokesman and in his heart decided to tempt the brigadier three times.

"Do you know, Brigadier, that we orphans, the whole town of us, are dying?" So he began his first temptation.

"I do," the brigadier replied.

"And do you know whose worthless thievery caused such a thing to happen to us?"

"No, I don't."

The first temptation was over. Evseich returned to the belfry and gave a detailed report to the people. "The brigadier, seeing such harshness in Evseich, was very frightened," the chronicler tells us.

Three days later Evseich came to the brigadier a second time, "but now he had lost his former firm look."

"With justice I'll live well anywhere!" he said. "If my cause is right, you may send me even to the end of the earth—there, too, I'll be well with justice!"

"True, you can live well with justice," the brigadier replied, "only here is what I'll tell you: it would be better for you, old man that you are, to sit at home with your justice, rather than call down trouble on your head!"

"No! I'm not going to sit at home with justice, because our mother justice is fidgety! You think of getting home and into a warm bed, and she, mother justice, is driving you out . . . that's what!"

"Well, then! I'm not against it! Only there's a chance that you and your justice are kicking against the pricks!"

The second temptation was over. Evseich again returned to the belfry and gave another detailed report to the people. "And the brigadier, seeing that Evseich needlessly discussed justice, now feared him less than before," adds the chronicler. In other words, Ferdyshchenko realized that if a man begins a roundabout talk about justice, it means he is not quite sure he will not be flogged for this same justice.

After another three days, Evseich came to the brigadier the third time and said:

"And do you know, old cur—"

But before he had time to properly open his mouth, the brigadier, in his turn, barked:

"Put the fool in fetters!"

They dressed Evseich in prisoner's garb and led him, "like a bride going to meet her bridegroom," to the police station, accompanied by two old veterans. As the procession moved on, the crowds of Foolsburgers stepped back, making way for them.

"Never fear, Evseich, never fear!" came from the crowd. "You'll live well anywhere with justice."

He bowed to all sides, saying:

"Forgive me, fine boys, if I offended anyone, and if I sinned before anyone, and if I said an unjust word to anyone . . . forgive me everything!"

"God will forgive!" the people responded.

"And if I was rude to the superiors . . . and if I was an instigator . . . forgive me that, for Christ's sake!"

"God will forgive!"

From that moment on old Evseich vanished as if he had never existed, vanished without a trace, as only the zealots of the Russian land are able to vanish. Even so, the brigadier's severity was only temporarily effective. For a few days the town grew quieter, but since there was still no bread ("No need is more grievous!" says the chronicler), willy-nilly the Foolsburgers again had to gather by the belfry. From his porch the brigadier watched this Foolsburgian "rebellious frenzy," thinking: "Shoot some now—paf-paf-paf—and that's it for them!" But the Foolsburgers were beyond rebelling. They gathered and quietly began to discuss how "to provide for themselves," but, unable to think up anything new, they again elected a spokesman.

The new spokesman, Pakhomych, looked at the matter differently than his unfortunate predecessor. He realized that the surest thing now was to begin writing petitions to all places.

"I know a little fellow," he said to the Foolsburgers. "Maybe we should first go and beg for his help?"

Most of them were happy to hear that. However great their "want," they all felt relieved at the thought that there was somewhere a man who was ready "to be zealous" on their behalf. That they could not do without "zeal" they all realized; but to each of them it seemed far more suitable that someone else be "zealous" for him. Therefore the crowd was just about to move ahead and follow Pakhomych's advice when the question arose of where to go: to the right or to the left. Those of the party of restraint took advantage of this moment of indecision.

"Wait, fine boys!" they said. "What if the brigadier just thrashes us on account of this man? Let's find out beforehand who the man is?"

"This is a man who knows all the ins and outs! A hard-boiled fellow, in short!" Pakhomych reassured them.

On closer look it turned out that the "little fellow" was none other than the retired clerk Bogolepov, dismissed from service "for the tremor of his right hand," which tremor was caused by drink. He lived somewhere "on the swamp" in the dilapidated hut of a town wench nicknamed "the nanny goat" and "a public cup" for her frivolity. He had no real occupation, and was busy day and night writing pettifogging letters, steadying his right hand with his left. There was no other information about "the little fellow," and apparently there was no need for it, because the majority were predisposed beforehand to trust him unconditionally.

Nevertheless, the question of the "restrainers" was not wasted. When the crowd finally moved according to Pakhomych's directions, several persons separated themselves and went straight to the brigadier's quarters. A schism took place. The so-called "fallen away" appeared, that is, the farsighted ones whose task was to preserve their backs from anticipated future commotions. Those "fallen away" came to the brigadier's premises, yet did not say anything, but just shuffled about there a little so as to witness.

However, in spite of the schism, the thing undertaken "on the swamp" took its course.

Bogolepov pondered for a moment, as if needing to push the old drunkenness out of his head. But this was a momentary pondering. Following which he quickly took a pen out of an ink-stand, sucked on it, spat, clutched his right hand with his left, and began to scribble:

To All Places of the Russian Empire

We, the lowliest and most suffering people of all estates and ranks inhabiting the most unfortunate town of Foolsburg beg the following points:

(1) We hereby inform all places and persons of the Russian Empire: we orphans are dying, all of us to a man. The superiors we see around us are inefficient, strict in exacting taxes, unhurried in providing assistance. And we also inform you: the cabbie's wife Alenka, who is with that brigadier Ferdyshchenko, is undoubtedly the source of all our calamities, and we see no other reason. While Alenka lived with her

husband Mitka the cabbie, everything was quiet in our town and we lived in plenty. Although we accept to suffer longer, we have an apprehension: if we all die, the brigadier and his Alenka may slander us before the authorities and present us as dubious.

(2)   There are no more points.

To this petition the illiterate people of the town of Foolsburg put two hundred and thirty crosses by way of signatures.

When this petition was read and signed with crosses, everyone felt easier at heart. They put the letter in an envelope, sealed it, and sent it in the mail.

"See it trudging!" the old men said, watching the troika carrying their petition into the unknown distance. "Now, fine boys, we won't have to hold out for long!"

And indeed the town again became quiet; the Foolsburgers did not think of any new riots, but sat by the gates waiting. When passersby asked how things were, they answered:

"Now our business is assured! We've sent a petition, brother!"

But a month went by, then another—there was no resolution. The Foolsburgers went on living, went on chewing something. Their hopes were growing and acquired greater probability with every new day. Even the "fallen away" began to be convinced that their apprehensions were mistaken and insisted on being written down as instigators. Quite possibly this would have ended by wearing everyone out, if the brigadier had not stirred up public opinion by his administrative ineptitude. Deceived by the ostensible peacefulness of the townsfolk, he found himself in a most ticklish situation. On the one hand he sensed that there was nothing he could do;

on the other hand he also sensed that it was impossible to do nothing. Therefore he undertook something in between, something that partly resembled the game of jackstraws. He would get his hook into the thick of things, fish out a malefactor, and jail him. Then he would do it again, fish out another one, and again jail him. And all the while he wrote and wrote. The first one to be jailed was, of course, Bogolepov, who in his fright denounced a whole lot of malefactors. Each of those, in turn, denounced a lot of other malefactors. The brigadier luxuriated in it, but the Foolsburgers were not only not frightened, but laughed and said among themselves: "What's this new game the old cur has started?"

"Wait!" they reasoned. "The paper's going to come!" But the paper would not come, and the brigadier was weaving and weaving his net and gradually weaved it until the whole town was caught in it. Nothing is more dangerous than roots and threads, when the authorities get hold of them.[2] With the help of the two veterans, the brigadier fettered and dragged to jail almost the entire town, so that there was no household left without one or two malefactors.

"This way, brothers, he'll guilt us all!" the Foolsburgers figured, and this apprehension was enough to pour more oil into the dying fire.

All at once, without any preliminary arrangement, the hundred and fifty "crosses" that had escaped the brigadier's claws turned up on the square ("the fallen away" again wisely disappeared), and reaching the brigadier's house, they stopped.

"Hand over Alenka!" the crowd droned.

The brigadier realized that matters had gone too far, and he had nothing left but to hide in the archive. He did just that. Alenka rushed after him, but, as chance would have it, the door of the archive slammed shut the moment the brigadier crossed its threshold. The lock clicked, and Alenka remained outside with her arms spread wide. In this pose she was found by the crowd, found pale, her whole body trembling, all but crazed.

"Have pity, fine boys, on my fair body!" Alenka said in a voice weak with terror. "You know that he took me from my husband by force!"

But the crowd no longer heard anything.

"Tell us, witch," they boomed, "how did you bring drought on our town with your witchcraft?"

Alenka was beside herself. She thrashed about and, as if sure of her inevitable end, only repeated: "Wretched me! Oh Lord, wretched me!"

Then an unheard-of thing happened. They carried Alenka, like a feather, to the top tier of the belfry and threw her down onto the rampart from a height of more than a hundred feet . . .

"And not a shred remained of the brigadier's sweet joy. In the twinkling of an eye, hungry stray dogs tore her up."

And just as this senseless, bloody drama was taking place, a thick cloud of dust arose far down the road.

"Bread is coming!" cried the Foolsburgers, instantly going from fury to joy.

"Rooty-toot! Rooty-toot!" sounded clearly from within the cloud of dust . . .

Come running
In a column!
Bayonets, clang!
Quick! quick! quick!

The Straw Town

The town had barely begun to recover when a new flightiness descended upon the brigadier: he was seduced by the accursed musketeer girl Domashka.[1]

At the time the musketeers were no longer those pre-Peter musketeers, but they still remembered a thing or two. Their sullen and somewhat sarcastic ways yielded with difficulty to the civilizing efforts of the authorities, however much the latter tried to bring it home to them that ruckus and sedition can in no way be tolerated as a "permanent occupation." The musketeers lived in a separate suburban settlement, named Musketeers' after them, and at the opposite end of town was the Cannoneers' suburb, inhabited by Peter's disgraced cannoneers and their descendants. However, common disgrace did not unite these people, and the two suburbs constantly warred with each other. It seemed there were some old accounts between them that they were unable to forget and which each side formulated thus: "Were it not for your mutual thievery then, we would be enjoying life in Mother Moscow to this day." These accounts surfaced particularly during the mowing season. Each suburb owned its special meadows, but the boundaries of these meadows were defined thus: "In the hollow 'where Long Pyotr was flogged' there's a wedge of land and that by two." Every year around Saint Peter's Day[2] both musketeers and cannoneers came to this place; first they sensibly looked for some gully, some brook, and also some crooked birch tree that had been a very clear boundary sign, but had been cut down thirty years earlier; then, having found nothing, they would start talking about "thievery" and end by gradually applying the scythes. Serious massacres took place, but the Foolsburgers were so used to this phenomenon that they were not in the least embarrassed by it. Later on the authorities became worried and ordered the scythes taken away. There was no mowing, and the cattle began to die of hunger. "There was no gain for the musketeers or the cannoneers, but only great glee for the land surveyors," adds the chronicler on this occasion.

Ferdyshchenko personally showed up at one of these massacres with a fire pump and a barrel of water. At first he took charge very actively and even sent a big jet of water at the fighters; but when he saw Domashka working in nothing but her shift at the head of everybody, hay-fork in her hands, his "malignant" heart was so inflamed that he instantly forgot both the force of his oath and the purpose of his arrival. Instead of gradually reinforcing the water-pouring tactics, he most calmly sat down on a hammock and, smoking his pipe, struck up a piquant conversation with the surveyors. Thus he sat, devouring Domashka with his eyes, till evening, when the gathering darkness forced the fighting sides to go home.

The musketeer girl Domashka was of a completely different kind than Alenka. As much as the latter was smooth and feminine in all her movements, so the former was abrupt, resolute, and masculine. Unwashed, disheveled, bedraggled, she was a typical hellcat, casually cursing and using any occasion to adorn her speech with some obscene gesture. From morning till evening her voice rang out in the suburb, cursing and invoking all sorts of evil, and ceasing only when vodka calmed her to the point of unconsciousness.

The young musketeers pursued her with passion, though without hostility among themselves, and generally everybody called her "a sugar bowl" and "an open road." The cannoneers feared her, but secretly lusted after her as well. She was extraordinarily bold. She seemed to accost you directly, as if saying: "Come on, let's see if you can subdue me"—and, of course, it was flattering to prove to this "termagant" that you could "subdue" her. She was careless about her dress, as if she felt instinctively that her power was not in colorful sarafans, but in that inexhaustible stream of youthful shamelessness which broke out irrepressibly in her every movement. Rumor had it that there was a husband, but since she rarely spent nights at home but slept in barns and sheds, and had no children besides, this husband of hers was completely forgotten, as if she had come into this world as everybody's wench and a barren one besides.

But in fact it was precisely this altogether brazen ignoring of all conventions that attracted the "malignant" heart of the finicky old man. Alenka's sweet, melting shamelessness was forgotten; he needed a more acute excitement, more capable of affecting his old, somnolent sensuality. "We've tried a sweet wench," he said to himself, "now let's try a shrewish one." And, having said this, he dispatched a police officer to the Musketeers' suburb, providing him, for form's sake, with a register. The officer found Domashka drunk, lying behind the kitchen garden, by a barn, surrounded by a crowd of young musketeers. Hearing a request to present herself, she was as if astonished, but since in fact she did not care, and to her "one horse is as good as another," after a moment's hesitation she started getting up to follow the policeman. But the musketeers protested and took the wench away from him.

"That's much too sweet for him!" they shouted. "First he takes Alenka away from Mitka, and now he's of a mind to take a woman from our people's communality!"

The brigadier certainly ought to have been ashamed this time, but he was as if possessed. He ran around town like a madman, shouting and screaming. Of no benefit to him were the lessons of the past or the remorse of his own conscience, which clearly warned the inflamed old man that it was not he who would have to pay for his sins, but the same totally innocent Foolsburgers. No matter how the musketeer boys protested, no matter how Domashka herself insisted that she "dared not go against the people's communality," force got the upper hand as usual. The brigadier had the stubborn wench whipped twice, and twice she quite steadfastly endured the undeserved punishment, but the third time she surrendered . . .

Then the cannoneers stepped forth and started pestering and mocking the musketeers for failing to defend their woman against the brigadier's knouts. "The cannoneers were stupid," explains the chronicler. "They were unable to understand that while laughing at the musketeers, they were laughing at themselves." But the musketeers were beyond explaining the actions of the cannoneers by stupidity or some other reason. Like all mortally insulted people who are unable to take revenge on the direct culprit, they vented their anger on those who reminded them of it. There were fights, outrages, and injuries; they fought one to one and band to band, and it was the town that suffered most of all from that hatred, being situated exactly in between the warring sides. The brigadier no longer listened to anything or paid attention to anything. He took Domashka up to his quarters, and celebrated the first day of his triumph by getting dead drunk together with the new victim of his sensuality . . .

A new and terrible calamity was not slow in befalling the town . . .

The fire began on July 7, the eve of the feast of the Kazan Mother of God.

Until the first days of July things could not have been better. There were occasional rains, and they were so gentle, warm, timely that everything that could grow grew with extraordinary speed, swelled and ripened, as if brought out of the depth of the earth by magic. But then came the heat and the drought, which were also beneficent, because this was the time for the field work. The people rejoiced, hoping for an abundant harvest, and hastened with the work.

In the morning of the 6th the holy fool Arkhipushko came out to the marketplace, stood in the middle, and began to wave his homespun shirt in the wind.[3]

"I'm burning! I'm burning!" the holy fool shouted.

The old men who were chatting next to him fell silent, surrounded him, and asked:

"Where, dear man?"

But the prophet muttered something incoherent.

"A musket shoots, scorching with fire, stifling with stench and smoke. You'll see the sword of fire, hear the voice of an archangel . . . I'm burning!"

They could not get anything else from him, because, having uttered this nonsense, the holy fool vanished at once (as if falling through the earth), and no one ventured to stop the blessed man. Nevertheless, the old men fell to thinking.

"He mentioned a musket!" they said, nodding in the direction of the Musketeers' suburb.

But this was not the end. Before an hour was out, the holy fool Anisyushka appeared on the same marketplace. She carried a tiny bundle in her hands and, sitting amidst the market, began to dig a hole in the ground with her finger. The old men surrounded her, too.

"What are you doing, Anisyushka? What's this hole you're digging?" they asked.

"Burying my fineries!" the blessed woman replied, looking at the inquirers with a mindless smile, as if frozen on her face since the day she was born.

"Why bury it? No one's going to profit from a godly woman like you."

But the blessed fool muttered:

"Burying my fineries . . . eight ribbons . . . eight scraps of cloth . . . eight silk kerchiefs . . . eight golden cuff links . . . eight ruby earrings . . . eight emerald rings . . . eight amber necklaces . . . eight strings of pearls . . . the ninth—a crimson ribbon . . . hee-hee!" she laughed her quiet, infantile laugh.

"Lord God! What's coming!" the frightened old men whispered.

They turned and saw the brigadier, totally drunk, looking at them from the window, unable to bring out a word. And Domashka drawing on his face with a piece of charcoal.

"An ill wind has brought us this hungry cur again!" people were about to say, but the brigadier seemed to guess their thoughts and bawled in a voice not his own:

"More rioting? Didn't catch on last time?"

With heavy hearts the Foolsburgers trudged home, and that day there was no laughter, no singing, no talking in the streets.

The next morning the weather took a turn for the worse; but the work was urgent (the beginning of the harvest), and everybody went to the fields. The work went sluggishly.

Whether because it was the eve of the feast, or because everybody was oppressed by some vague premonition, people moved as if in sleep. So it went on till five o'clock, when they began to leave for home, to dress for the vigil. Toward seven in the evening the bells began to ring, and the streets were filled with motley crowds. There was only one cloud in the sky, but the wind was growing stronger, intensifying the general premonitions. Before the third bell-ringing the sky became completely overcast, and there was such a deafening roll of thunder that all the churchgoers shuddered. The first roll was followed by a second, then a third; then the sound of an alarm came from somewhere, not too close. People poured out of all the churches at once. They crowded, crushing one another in the doorways, especially the women, who bewailed their lives and property in advance. The Cannoneers' suburb was burning, and from there a whole wall of sand and dust was blowing in the direction of the crowd.

Although it was just eight o'clock, the sky was so covered with thunderclouds that it was totally dark outside. Above was a black, boundless abyss, cross-cut by lightning; the air around was filled with swirling atoms of dust—it all presented an unimaginable chaos, and a terrible background against which there was a no less terrible silhouette of the fire. One could see people stirring in the distance, and it seemed as if they were unconsciously swarming in one place and not rushing about in anguish and despair. One could see wisps of burning straw torn off the roofs and whirling in the air, making the impression of some fantastic spectacle and not the bitterest of evils the unconscious forces of nature produce in such abundance. Gradually, one after another, the wooden buildings caught fire and as if melted away. In one place the fire was in full play; the whole building was engulfed by the flames, and its size diminished with every minute, and the silhouette acquired some fanciful forms, chiseled and gnawed out by the terrible element.

Now another bright dot flashed to the side, was covered by thick smoke; a moment later a fiery tongue surfaced among its billows; then the tongue again disappeared, again surfaced—and gathered strength. A new dot, another dot . . . first black, then bright orange; a whole pattern of shining dots forms, and then—a real sea, in which all separate detail is drowned, and which spins within its shores by its own power and produces its own crackle, roar, and hiss. You cannot tell what is burning here, what is weeping, what is suffering; everything here is burning, everything is weeping, everything is suffering . . . You cannot even hear any separate moans.

People moaned only in the first moments, when, beside themselves, they ran to the scene of the fire. They remembered everything that used to be dear to them: everything they cherished, warmed, clung to, everything that helped them to reconcile with life and bear its burden. So used is man to these eternal idols of his soul, for so long he has placed his best hopes in them, that the possibility of losing them has never presented itself clearly to his mind. And now comes the moment when this thought appears not as an abstract phantom, not as the fruit of a frightened imagination, but as a naked reality against which there cannot be any protests. At the first encounter with this reality, a human being cannot endure the pain that strikes him; he moans, stretches out his arms, complains, and swears, but at the same time there is still hope that the evil may pass by. But once he is certain that the evil has already been accomplished, his feelings suddenly calm down, and one desire alone settles in his heart— the desire for silence. A man comes to his house, he sees that it is shot through with light, that thin fiery snakes crawl out from all the cracks, and he begins to realize that this is that very *end of everything* which he used to imagine only vaguely, and the expectation of which, imperceptibly for his own self, permeated his whole life. What is left to be done? What can he still undertake? He can only say to himself that the past is over and that he has to begin something new, something he would willingly avoid, but which cannot be gotten rid of, because it will come of itself and will be called "tomorrow."

"Are you all here?" a woman's voice comes from the crowd. "One, two . . . where's Nikolka?"

"I'm here, Mommy," prattles the frightened child, hiding behind his mother's sarafan.

"Where's Matrenka?" a voice comes from another place. "Matrenka stayed in the cottage!"

To this call a lad steps forth from the crowd and rushes headlong into the flames. An agonizing minute passes, then another. Beams collapse one by one, the ceiling is cracking. At last the lad appears amidst the clouds of smoke; his hat and jacket are smoldering, his arms are empty. A scream of "Matrenka! Matrenka! Where are you?" follows; then come words of comfort, accompanied by suggestions that Matrenka probably got frightened and hid in the kitchen garden . . .

Suddenly to one side, from within an empty shed, comes an inhuman scream, which makes this panic-stricken crowd cross themselves and cry out: "Lord, save us!" All or almost all the people rush in the direction of this shout. The barn had only just caught fire, but it was already impossible to go near it. Fire took over the wattle walls, twined around each twig, and in one minute turned the dark smoking mass into a glowing, brightly transparent fire. A man could be seen inside, rushing here and there, tearing off his shirt, scratching his chest with his nails, then suddenly stopping and stretching tall, as if inhaling. Sparks could be seen spraying onto him, as if pouring, then his hair caught fire; he tried to put it out, then suddenly started spinning in one place . . .

"Good Lord! That's Arkhipushko!" people finally made him out.

Indeeed it was he. Surrounded by the glowing brushwood, his dark, semi-savage figure looked luminous. In people's eyes he was not the dirty Arkhipushko with the wandering dull gaze, as they usually saw him, not Arkhipushko in the throes of death, struggling strengthlessly, like any other mortal, against the imminent end, but some sort of an enthusiast wearying under the burden of an overflowing rapture.

"Open the door, Arkhipushko! Open it, dear man!" people cried from a distance, pitying him.

But Arkhipushko did not hear them and went on spinning and shouting. Obviously he already had difficulty breathing. Finally the posts supporting the straw roof burned down. A whole cloud of flame and smoke collapsed on the ground, engulfed the man, and whirled. The glowing point turned back into a dark one; everybody instinctively crossed themselves . . .

The cannoneers had barely come to their senses after that spectacle when something new horrified them: the bells in the cathedral belfry hummed and the biggest of them crashed to the ground. They rushed there, and seeing that their whole suburb was already in flames, began to think of saving themselves. The crowd of people left without a roof, food, and clothing, thronged to the town, but there, too, they met with general turmoil. Although it was obvious that the flames had taken everything they could, for the townsfolk watching the fire from across the river it looked as if the fire was growing and the glow was getting brighter and brighter. The air was all filled with the luminous mass, in which the separate dots of faggots and burning wisps of straw spun and whirled. "Where will they fly to? Who will they fall upon?" wondered the petrified townsfolk.

This question caused general panic; everyone rushed to his own house to save his possessions. The streets were clogged with carts and walking people, packed and loaded with household chattels. The string of them moved hastily but without any special noise toward the common and, having gone a safe distance from the town, began to settle. At that moment a long-awaited rain came down and dissolved the quickly yielding black soil of the common.

Meanwhile, the cannoneers stopped at the town square and decided to wait for morning. Some Bible-lover began to sing "By the Waters of Babylon," burst into tears, and was unable to finish;[4] someone mentioned the name of the musketeer woman Domashka, but no response came to that. Everyone seemed to forget about the brigadier, though some insisted they had seen him hanging around with the only fire pump, trying to protect the priest's house. The priest was right there with everybody and murmured:

"We have transgressed!" he repeated.

"You, long skirt, you should have prayed to God more and lolled less with your wife!" came an immediate answer, and the conversation never returned to this subject.

By morning the fire was indeed dying down, partly because there was nothing left to burn, partly because of the pouring rain. The cannoneers trudged back to the scene of the fire and saw heaps of ashes and charred beams with fire smoldering under them. They found some hooks, brought a pump from the town, and began unhurriedly to take away what still could be of use and to extinguish the burning remnants. Each of them rummaged by his house, looking for things; many did find things and crossed themselves.

It turned out that some dozen persons had burned up, two adults among them. The girl Matrenka they had talked about the previous night was found sleeping in the kitchen garden between the beds. The day gradually took on its usual working shape. Few people counted their losses; each tried first of all to determine not what he had lost, but what he still had. One had an untouched cellar, and rejoiced that there was some kvass and a previous day's loaf of bread in it. Another man's barn with a cow locked in it by some miracle had been spared by the fire.

"Attagirl, Brownie! Smart girl!" they praised her.

The townsfolk, too, began little by little to return to their dens from the forced encampment; but that did not last. Around noon an alarm sounded again at the Church of Elijah the Prophet on the Swamp. The fire began at the barn of that "nanny goat" with whom the chronicler acquainted us in his story of the clerk Bogolepov. There was a surmise that Bogolepov, being drunk, was smoking his pipe and a spark fell into the hay dust; but since he himself happened to have burned up, this surmise was never pursued and made known. In fact, the fire was not very important, and could easily have been stopped, but people were so worn out and shaken by the events of the last sleepless night that the word "fire!" was enough to cause a new general panic. Everybody again rushed to their houses, picked up whatever they could, and ran to the common. Meanwhile, the fire kept growing.

We will not describe the further vicissitudes of this calamity, the less so as they are quite similar to those we have described above. Let us say only that the town was burning for two days and during this time two neighborhoods burned down completely: the Swamp and Naughties, so called because it was inhabited by soldiers' wives who practiced a shameful trade.[5] Only on the third day, when the fire began to approach the cathedral and the merchants' arcades, did the Foolsburgers come to their senses somewhat. Urged by the mutinous musketeers, they set forth from the camp, and the crowd of them came to the mayor's house and asked Ferdyshchenko to come out.

"Are we going to be burning for long?" they asked him, when, after some hesitation, he appeared on the porch.

But the shifty brigadier only hemmed and hawed and said that he could not argue with God.[6]

"We don't mean that you should argue with God," insisted the Foolsburgers. "Mangy as you are, how can you go against God! Just tell us this: for whose outrages should we orphans now be dying?"

Then suddenly the brigadier became ashamed. His heart was aflame with great regret, and he stood before the Foolsburgers and shed tears. ("And those tears of his were all crocodile tears," anticipates the chronicler.)

"Weren't all your last year's tortures enough for us? Haven't enough of us suffered death from your stupidity and your knout?" the Foolsburgers went on, seeing that the brigadier was repentant. "Think better, old man! Leave off your foolishness!"

Then the brigadier knelt before all the people and began to repent. ("And his repentance was like a viper's," again anticipates the chronicler.)

"Forgive me, for Christ's sake, fine boys!" he said, bowing to the ground before the people. "I abandon my foolishness forever and ever, and I'll hand over this foolishness of mine into your own hands! Only, for Christ's sake, don't do her any violence, but take her honorably to the Musketeers' suburb!"

And, having said that, he brought Domashka out to the crowd. The Foolsburgers saw the perky wench and gasped. She stood before them the same as ever: unwashed, uncombed—she stood with a drunken smile wandering over her face. And they liked this Domashka so much, so much that words could not tell.

"Greetings to you, Domashka!" the townsfolk barked as one man.

"Hello there! Have you come to free me?" responded Domashka.

"Are you willing to come back to our communality?"

"With the greatest pleasure!"

They took Domashka under the arms and brought her to the same barn from which she had been taken by force some time before.

The musketeers rejoiced, ran around the streets, banged on pots and pans, and shouted their usual war cry:

"We've shamed him! We've shamed him!"

There began a great rejoicing and cheer among the Foolsburgers. Everybody felt the burden fall from their hearts, and from now on there was nothing else to do but prosper. With the brigadier at their head, the townsfolk went to meet the fire and within a few hours dismantled a whole street of houses and dug a deep ditch around the fire on the side of the town. The next day the fire died out of itself, owing to a lack of nourishment.

But it was not without reason that the chronicler anticipated the events with insinuations: the brigadier's tears indeed turned out to be crocodile, and his repentance was that of a viper. As soon as the danger was over, he sat down in his office and began to write reports to all places. For ten hours in a row he dipped his pen into an inkstand, and the more he dipped, the more venomous it became.

"This July 10th," he wrote, "a great riot of all Foolsburg citizens against me took place. On the occasion of the great fire that happened in the village of Naughties, people of all estates gathered in my, the brigadier's, premises and began forcing me to kneel before them, so that I would ask forgiveness before those worthless people. I fearlessly declined to do so. And it is my thinking now: if these worthless people are condoned now and tolerated in the future, could it not be repeated and become less amenable to calming down?"

Having written this, the brigadier sat by the window and began waiting to hear the approaching rooty-toot! rooty-toot! But at the same time he was pleasant and friendly, so that he even charmed them by his amiability.

"My dear, darling people!" he said to them. "Why are you so angry with me? As God took, so He will give again! He is the King of Heaven, He has mercy in abundance! That's how it is, brothers dear!"

Occasionally, however, some sort of dubious smile appeared on his face that did not bode anything good . . .

And so one bright morning a cloud of dust appeared on the road, which, gradually approaching, finally came close to Foolsburg.

Rooty-toot! rooty-toot! clearly sounded from inside the mysterious cloud.

> *Horns sound!*
> *Now's the time*
> *To beat the enemy!*

The Foolsburgers froze.

A Fantastic Traveler

The Foolsburgers had barely recovered, when the brigadier's frivolity all but brought a new calamity upon them.

Ferdyshchenko decided to travel.

This was a very strange intention, since Ferdyshchenko's whole domain consisted of the town common, which did not contain any treasures either on the surface of the earth or in its bosom. Of course there were heaps of dung in various places, but even in the archaeological respect they did not represent anything remarkable. "To travel where and with what purpose?" All sensible people asked themselves this question, but they were unable to answer it adequately. Even the brigadier's housekeeper—even she was greatly perplexed when Ferdyshchenko announced his intention to her.

"What's this urge to go wandering?" she said. "You'll get stuck in the first pile you come upon! Stop this mischief, for Christ's sake!"

But the brigadier stood firm. He imagined that the grass would become greener and the flowers would blossom brighter as soon as he drove out to the common. "The fields will get fat, the rivers will flow abundantly, the boats will race, the cattle will multiply, routes of communication will turn up," he muttered to himself, and cherished his plan like the apple of his eye. "He was a simple man," explains the chronicler, "so simple that even with so many troubles he did not lose his simplicity."

Obviously, in this he imitated his patron and benefactor, who was also fond of driving around (in the brief register of mayors, Ferdyshchenko is mentioned as a former orderly of Prince Potemkin) and liked to be fêted everywhere.

A vast plan was drawn up: first to go to one corner of the common; then, cutting across it, to descend to the other corner; then to wind up in the middle; then again to go straight, and then wherever your feet take you. To receive congratulations and gifts everywhere.

"Look out!" he said to the inhabitants. "As soon as you see me, start banging on pans at once, and start congratulating me as if I've arrived from God knows where!"

"Yes, dear Pyotr Petrovich!" the Foolsburgers said, having learned their lesson; but to themselves they thought: "Lord, he may just go and burn down the town!"

He set out on Saint Nicholas Day, right after the early liturgy, and said he would not be home soon. He had his orderly Vassily Blackfeet with him and two veterans. The procession slowly headed to the righthand corner of the common, but since the distance was short, they made it in half an hour, no matter how slowly they tried to move. The Foolsburgers who awaited them there, four in number, banged on the pans, and one of them shook a tambourine. Then they offered him gifts: a pickled sturgeon belly, a smaller jerked sturgeon, and a piece of ham. The brigadier got out of the britzka and began to argue that those were few gifts, "and not real ones, but stale," and were belittling for his honor. Then the Fools-burgers produced fifty kopecks each and the brigadier was pacified.

"Well, old boys," he said amiably, "show me what interesting things you've got here."

They began to walk back and forth on the common, but did not find anything interesting except for one dung heap.

"Last year, when we camped here during the fire, there was a whole lot of cattle here!" one of the old boys explained.

"It would be good to found a town here," the brigadier said, "and call it Domnaglory, in honor of Domashka, who you troubled for nothing at the time!"

And then added:

"And what about the bosom of the earth?"

"That is unknown to us," the Foolsburgers replied. "We think there should be a lot of everything, but we're afraid to explore it: what if someone sees it and informs the authorities!"

"Afraid?!" the brigadier grinned.

In short, the whole inspection was finished in half an hour, and even that was more than necessary. The brigadier saw that there was a lot of time left (the departure from that spot had been planned only for the next morning), and he began to lament and reproached the Foolsburgers for having neither navigation, nor shipping, nor mining, nor minting, nor transportation, nor even statistics—nothing to gladden a superior's heart. And above all, no enterprise.

"You should've gotten yourselves ships to carry coffee and sugar," he said. "Where are they?"[1]

The old boys looked at one another; they could see that the brigadier spoke as if to the point, but then as if beside the point; they wavered a bit and then each took out another fifty kopecks.

"For this I thank you," said the brigadier, "and as to my slip about navigation, forgive me for that!"

Then one of the townsfolk stepped forward and obligingly said that he had brought a little wooden cannon on wheels and a small stash of dry peas. The brigadier was very happy for that amusement, sat down on the green, and began to fire the toy cannon. They spent much time firing it, and even got tired, but it was still a long time till dinner.

"Ah, drat it all! It seems like the sun is moving backwards here!" said the brigadier, indignantly glancing at the luminary which slowly sailed toward the zenith.

At last, however, they sat down to dinner, but the brigadier, who since his time with Domashka had taken to drinking, right away got disgustingly drunk. He talked indecently and pointed at the "little wooden cannon," threatening to gun down all his hosts. Then his orderly Vassily Blackfeet interceded for them: he was also drunk, but not as much.

"You'd better stop all this nonsense!" he cut the brigadier short. "If I weren't here to look after you, mangy as you are, you wouldn't be able to peep, much less use such a weapon!"

Meanwhile, time went on hopelessly slowly. They ate and ate, drank and drank, and the sun was still high. They began to sleep. They slept and slept, slept all the drink out, and then began to get up.

"The sun is really high this morning!" the brigadier said, waking up and taking the west for the east. The mistake was so obvious that even he realized it. They sent one of the old boys to Foolsburg to fetch some kvass, hoping to while away the time in waiting; but the old boy came back in a trice, bringing a whole jug on his head without spilling a single drop. First they drank kvass, then tea, then vodka. Once it became dark, they lit an oil lamp and illumined the dung heap. The lamp blinked, fumed, and spread stench.

"Thank God! The day has ended before we knew it!" said the brigadier, wrapped himself in his overcoat, and went to sleep for the second time.

The next day they went across the common and, fortunately, met a shepherd. They started asking him who he was and why he was loitering on this common, and whether there was some intent in his loitering. The shepherd was frightened at first, but then confessed everything. Then they searched him and found a small chunk of bread and a scrap of footcloth.

"Tell us what the intent of your loitering was," the brigadier went on with his pointed questioning.

But the shepherd answered all the questions with grunting, and the travelers were forced to take him along for further questioning, and thus they arrived to the other corner of the common.

Here, too, they banged on pans and gave gifts, but time went more quickly because they questioned the shepherd and, truth be told, fired the little cannon at him. In the evening they lit the oil lamp again, and everybody got a headache from the fumes.

On the third day they released the shepherd and went to the center, and here the brigadier's reception was a real triumph. The rumor of his traveling grew by the hour, and since it was Sunday, the Foolsburgers decided to celebrate it in a special way. Having put on their best clothes, they formed into a square and waited for their superior. They banged on the pans, shook the tambourines, and there was even a fiddle. Cauldrons smoked nearby, in which such quantities of pigs, geese, and other creatures were cooked and roasted, that even the priests would have been envious.[2] The brigadier realized for the first time that popular love is a power that means something edible. He got out of the britzka and burst into tears.

Everybody wept there, wept from pity, and wept also from joy. Especially tearful was a very ancient woman (of whom they told that she was the granddaughter of the illegitimate daughter of Marfa the Mayoress).[3]

"Why're you weeping so, dear old woman?" asked the brigadier, gently patting her on the shoulder.

"Ah, our father! our provider! How can we not weep! We're always weeping . . . all our life we're weeping!" the old woman sobbed in response.

At noon tables were set up and dinner was served; but the brigadier committed the imprudence of downing three glasses of vodka. His eyes suddenly became fixed and stared at one spot. Then, having eaten the first course (cabbage soup with corned beef), he drank two more glasses and started saying that he had to run.

"Why this urge to run, and where to?" the honored Foolsburgers sitting around tried to talk sense into him.

"Wherever my feet take me!" he muttered, obviously recalling this phrase from his itinerary.

After the second course (suckling pig in sour cream sauce) he felt ill, but he overcame it and ate some goose with cabbage. After that his mouth became twisted.

They could see a certain administrative nerve twitching on his face; it twitched for a while and suddenly became still . . . The Foolsburgers, perturbed and frightened, jumped up from their seats.

It ended . . .

Ended the glorious mayorship, darkened in the later years by two corrective actions on the Foolsburgers. "Was there any need for these corrective actions?" the chronicler won-

ders and, unfortunately, leaves the question without any answer.

For some time the Foolsburgers were immersed in expectation. They feared that they might be accused of deliberately
overfeeding the brigadier, and that again they might hear the
"rooty-toot, rooty-toot" coming from God knows where.

Close your ranks!
The better
To beat the enemy!

Luckily, however, this time these apprehensions proved
ungrounded. A week later a new mayor arrived from the
provincial capital, and the superiority of the administrative
measures he took made the Foolsburgers forget all the old
mayors, Ferdyshchenko included. This was Basilisk Semyonovich Wartbeardin, with whom, in fact, the golden age
of Foolsburg began. Fears dissolved, one good harvest followed another, there were no comets, and people had money
enough to burn. Which would have been easy to do since it
was all paper money.[4]

The Wars for Enlightenment

Basilisk Semyonovich Wartbeardin, who came to replace the brigadier Ferdyshchenko, was the exact opposite of his predecessor. As much as the latter had been loose and flabby, so the former was strikingly efficient and possessed some unprecedented administrative meticulousness, which manifested itself with particular energy in questions not worth a tinker's damn.

Always neatly buttoned up and having his visored cap and gloves ready, he presented the type of a mayor whose legs were ready any moment to run God knows where. During the day he flitted about town like a fly, making sure that the townsfolk looked cheerful and happy; during the night he was busy extinguishing fires, giving false alarms, and generally taking people unawares.

He shouted all the time, and his shouting was extraordinary. "Such a quantity of shouting he had in him," the chronicler says, "that it caused many Foolsburgers to be permanently frightened, for themselves and for their children."

This is a remarkable observation, and it is confirmed by the fact that later on the authorities were obliged to grant the Foolsburgers all sorts of benefits, precisely "on account of their fright." He had a good appetite, but he ate hastily, mumbling all the while. He slept with only one eye shut, which caused great consternation in his wife of twenty-five years, who, in spite of such long cohabitation, was unable to look without shuddering at his other, unsleeping eye, perfectly round and directed at her with curiosity. When there was absolutely nothing to do—that is, there was no need to flit about, to catch people unawares (there are such difficult moments in the life of the most efficient administrators)—he either issued laws or marched around his study, watching the play of his boot's toe, or refreshing military commands in his memory.

There was yet another particularity in Wartbeardin: he was a writer. Already ten years before his arrival in Foolsburg, he had begun writing a proposal "on the greater expansion of the armies and fleets in all places, so as thereby hopefully to achieve the return (*sic*!) of ancient Byzantium under the sway of the Russian State," and to this proposal he added one line every day.[1] This way a voluminous notebook was formed, which contained three thousand six hundred and fifty-two lines (there were two leap years), at which he pointed to visitors not without some pride, therewith adding:

"See, my dear sir, how far my plans have extended!"

Generally, political woolgathering was very much in vogue just then, and so Wartbeardin did not escape the general tendencies of the time. Very often the Foolsburgers saw him sitting on the balcony of the mayor's house, his eyes filled with tears, gazing at the fortresses of Byzantium bluing in the distance. The pasturelands of Byzantium and Foolsburg were adjacent to such a degree that Byzantine herds almost constantly mixed with the Foolsburgers' herds, causing ceaseless disputes. It seemed as if all that was needed was a call to arms . . . And Wartbeardin waited for this call, waited with passion, with an impatience that bordered almost on indignation.

"First we'll finish with Byzantium, sirs," he dreamed, "and then, sirs . . .

To the Drava, to the Morava, to the distant Sava
And to the quiet blue Danube.

Yesss, sirs!"

To tell the whole truth, in secret he even prepared a very strange memorandum addressed to our famous geographer K. I. Arseniev.[2] "I hereby propose to Your Honor," he wrote, "that in all future textbooks of geography the city known to you as Byzantium be listed thus: 'Constantinople, formerly Byzantium, now the provincial capital Ekaterinograd, located on the strait uniting the Black Sea to the sea formerly called Propontis, which city was brought under the sway of the Russian State in the year 17--, with the unity of treasuries extended to it (which unity consisted in the use of Byzantine currency in the capital city of Saint Petersburg). The city being vast, its administration is realized by four mayors, who are in a state of ceaseless dispute. The city trades in walnuts, has one soap factory and two tanneries.'" But alas! the days went by, Wartbeardin's dreams were growing, but no call came. Infantry troops passed through Foolsburg, cavalry passed through Foolsburg.

"Where to, dear boys?" Wartbeardin asked the soldiers excitedly.

But the soldiers blew trumpets, sang songs, raised the street dust with the toes of their boots, and went on, went on.

"There's droves of them soldiers!" said the Foolsburgers, and it seemed to them that they were some special people made by nature to walk and walk endlessly in all directions. That they descended from one plateau in order to climb onto another plateau, crossed one bridge in order to go on from there to another bridge. And another bridge, and another plateau, and yet another, yet another ...

In this extremity Wartbeardin realized that the time of political undertakings had not yet come and that he had to limit his tasks only to the so-called essential needs of the land. Among these needs the first place belonged, of course, to civilization; or, as he himself defined this word, "the science of how in the Russian Empire every valiant son of the fatherland should be firm in adversity."[3]

Filled with these vague dreams, he arrived in Foolsburg and first of all subjected the intentions and deeds of his predecessors to strict scrutiny. But when he looked at the records, he simply gasped. A procession passed before him: Klementy, and Gigantov, and Lamvrokakis, and Blockheadov, and the Marquis de Sanglotte, and Ferdyshchenko, but what these people did, what they thought about, what their pursuits were—that was impossible to define in any way. It seems as if this line of people is nothing but a dream in which some faceless images flash, some vague cries ring out, similar to the distant hubbub of a drunken crowd ... Now a shadow steps out of the darkness, claps—one, two!—and disappears, no one knows where; then another shadow comes in its place, also claps somehow, and disappears ... All one hears on all sides is "Smashitall!," "Insufferable!"—and precisely what is to be smashed, what is insufferable, is quite impossible to figure out. You are glad to step aside, to huddle in a corner, but you cannot step aside or huddle, because from every corner you hear the same "Smashitall!," which drives you into another corner and there, again, it catches up with you. It was some sort of wild energy deprived of all content, so that even Wartbeardin, with all his efficiency, had some doubts of its merit.[4] The state councillor Epikurov alone stood out favorably from this motley crowd of administrators, showing a fine and perceptive intellect and generally manifesting himself as the successor of the reforms that marked the beginning of the eighteenth century in Russia. It was him, of course, that Wartbeardin took as an example.

Epikurov accomplished a great deal. He paved Noble and Grand Streets, collected all the arrears, was the patron of learning, and petitioned to establish an academy in Foolsburg. But his main achievement consisted in introducing the use of mustard and bay leaf. This last enterprise struck Wartbeardin so much that he immediately had the bold thought of doing exactly the same with regard to olive oil. He began to research the measures used by Epikurov to succeed in his undertaking, but since it turned out that the archive records, as usual, had burned up (or maybe were deliberately destroyed), he had to make do with oral traditions and stories.

"There was a lot of noise here!" the old-timers told him. "There was flogging by soldiers, and simple flogging... Many even went to Siberia over this same thing!"

"Meaning there were rebellions?" asked Wartbeardin.

"As if there weren't rebellions! We have a clue about it, sir: If there's flogging, then sure thing there's a rebellion!"

Further inquiries revealed that Epikurov was a stubborn man, and having once planned to do something, he brought it to an end. He always acted sweepingly—that is, he suppressed and dispersed thoroughly—but at the same time he realized that this one means was not enough. Therefore, independently of general measures, over the course of several years, he ceaselessly and tirelessly performed separate raids on townsfolks' homes and suppressed each person individually.

Generally there is one astonishing fact in the whole history of Foolsburg: today the Foolsburgers are dispersed and destroyed to a man, and tomorrow, lo and behold, again some Foolsburgers appear, and the so-called old-timers (probably the former "young and feisty"), as their custom is, speak out at gatherings. How they emerged was a mystery, but Epikurov perceived this mystery perfectly well, and therefore did not spare the birch rods. As a true administrator, he distinguished two sorts of flogging, flogging without investigation and flogging with investigation, and was proud of being the first in the line of mayors to introduce flogging with investigation, whereas all his predecessors flogged any old way and often even those whom there was no reason to flog. And indeed, acting reasonably and consistently, he obtained the most brilliant results. Throughout his mayorship, the Foolsburgers not only never sat down to eat without mustard, but even cultivated vast mustard plantations to satisfy the demand of the trade. "And this town flourished like a lily of the field,[5] sending this bitter product to the farthest parts of the Russian Empire and getting in exchange precious metals and furs."

But in 1770 Epikurov died, and the two mayors who succeeded him not only did not support his reforms, but even, so to speak, fouled them up. And what is most remarkable, the Foolsburgers turned out to be ungrateful. They did not regret in the least the abolition of authoritative civilization, but even seemed to be glad. They stopped eating mustard altogether, dug up their plantations, and planted cabbage and sowed peas in them. In short, what happened was what always occurs when enlightenment comes too early to people in infancy and immature in a civic sense. Even the chronicler mentions this circumstance, not without irony. "He [Epikurov] spent many years erecting this sophisticated edifice, but he did not understand that he was building on sand." But the chronicler, in his turn, obviously also forgets that the whimsicality of human actions consists precisely in this: to build an edifice on sand today, and tomorrow, when it collapses, to start erecting another edifice on the same sand.

Thus it transpired that Wartbeardin arrived at just the right moment to save the perishing civilization. In him the passion for building on sand reached the point of frenzy. He kept thinking day and night about what he could possibly build so that once built, it would suddenly come crashing down and fill the universe with dust and litter. He thought this way and that, but he really could not think up anything. Finally, for lack of original thoughts, he decided to literally follow in the tracks of his famous predecessor.

"My hands are tied," he complained bitterly to the Foolsburgers. "Otherwise I'd show you a thing or two!"

He also found out just then that the Foolsburgers in their negligence had completely abandoned the use of mustard, and therefore, to begin with, he confined himself to making this use mandatory; and he added olive oil to it as a punishment for disobedience. At the same time he resolved in his heart not to lay down weapons as long as there was a single perplexed person left in the town.

But the Foolsburgers, too, kept their own counsel. To the energy of action they, with great resourcefulness, opposed the energy of inaction.

"Do what you like to us!" some said. "Cut us to pieces if you like, chew us up if you like—but we won't accept it!"

"You can't do anything to us, brother!" said others. "We've got no flesh, you can't even pinch us!"

And they went on kneeling all the while.

Apparently, when these two energies meet, something quite curious always happens. There is no rebellion, but there is no real obedience, either. There is something in between, of which we had seen examples under serfdom. Say a lady finds a cockroach in the soup: she summons her cook and tells him to eat the cockroach. The cook puts the cockroach into his mouth, it looks as if he is chewing it, but he does not swallow. It was exactly the same with the Foolsburgers: they chewed well enough, but swallowing there was none.

"I'll break this energy!" Wartbeardin kept saying, while he thought his plan over slowly and unhurriedly.

And the Foolsburgers went on kneeling and waiting. They knew that this was rebellion, but they could not help kneeling. Lord, the things they mulled over all the while! They thought: If they start eating mustard now, what other vileness will they be forced to eat in the future? If they don't, it might mean tasting the whip. It seemed to them that kneeling in this case presented a middle way that might reconcile the two sides.

And suddenly the trumpet sounded, the drum banged. Wartbeardin, fully buttoned and filled with courage, rode out on a white horse. He was followed by cannoneers and musketeers. The Foolsburgers thought that their mayor was going to vanquish Byzantium, and it turned out that he intended to vanquish them . . .

Thus began the extraordinary series of events which the chronicler describes under the general name of "the Wars for Enlightenment."

The first war "for enlightenment" was, as has already been said, on the occasion of mustard, and began in the year 1780—that is, almost immediately upon the arrival of Wartbeardin in Foolsburg.

Nevertheless Wartbeardin did not venture to start shooting right away; he was too much of a pedant to fall into such an obvious administrative error. He acted gradually and, with that purpose in mind, summoned the Foolsburgers and began to entice them. In the speech he delivered on that occasion, he developed in great detail the question of accompaniment in general, and mustard as accompaniment in particular; but either because his words presented more personal faith in the rightness of the cause than actual persuasion, or because he did not speak but shouted, as was his custom, in any case the result of his talk was that the Foolsburgers were frightened and again, as a whole community, fell on their knees.

"They did have reason to be frightened," says the chronicler on the occasion. "There was this little fellow standing before them, not much to look at, and he did not speak words, but only shouted his head off."

"Did you get it, old boys?" he asked the townsfolk, who stood there stunned.

The people bowed to the ground and were silent. Naturally this blew him up even more.

"Am I sending you to death . . . or what? . . . Sscoundrrels!"

But as soon as this new burst of thunder came from his lips, the Foolsburgers instantly jumped up and ran in all directions.

"Smashemall!" he shouted in their wake.

Wartbeardin spent that whole day grieving. He silently paced the rooms of the mayor's house and only repeated softly: "Bastards!"

Most of all he was concerned with the Musketeers' suburb, which had distinguished itself with the most insuperable stubbornness even in the time of his predecessors.[6] The musketeers brought the energy of inaction to the point of refinement. They not only did not come to the gatherings at Wartbeardin's invitations, but, seeing him approach, they disappeared somewhere as if falling through the earth. There was no one to persuade, no one to ask. One could hear someone trembling somewhere, but where the trembling was and why was impossible to find out.

Meanwhile, there could be no doubt that the source of all evil was in the Musketeers' suburb. The most cheerless rumors reached Wartbeardin about this nest of sedition. A preacher appeared who transposed the name Wartbeardin into numbers and proved that, if you omit the letter *r* you will get 666, which is the number of the Prince of Darkness.[7] Polemical tracts circulated in which it was explained that mustard was an herb that grew out of the body of a harlot, who was called a "muss" for her loose behavior, and that was where the word "mustard" came from. A poem was even written in which the author alluded to the mayor's mother, referring very disapprovingly to her behavior. Paying heed to this singing and talking, the musketeers reached an almost ecstatic state. They wandered arm in arm around the town and, to drive the spirit of cowardice forever from their midst, bawled at the top of their lungs.

Wartbeardin felt his heart filling drop by drop with bitterness. He did not eat or drink, and only uttered foul words, as if trying to cheer himself up. The thought of mustard seemed so simple and clear that its nonacceptance could not be interpreted in any other way than as malevolence. The more painful this awareness was, the more effort Wartbeardin needed to harness the impulses of his passionate nature.

"My hands are tied!" he repeated, broodingly chewing his dark mustache. "Otherwise I'd show you a thing or two!"

Yet he thought, not without reason, that the natural outcome of any collision was flogging, and this awareness sustained him. While waiting for this outcome, he occupied himself with his affairs and was quietly drafting a regulation, "On the Nonconstraint of Mayors with Laws." The first and only paragraph of this regulation stated: "If you feel that a law hinders you, take it from your desk and put it underneath you. Thus the law is made invisible, and you will acquire great freedom of action."[8]

However, this regulation had not yet been confirmed and, consequently, it was impossible to evade constraints. A month later Wartbeardin summoned the townsfolk again and again shouted at them. But he had barely managed to utter the first two syllables of his greeting ("which I omit to mention for reasons of shame," remarks the chronicler), when the Foolsburgers scattered again, before even having time to kneel. Only then did Wartbeardin decide to make use of real civilization.

He set out on his campaign early in the morning and made it look as if this were a simple military parade. The morning was clear, fresh, slightly chilly (it was the middle of September). The sun played on the soldiers' casques and rifles; the roofs of the houses and the streets were covered by a light layer of hoarfrost; stoves were burning everywhere, and merry flames could be seen through the windows of every house.

Although the main goal of the campaign was the Musketeers' suburb, Wartbeardin acted slyly. He did not go either straight ahead or to right or left, but began maneuvering. The Foolsburgers poured outside and encouraged the evolutions of the skillful leader with loud approvals.

"Thank God! It seems he's forgotten about the mustard!" they said, taking off their hats and piously crossing themselves in the direction of the belfry.

And Wartbeardin kept maneuvering, and around noon

reached the Naughties, where he halted. The participants of the campaign all received a glass of vodka and were ordered to sing songs, and in the evening they took captive a town girl, who happened to stray too far from the gates of her house.

The next day, getting up early, they began looking for a prisoner to interrogate. They did it in earnest, without batting an eye. They brought in some Jew and first wanted to hang him, but then remembered that that was not the idea and forgave him. The Jew testified under oath that they should first go to the Dung settlement, then circle around the field until they came to the place called Dunka's Ravine. And from there, passing three checkpoints, follow their noses.

That is what Wartbeardin did. But before his people had walked a quarter of a mile they felt that they were lost. Nothing could be seen—neither land, nor water, nor sky. Wartbeardin sent for the treacherous Jew in order to hang him, but the tracks were already cold (later it turned out that he had fled to Petersburg, where he instantly succeeded in obtaining a railroad concession).[9] They spent quite a long time in broad daylight, and it was as if the people had some sort of darkening, because the Dung settlement was obviously before their eyes, but no one saw it. Finally a real evening darkness descended and someone shouted: "Robbery!" It was some drunken soldier, but the people were confused and, thinking that the musketeers were coming, went into battle.

They fought hard all night, they fought without seeing, at random. There were many wounded and many killed. Only when day broke did they see that they had been fighting against their own, and that the scene of this misunderstanding was right at the edge of the Dung settlement. They decided to bury the fallen and set up a monument at the place of the battle, honoring the day it had taken place as "the Day of the Born-blind," and in memory of it to institute annual festivities with rollicking singing and dancing.[10]

On the third day they halted in the Dung settlement. Here, taught by experience, they demanded to have hostages. Then, having caught local people's chickens, they organized a memorial party for the fallen soldiers. The locals thought it strange that the mayor was playing a game and at the same time catching their chickens; but since Wartbeardin did not divulge his secret, they decided that such were "the rules of the game" and kept quiet.

But when, after the memorial party, Wartbeardin ordered the soldiers to trample an outlying field of winter wheat, the people fell to thinking.

"Can there really be such rules, brothers?" they said among themselves, but so softly that even Wartbeardin, who keenly followed the trends of thinking, did not hear anything.

On the fourth day, at dawn, they went to Dunka's Ravine, fearing to be late, because the march was long and fatiguing. They walked for a long time and constantly asked the hostages: "How soon?" Great was the general amazement when suddenly, in the middle of an open field, the hostages cried out: "Here!" And well they might be amazed: there was no sign of any dwellings; the bare field stretched far and wide, and only in the distance was there a deep depression into which, according to legend, the girl Dunka once fell as she hurried, drunk, to an amorous tryst.

"So where's the settlement?" Wartbeardin asked the hostages.

"There isn't any settlement here!" said the hostages. "There used to be one, there were settlements everywhere before, but the soldiers destroyed everything!"

Wartbeardin did not believe these words, and it was decided to flog the hostages until they showed where the settlement was. But—strangely enough—the more they flogged, the weaker was the hope of finding the desired settlement! This was so unexpected that Wartbeardin tore his uniform and, raising his right hand to the sky, shook his finger at it and said:

"Ah, you all!"

The situation was awkward; it was dark, cold, and damp, and wolves appeared in the field. In a fit of reasonableness, Wartbeardin issued an order: Don't sleep all night, and tremble.

On the fifth day they went back to the Dung settlement and on the way trampled down another field of winter wheat. They walked a whole day and only in the evening, tired and hungry, reached the settlement. But they did not find anybody in it. The inhabitants, seeing the approaching army in the distance, ran away, taking all the cattle with them, and entrenched themselves in an unassailable position. The army was to give battle for this position, but, since their powder was fake, they were unable, fire all they might, to cause any harm except for an unbearable stench.

On the sixth day, Wartbeardin wanted to continue the bombarding, but he noticed some treason. During the night the hostages had been released and many real soldiers had been dismissed and replaced by tin ones. When he asked why the hostages had been released, he was referred to a regulation which supposedly said: "Hostages should be flogged and, once flogged, not kept for longer than twenty-four hours, but sent home for recovery." Like it or not, Wartbeardin had to agree that they had acted correctly, but then recalled his regulation "On the Nonconstraint of Mayors with Laws" and wept bitterly.

"And what is this?" he asked, pointing at the tin soldiers.

"That's for ease, Your Honor!" came the answer. "They don't ask for provisions, but they can march like anything!"

This, too, had to be accepted. Wartbeardin withdrew into a cottage and held a military council with himself. He would have liked to punish the "Dung people" for their impudence, but, on the other hand, he recalled the siege of Troy, which lasted a whole ten years, even though Achilles and Agamemnon were among the besiegers. It was not privations that he feared, not the separation from his dear spouse that distressed him, but that in the course of those ten years his absence from Foolsburg might be noticed, and that without any particular advantage for him. He also recalled on this occasion a lesson from history that upset him very much. "Despite Menelaus's good-nature," the teacher of history had said, "the Spartans had never been so happy as during the siege of Troy; for although many documents remained unsigned, instead many backs remained unflogged, and the latter privation amply rewarded them for the former ..."

On top of that, continuous autumn rains began to pour down, threatening to ruin communications and stop the delivery of provisions.

"Why the devil didn't I go straight for the musketeers!" Wartbeardin exclaimed ruefully, looking out the window at the puddles that were growing by the minute. "I'd have been there in half an hour!"

And for the first time he understood that in some cases too much wit is tantamount to witlessness, and the result of this awareness was the decision to retreat and form a reliable reserve out of the tin soldiers.

On the seventh day they set off at dawn, but, since the road had become eroded overnight, the men proceeded with difficulty and the cannons sank into the yielding black soil.

On the way they had to attack Whistling Wench Hill. At the command "Charge!" the front rows valiantly rushed ahead, but the tin soldiers did not follow them. And since the features of their faces had merely been outlined "in haste" and that not very distinctly, it seemed from a distance that the soldiers were smiling ironically. And there was only one step from irony to sedition.

"Cowards!" Wartbeardin muttered through his teeth, but was embarrassed to say it aloud and was forced to retreat from the hill with losses. They went in a roundabout way, but here they encountered a swamp the existence of which no one had suspected. Wartbeardin looked at the map of the common: it was all plowland, and wet meadows, and some small shrubs, and also stones, but no swamp, and that was that.

"There's no swamp here! It's all lies! March on, you bastards!" Wartbeardin commanded, and he climbed onto a hummock to closely observe the crossing.

His men got into the mire and immediately drowned all their artillery. They themselves managed to climb out, covered all over with mud. Wartbeardin, too, got all muddy, but he could not worry about that. He looked at the lost artillery and saw his cannons half-sunk, their muzzles turned up to the sky as if threatening to shoot at it. And he began to lament and grieve.

"So many years of amassing, cherishing, caring!" he complained. "What am I going to do now! How will I govern without cannons!"

The army was utterly demoralized. When they got out of the mire, before their eyes again was a vast plain and again without any sign of habitation. In places there were human bones lying about and some bricks piled high; there was every evidence that once a very strong and original civilization had existed here (later it turned out that the former mayor Urus-Kugush-Kildibaev, being in a drunken state, had taken this civilization for a rebellion and destroyed it), but many years had passed since then and not a single mayor had bothered to restore it. Some strange shadows flitted across the field; mysterious sounds reached one's ear. Some sorcery was going on, similar to what is usually presented in the third act of *Ruslan and Ludmila*, when frightened Farlaf rushes onstage. Although Wartbeardin was braver than Farlaf, even he shuddered at the thought that wicked Naïna was just about to come out to meet him . . . [11]

Only on the eighth day, around noon, did the exhausted soldiers see the hills of the Musketeers' suburb and joyfully blow their horns. Wartbeardin remembered that the prince Sviatoslav Igorevich, before going to defeat his enemies, always sent to tell them: "I'm going against you!"—and, guided by this example, dispatched his orderly to the musketeers with the same greeting. [12]

The next day, as soon as the sun gilded the tops of the thatched roofs, the army, with Wartbeardin at its head, already entered the suburb. But there was no one in it besides a retired priest, who at that moment was deliberating within himself the possibility of joining the schismatics. [13] The priest was an ancient man, more capable of instilling melancholy than filling a soul with courage.

"Where are the inhabitants?" Wartbeardin asked, flashing his eyes at the priest.

"They were just here!" the priest mumbled indistinctly.

"What do you mean, 'just'? Where have they escaped to?"

"Why 'escaped'? What's the need to escape from their own homes? They must have hidden from you somewhere around here!"

Wartbeardin stood where he was, digging the ground

with his feet. There was a moment when he began to believe that the energy of inaction was going to triumph.

"I should have started the campaign in the winter!" he regretted in his heart. "Then they wouldn't be able to hide from me."

"Hey! Who's there! Come out!" he shouted in such a voice that even the tin soldiers trembled.

But the place was silent as if it had died. Some sighs broke out from somewhere, but the mysteriousness with which they came from invisible organisms vexed the upset mayor still more.

"Where are these brutes sighing?" he shouted furiously, looking around in despair and evidently losing any ability to reason. "Go and find the brute who's sighing there and bring him to me!"

There was a search, but no matter how they looked, they found no one. Wartbeardin walked up and down the street peeking into all the chinks—there was no one!

This puzzled him so much that the most incongruous thoughts suddenly flooded his head.

"If I dessstroy them now by fire ... no, I'd do better to starve them! ..." he thought, passing from one incongruous idea to another.

Suddenly he stopped, struck dumb before the tin soldiers.

Something quite extraordinary was happening to them. In front of everyone, the soldiers began to fill with blood. Their eyes, fixed until then, suddenly began to roll and express anger; their mustaches, painted haphazardly, straightened out and began to move; their lips, which had been just a thin pink line almost washed off under the rain, puffed up and expressed the intention to utter something. Nostrils, which earlier had been completely nonexistent, appeared and began to swell up and show impatience.

"What is it, my good men?" asked Wartbeardin.

"Cottages . . . cottages . . . break them down!" the tin soldiers uttered indistinctly and somehow gloomily.

The remedy had been found.

They started with the first one in the row. Whooping, the "tin men" rushed onto the roof and instantly went berserk. Bundles of straw, planks, wooden cogs flew down. Whole clouds of dust whirled up.

"Stop! Stop!" shouted Wartbeardin, suddenly hearing a moan just next to him.

The whole suburb was moaning. It was a vague but constant hum, in which it was impossible to distinguish a single separate noise, but which as a whole presented a barely contained heartache.

"Who's there? Come out!" Wartbeardin shouted again at the top of his voice.

The suburb fell silent, but no one came out. "The musketeers hoped," says the chronicler, "that this new method (that is, suppression by way of the destruction of houses), like all others, was only a passing dream, but they did not comfort themselves with this sweet hope for long."

"Keep going!" Wartbeardin said firmly.

There was crash and smash; one by one the beams were broken from the frame, and as they fell to the ground, the moaning grew more and more. After several minutes the end cottage ceased to exist, and the "tin men," with still greater cruelty, were already attacking the second one. But when, after a short break, the hiding inhabitants again heard the sounds of an axe continuing its deed of destruction, their hearts wavered. They crept out all at once, old and young, male and female, and, their hands raised to the sky, fell on their knees in the middle of the square. Wartbeardin, though carried away at first, recalled the words of the instruction:

"While suppressing, care not so much about destroying as about correcting," and grew quiet. He realized that his hour of triumph had already come, and it would be the more complete if, in the final end, there were no bloodied noses or dislodged cheekbones.

"Do you accept mustard?" he asked distinctly, trying as well as he could to remove the menacing notes from his voice.

The crowd silently bowed to the ground.

"Do you accept it or not, I'm asking you!" he repeated, already beginning to seethe.

"We do! We do!" the crowd droned softly, as if sighing.

"Very well. Now tell me, which of you insulted the memory of my dearest mother in verses?"

The musketeers faltered; they did not think it right to betray the one who in a bitter moment of their life had comforted them; however, after a moment's hesitation, they decided to fulfill this request of the superior as well.

"Come out, Fedka! Nothing to be done! Come out!" voices said in the crowd.

A blond fellow stepped forth and stood before the mayor. His lips twitched as if wishing to smile, but his face was white as a sheet and his teeth chattered.

"So it's you?" Wartbeardin laughed and, stepping back as if wishing to examine the culprit in full detail, he repeated: "So it's you?"

Apparently an inner struggle was going on in Wartbeardin. He was pondering whether he should smack Fedka's face or punish him in some other way. He finally came up with, so to speak, a mixed measure.

"Listen!" he said, straightening Fedka's jaw a little. "Since you dishonored the memory of my dearest mother, henceforth you shall glorify that memory so precious to me in verse every day, and bring those verses to me!"

With this he gave the all-clear signal.

The rebellion was over; ignorance had been suppressed, enlightenment was put in its place. Half an hour later Wartbeardin, loaded with booty, made a triumphant entry into the town at the head of many captives and hostages. Since among them were some officers and other persons of the first three ranks, he ordered that they should be treated gently (having had their eyes put out just to be sure), and all the rest be sent to hard labor.[14]

That same evening, having shut himself in his office, Wartbeardin made the following note in his diary:

"On the 17th of this September, after a difficult but glorious nine-day campaign, a most joyful and desirable event took place. Mustard has been established everywhere and forever, without shedding a single drop of blood."

"Except," the chronicler adds with irony, "for the blood spilled by the gate of the Dung settlement, in memory of which to this day we celebrate a feast with rollicking dancing . . ."

It may very well be that much of what I have recounted above will seem far too fantastic to the reader. What need had Wartbeardin to undertake a nine-day campaign, if the Musketeers' suburb was close at hand and he could reach it in half an hour? How could he get lost on the town common, which he, being the mayor, should have known very well? Can we believe the story about the tin soldiers, who supposedly not only marched, but in the end even filled with blood?

Realizing the importance of these questions, the publisher of this chronicle thinks it possible to give the following reply: The history of Foolsburg, first of all, portrays a world of miracles, which we can reject only if we reject the existence of miracles in general. But that is not all. There are miracles in which, on close inspection, one can notice a very vivid real basis. We all know the tales about Baba Yaga of the bone leg, who moved around in a mortar, driving it with a broom. We consider her way of traveling a miracle created by popular fantasy. But no one asks why popular fantasy produced precisely this and not some other fruit. If the explorers of our past paid due attention to this subject, one could be certain beforehand that many things would be discovered that until now had been shrouded in mystery. Thus, for instance, it would be discovered that the origin of this legend is purely administrative, that Baba Yaga is none other than a mayoress, or perhaps a lady governor, who, to evoke a saving fear in the townsfolk, traveled around the country of her jurisdiction in precisely that manner, and that she captured the Ivanushkas she met on her way and, returning home, cried: "I'll roll about, and I'll loll about, having had my fill of Ivanushka's sweet flesh."[15]

It seems this is quite sufficient to persuade the reader that the chronicler treads ground that is far from fantastic, and that everything he has told about Wartbeardin's campaigns can be taken as a reliable document. Of course, at first sight it might appear strange that Wartbeardin spent nine days in a row circling the common; but we should not forget that, first, he had no need to hurry, since it was predictable beforehand that his undertaking would end with success in any case, and, second, any administrator willingly resorts to maneuvering in order to impress the townsfolk. If it were possible to imagine so-called bodily correction without the rites that precede it—such as removal of clothing, admonishment by the person who does the correction, and soliciting forgiveness on the part of the person being corrected—what would remain of it? Merely an empty formality, the meaning of which would be clear only to the one who undergoes it! Exactly the same should be said about any campaign, whether it is undertaken with the purpose of subduing kingdoms or simply exacting arrears. Take "maneuvering" away and what will remain?

There is certainly no doubt that Wartbeardin could have avoided many very serious mistakes. For instance, the episode which the chronicler calls "born-blind" is really bad. But let us not forget that success never comes without sacrifices, and that if we strip the carcass of history of the lies and prejudices it gets overgrown with in time, the result will always be a bigger or smaller number of "the fallen." Who are these "fallen"? Were they right or wrong, and to what extent? How is it that they received the name of "the fallen"? All this will be sorted out later. But they are necessary, because without them there would be no one to commemorate.

Thus it is only the question of the tin soldiers that remains unanswered. But the chronicler does not leave it unclarified. "We notice very often," he says, "that objects which are apparently perfectly inanimate (like a stone) begin to feel a yearning as soon as they encounter a spectacle that affects their inanimateness." And he gives the example of some neighboring landowner who had a stroke and spent ten years immobile in an armchair. With all that he emitted a joyful grunting when the quitrent was brought to him ...

There were four Wars for Enlightenment. One of them is described above; of the other three, the first had as its purpose to explain to the Foolsburgers the benefit of making stone foundations under their houses; the second emerged as the result of the refusal of the townsfolk to cultivate Persian chamomile,[16] and the third, finally, was caused by the rumor that spread in Foolsburg about the establishing of an academy. Generally, it is obvious that Wartbeardin was a utopian, and had he lived longer, he would probably have ended by being exiled to Siberia for freethinking, or for having set up a phalanstery in Foolsburg.[17]

There is no need to describe this series of brilliant feats in detail, but it will not hurt to point here to their general character.

Wartbeardin's further campaigns are marked by considerable advanced planning. He prepared material for uprisings with great care and crushed them with great speed. The most difficult campaign, caused by the rumor about establishing the academy, lasted only two days; the others no longer than a few hours. Usually, after his morning tea, Wartbeardin would sound the call; the tin soldiers would come running, instantly filled with blood, and rush to the spot at top speed. By dinnertime Wartbeardin would return home and sing a hymn of thanksgiving. Thus he finally achieved that in a few years there was not a single Foolsburger left who could point to a place on his body that had not been flogged.

On the part of the townsfolk there reigned, as before, complete bewilderment. One can see from the stories of the chronicler that they would have been glad not to rebel, but could not organize it, simply because they did not know what rebellion consists in. Indeed, Wartbeardin very cleverly got them ensnared. Usually he did not explain anything properly, but made his wishes known by means of leaflets that secretly, during the night, were glued onto the corner houses of all the streets. These leaflets were written in the spirit of the present-day advertisements by Kach's samovar shop, in which inessential words were all printed in big letters, and everything of essence was presented in the smallest type. Besides, the use of Latin names was permitted; so, for instance, Persian chamomile was called not Persian chamomile but "Pyrethrum roseum," or else "salivant," belonging to the family of "compositas," et cetera. The result of it was that the literate fellows entrusted with reading the leaflets aloud, read only the words written in capital letters, indistinctly mumbling all the rest. As, for example (see the leaflet about Persian chamomile):

IT IS KNOWN TO ALL

What devastation is produced by bedbugs, fleas, etc.

FINALLY FOUND

Enterprising people have brought from the Far East, etc.

Of all these words people grasped only "known to all" and "finally found." And when the readers shouted these words, men took their hats off, sighed, and crossed themselves. Clearly this was no rebellion, but rather the carrying out of the authorities' requirements. The people were driven to sighing—what other ideal could anyone demand!

And so the whole thing was a misunderstanding, and this is all the more plausible since even to this day the Foolsburgers are unable to explain the meaning of the word "academy," though it was this word that Wartbeardin had printed with capital letters (see the complete collection of leaflets, No. 1089). Moreover, the chronicler demonstrates that the Foolsburgers even insisted that Wartbeardin shed some light into their ignorant heads, but did not succeed, and that was the fault of the mayor himself. They often went all together to his premises and said to him:

"Explain it to us, please! Tell us what it's all about!"

"Away with you, ruffians!" Wartbeardin usually answered.

"We're no ruffians! It must be you've never seen real ruffians! Please, tell us what to do!"

But Wartbeardin said nothing. Why? Was it because he regarded the lack of understanding in Foolsburgers as no more than a ruse to conceal their stubborn resistance, or because he wanted to give them a surprise—a plausible answer cannot be given. But it must be that it was partly both. No administrator who clearly understands the benefit of the offered measure ever thinks that this measure can be dubious or incomprehensible to anyone. On the other hand, every administrator is always a fatalist and firmly believes that, if he continues his administrative course, in the end he will find himself face-to-face with the human body. Therefore, to forestall this inevitable denouement with preliminary perorations would only exacerbate it and make it still more embittered. And, finally, every administrator strives to be trusted, and what better way is there to show trust than by unquestioningly doing something one does not understand?

Be that as it may, the Foolsburgers always learned the object of the campaign only once it was over.

However brilliant the results obtained by Wartbeardin seemed, in effect they were far from beneficial. True, obduracy was destroyed, but at the same time contentment was also destroyed. The townsfolk hung their heads and as if withered; they went out to work in the fields unwillingly, came back home unwillingly, sat down to their meager meals unwillingly, and then wandered from corner to corner as if they were sick of everything.

To crown it all they cultivated mustard and Persian chamomile in such quantities that the price of these products fell incredibly low. An economic crisis ensued, and there was no Molinari or Bezobrazov to explain to the Foolsburgers that that was in fact true prosperity.[18] Not only did they not receive precious metals and furs in exchange for their produce, but they did not have enough to buy bread.

Even so, things went on somehow till 1790. From full rations the inhabitants passed to half rations, but did not fall behind with taxes, and even showed some taste for enlightenment. In 1790 they took their produce to all the big markets, but no one bought anything: everyone felt sorry for the bedbugs. Then the Foolsburgers passed on to a quarter ration and withheld their taxes. Just then, as if for the fun of it, the revolution broke out in France, and everyone clearly realized that "enlightenment" is good only when it has an unenlightened nature. Wartbeardin received a letter in which it was recommended to him: "On the occasion of the event known to you, please keep watch diligently, so that this incorrigible evil is rooted out with no omissions."

Only then did Wartbeardin suddenly realize that he had been progressing much too quickly and not at all in the right direction. Having begun to collect taxes, he was astonished and indignant to discover that the yards and barns were empty, and if there was an occasional chicken somewhere, it was skinny and undernourished. But, as usual, he judged this fact not in a direct way, but from his own original point of view, meaning that he saw in it a rebellion, caused this time not by ignorance but by an excess of enlightenment.

"Ah, now it's the free spirit! You've grown fat!" he shouted, beside himself. "You're aping the French!"

And so a new series of campaigns began—this time against enlightenment. In the first campaign, Wartbeardin burned down the Dung settlement, in the second he devastated the Naughties, in the third he wiped out the Swamp. Still the taxes were withheld. The moment was coming when he would be left alone with his secretary among the ruins, and he was actively preparing for this moment. But Providence did not allow it to happen. By 1798 all the inflammable materials for burning down the whole town had been collected, when Wartbeardin suddenly passed away . . . "He scattered everybody," says the chronicler on the occasion, "so that there were even no priests left to perform the last rites, and a local police captain had to be invited to certify the departure of his rebellious spirit."

The Epoch of Relief from Wars

In 1802 came the fall of Blaggardov. He fell, as the chronicler tells us, because of his disagreements with Novosiltsev and Stroganov in regard to a constitution.[1] But this seems to have been merely a plausible pretext, for it is hardly possible that Blaggardov would have refused to introduce a constitution if the authorities had urged him to do so. Blaggardov belonged to the school of the so-called fledglings,[2] for whom it made no difference what was introduced. Therefore the true reason of his disgrace was most likely that he had at some point been a stoker in Gatchina, and consequently represented to a certain extent the Gatchina democratic principle.[3] Besides, the authorities were apparently aware that the Wars for Enlightenment, which later turned into wars against enlightenment, had so exhausted Foolsburg that there was a need to free it entirely from wars for a time. That the surmise about a constitution was no more than a rumor with no firm basis is proven, first, by recent research into the subject and, second, by the fact that the mayor Blaggardov was replaced by the Circassian Mikaladze, who hardly had a clearer notion of constitutions than Blaggardov.

Of course, it is impossible to deny that attempts at constitutional thinking did exist; but it seems that these attempts
were limited to policemen improving their manners to the
extent that they did not grab every passerby by the scruff of
the neck. This was the only sort of constitution considered
possible with society being then in an infantile state. First
it was necessary to accustom people to polite behavior, and
only then, once their morals were softened, could they be
given supposedly "real" rights.[4] From a theoretical point of
view, this way of thinking was, of course, perfectly correct.
On the other hand, it is no less probable that, however attractive the theory of polite behavior is, still, taken in isolation,
it by no means insures people against the sudden intrusion
of the theory of impolite behavior (as was later proven by
the appearance in the arena of history of such a personality
as Sullen-Grumble); and therefore, if we really wish to give
polite behavior a firm foundation, we must still, first of all,
provide the people with supposedly real rights. And this in
turn shows how flimsy theories are in general and how wise
are those army leaders who mistrust them.

The new mayor understood this, and therefore set it as
his goal to attract hearts solely by means of refined manners.
Though he was a military man himself, he disregarded form
and referred to discipline even with bitterness. He always
went about in an unbuttoned frock coat, under which could
be glimpsed an alluringly snow-white piqué waistcoat and
turndown collar. He readily offered his left hand to subordinates, readily smiled, and not only did not allow himself
to affirm anything too abruptly, but even liked, when receiving reports, to use phrases like "So, you were so good as to
say" or "I have already had the honor of telling you," and so
on. Only once, exasperated by the prolonged contrariness of
his assistant, did he allow himself to say, "I have already had

the honor of repeating to you, son of a gun"... but immediately checked himself and promoted the assistant to a higher rank. Being of a passionate nature, he was greatly drawn to the company of ladies, and this passion was the cause of his untimely demise. In an article he had written, "On the Attractive Appearance of Messieurs Mayors" (see further on in the supporting documents), he expounded his views on the subject in detail but, it seems, made a not entirely sincere connection between his successes with Foolsburg ladies and some political and diplomatic purposes. Most likely he was ashamed that he, like Mark Antony in Egypt, led an extremely sybaritic life,[5] and therefore he wanted to assure posterity that there are occasions when even a sybaritic life can have an administratively policing significance. This surmise is supported by the fact that there is no indication in the chronicler's account of frequent arrests taking place during Mikaladze's mayorship, or of someone being mercilessly thrashed, which certainly would have happened if his amorous activity was really directed toward protecting public security. Therefore it can be asserted with near certainty that he loved amorous adventures for their own sake and was a connoisseur of women's attractions just so, without any political purposes; and he invented the latter only as a cover before the authorities, who, despite their unquestionable liberalism, nevertheless did not omit asking every once in a while: Was it not time to start a war? "And he," the chronicler says on this subject, "pitying orphans' tears, always answered: 'No, it is not time yet, for the materials I am gathering for this purpose, in a way known to me, are not ready.' And before gathering them, he died."

Be that as it may, the appointment of Mikaladze was highly beneficial for the Foolsburgers. His predecessor, Captain Blaggardov, though not a man of what is called "essential" depravity, considered himself a man of conviction (the chronicler everywhere puts the word "willfulness" in place of "conviction"), and, in this quality, constantly tested whether the Foolsburgers were sufficiently firm in adversity. The result of his intense administrative activity was that by the end of his mayorship, Foolsburg consisted of a heap of blackened and decrepit huts, amid which only the police station proudly raised its watchtower to the sky. There was no real food, nor proper clothing. The Foolsburgers ceased to be ashamed, became overgrown with fur, and started sucking their paws.[6]

"How can you live this way?" the amazed Mikaladze asked the townsfolk.

"We live this way since we have no real life," replied the Foolsburgers with something that was either laughter or weeping.

Clearly, in view of such moral disarray, the new mayor's main care was directed first of all at the removal of the Foolsburgers' fear. And, to tell the truth, he acted quite skillfully in this sense. He undertook a whole series of measures that tended only towards the abovementioned goal. Their essence may be formulated as follows: (1) enlightenment and the punishments pertaining to it should be temporarily suspended, and (2) no new laws should be issued. The results were obtained immediately, and they were amazing. Before the month was out, the Foolsburgers had completely cast off the fur they had grown and began to be embarrassed of their nakedness. After another month they stopped sucking their paws, and six months later, following many years of silence, a first round dance took place in Foolsburg, at which the mayor was personally present, treating the female sex to decorated gingerbreads.

With these peaceful feats the Circassian Mikaladze marked his mayorship. Like every expression of truly fruitful activity, his governance was neither loud nor brilliant; it was distinguished neither by foreign conquests nor by internal disturbances; but it did respond to the need of the moment and fully reached the modest goals it had set for itself. There were few visible facts, but the consequences were countless. "You wise ones of this world!" exclaims the chronicler on this account, "reflect on it well, and let your hearts not be troubled at the sight of birch rods or other instruments, of which, in your high-minded opinion, the power and light of enlightenment supposedly consist!"

Those are all reasons why the Publisher of this history finds it quite natural that the chronicler, describing Mikaladze's administrative activity, is not very generous with details. This mayor is important not directly as an activist, but as the initiator of that peaceful path which Foolsburg civilization almost followed. The beneficent power of his actions was imperceptible, because such gestures as a handshake, as a gentle smile and generally meek behavior, can be felt only directly and do not leave vivid and visible traces in history. They do not produce a big change in either the economic or the intellectual state of the country, but if you compare these administrative actions with calling subordinates sons of guns, for instance, or with constant flogging, you would have to admit that the difference is enormous. Many, in considering Mikaladze's activity, find it not entirely impeccable. They say, for example, that he had no right to stop enlightenment, and that is so. But, on the other hand, if enlightenment is fatally connected with punishments, would it not be sensible to allow for short periods of rest even in this obviously beneficial thing? They also say that Mikaladze had no right not to issue laws—and that is certainly correct. But, on the other hand, do we not see that the best-educated people regard themselves as happiest on Sundays and feast days—

the days when superiors consider themselves free from writing laws?

It is hardly possible to neglect this evidence of experience. The story of the chronicler may well suffer from an absence of vivid and tangible facts, but this ought not to prevent us from recognizing that Mikaladze was the first in the succession of Foolsburg mayors to set up the most precious of all administrative precedents—the precedent of meek and unobscene rhetoric. Let us suppose that this precedent did not offer anything particularly firm; let us suppose that in its further development it was the object of various more or less cruel incidents; but it is impossible to deny that once introduced, it never died out completely, but from time to time even gave quite a persuasive reminder of its existence. Is that so little?

This worthy administrator had one weakness—an unrestrained, almost feverish craving for the female sex. The chronicler dwells on this peculiarity of his hero in great detail, but the remarkable thing is that there is no bitterness or anger in his story. Only once he puts it this way: "There was much damage from him for Foolsburg women and maidens," and by saying this he seems to imply that, in his opinion, it would have been better if there had been no damage. But he never expresses any indignation directly. However, we will not follow the chronicle in portraying this weakness, for those who wish to acquaint themselves with it can obtain everything necessary from the appended work "On the Seemly Appearance of Mayors," written by the exalted author himself. In all fairness we must say that this work omits one major circumstance mentioned in the chronicle. Namely, that one night Mikaladze got in with a local treasurer's wife, but he had just freed himself from his bonds (that is what the chronicler calls a uniform) when the jealous husband caught him unawares. A battle ensued in which Mikaladze did not so much beat as get beaten. But he washed himself immediately after and no traces of dishonor were left. This seems to be the only failure he suffered in this line, and it is understandable why he did not mention it in his work. This was such a negligible detail in the great succession of his formidable feats in this field that it did not even evoke in him any need for strategic considerations that could secure his campaigns in the future ...

Mikaladze died in 1806 from exhaustion.

Once the soil had been well prepared by polite behavior and the people had rested from enlightenment, the turn for the need of new laws came of itself. The state councillor Feofilakt Irinarkhovich Benevolensky, a friend and classmate of Speransky in the seminary, came to answer this need.[7]

From very early youth Benevolensky had felt an irresistible urge to lawmaking. Sitting in the classroom of the seminary, he had already outlined several laws, among which the following are to be noted: "Let every man's heart be contrite," "Let every soul tremble," and "Let every frog know his corresponding bog." But the older the highly gifted youth became, the more insuperable grew his inborn passion. That he would in any event become a lawmaker no one doubted; the question was what sort of lawmaker he would be—that is, would he resemble the thoughtfulness and administrative foresight of Lycurgus, or would he simply be firm as Draco?[8] The young man himself sensed the importance of this question, and in a letter to "a certain friend" (is Speransky not hiding behind this appellation?) describes his hesitations on the subject in the following manner.

"I am sitting in my dismal solitude," he writes, "thinking every moment of which laws are most beneficial. There are wise laws which contribute to human happiness (such as, for example, laws about supplying all people everywhere with food), but which in certain circumstances are not useful; there are laws that are not wise, which, though they contribute to no one's happiness, may be useful in certain circumstances (I do not give any examples: you know them yourself!); and there are, finally, middling laws, neither very wise nor very unwise, which, being neither useful nor useless, may be beneficial in the sense of having the best impact on human life. For example, when we forget ourselves and begin to imagine that we are immortal, how refreshing for us is the simple phrase: *memento mori*! There is also this: when we think that our happiness has no bounds, that wise laws do not concern us, and that we are not subject to the unwise ones, then the middling laws come to our help, and their role is to remind the living that there is no one on earth for whom at least some law has not been written at some appropriate time. And will you believe me, friend? The more I think, the more I incline toward the middling laws. They enchant my soul, because they are, in fact, not even laws, but, so to speak, the twilight of the laws.[9] Entering their area, you feel that you are in communion with legality, but what this communion is you do not understand. All this happens apart from any reflection; you do not think about anything, do not see anything definite, but at the same time you feel some sort of anxiousness, which seems vague because it is not based on anything in particular. It is, so to speak, an apocalyptic writing, which can only be understood by the one who receives it. The middling laws are convenient in that anyone who reads them says: how stupid! and yet everyone irrepressibly strives to obey them. If, for instance, a law is issued: 'Let everyone eat,' this will be precisely an example of those middling laws, which everyone strives to obey without the least amount of urging. You will ask me, friend: Why issue laws which everyone obeys anyway? To this I will respond that the aim of issuing laws is double: some are issued for the better organizing of peoples and countries, others so that the lawmakers do not stagnate in idleness"...

And so on.

Thus, when Benevolensky arrived in Foolsburg, his views of lawgiving had already been established, and that precisely in the sense which was most suitable for the needs of the moment. Consequently, the well-being of Foolsburgers, initiated by the Circassian Mikaladze, not only was not disrupted, but received an even greater confirmation. Foolsburg needed precisely "the twilight of the laws"—that is, such laws as, while usefully occupying the leisure time of the lawmakers, could be of no essential concern to any other people. Sometimes such laws are even called wise, and, in the opinion of competent people, there is nothing exaggerated or unmerited in this appellation.

But here an unforeseen circumstance emerged. When Benevolensky set about publishing the first law, it turned out that, being simply a mayor, he had no right to issue his own laws. At first, when the secretary informed Benevolensky of it, he did not even believe him. They began to search among the Senate edicts, and rummaged all through the archives, but found no laws that would authorize Wartbeardins, Epikurovs, Gigantovs, Benevolenskys, etc. to issue laws of their own invention.

"Without a law you can do as you like!" said the secretary. "But write laws you cannot, sir!"

"Strange!" said Benevolensky, and he immediately wrote to his superiors about the difficulty he had encountered.

"I arrived in the town of Foolsburg," he wrote, "and although I found its inhabitants enjoying the state of prosperity brought about by my predecessor, at the same time I discovered such a scarcity of laws that the people do not even conceive of any distinction between law and nature. And thus they wander in the dark of night, without any manifest light. In this extremity I ask myself: What if one of these wanderers happens to stumble and fall into an abyss, what can keep him from such a fall? Although there is an abundance of laws in the Russian state, they are all dispersed in various dossiers, and it is even quite possible that many of them burned up in past fires. And, owing to that, one can see the essential need for me, as a mayor, to be able to speedily issue laws of my own invention, even if they be not first-rate (I dare not dream of that!) but second- or third-. What confirms me in this thinking is that the town of Foolsburg, by its very nature, belongs, so to speak, to the realm of secondary legality, in which there is no need for burdensome or complicated laws. Expecting a positive response to this my petition, I remain . . ." etc.

The response to this submission came quickly.

"In response to your suggestion to regard the town of Foolsburg as a realm of secondary legality, we offer the following for your consideration:

(1) If there turn up a great number of regions where the mayors start writing secondary laws, will this not cause a certain amount of harm to the architecture of the Russian state? And

(2) If the mayors are allowed, as mayors, to write secondary laws, will the village headmen not then also, as headmen, ask to be allowed to issue laws, and of what sort will those laws be?

Benevolensky realized that these questions amounted to an indirect refusal, and was deeply distressed. The explanation of this distress by his contemporaries was that the poison of autocracy had already touched his soul. This was hardly so. When a man can do whatever he likes even without any laws, it is strange to suspect him of an ambition for something that not only does not expand, but in fact limits this possibility. For a law, whatever it might be (even such as, for example, "Let every man eat," or "Let every soul tremble"), does possess a limiting power which can never be to the liking of an ambitious man. It was thus obvious that Benevolensky was not so much an ambitious man as a kindhearted pedant to whom it even seemed objectionable to wipe his nose, unless the code of law clearly formulated that "if anyone is in need of wiping his nose, let him wipe it."

Be that as it may, Benevolensky was so distressed by this refusal that he withdrew to the house of the merchant's widow Raspopova (whom he respected for her art of baking savory pies) and, to give an outlet to the yearning for mental activity that consumed him, gave himself over with relish to the writing of sermons. For a whole month the priests read these masterfully written sermons in all the town churches, and for a whole month the Foolsburgers sighed listening to them—they had been written with such feeling! The mayor himself taught the priests how to deliver them.

"A preacher," he said, "should have a contrite heart and, consequently, a head slightly inclined to one side.[10] He should not bark, but speak in a languorous, as-if-sighing voice. He should not gesticulate frantically, but, placing his right hand initially on his heart (the true source of all sighing), gradually move it forward into space, and then back to the same source. In emotional passages, he should not shout or put in his own unnecessary words, but only sigh louder."

Meanwhile, the Foolsburgers were growing fatter and fatter, and Benevolensky was not only not distressed, but was even glad of it. It did not occur to him even once: What if these prosperous people were given a bloodletting? On the contrary, watching the townsfolk waddling about from the windows of Mrs. Raspopova's house, he even asked himself: Aren't these people so prosperous because they're not bothered by laws of any sort? However, this last suggestion was too bitter for his mind to stop at that. As soon as he tore his gaze from the exultant Foolsburgers, the longing for lawmaking came over him again.

"I'm even unable to describe it, my most esteemed Marfa Terentievna," he would say to Raspopova, "what I could do, and how prosperous these people would become compared to now, if I were permitted to issue at least one law a day!"

In the end he could not restrain himself anymore. One dark night, when not only the policemen but even the dogs were sleeping, he quietly snuck outside and scattered leaflets around with the first law he had composed for Foolsburg written on them. Though he understood that this way of publishing laws was rather reprehensible, the long-repressed passion for lawmaking so loudly demanded satisfaction that even the arguments of reason were silenced before its voice.

The law was apparently written in a hurry, and therefore was distinguished by extraordinary brevity. The next day, on their way to the market, Foolsburgers picked up the leaflets from the ground and read the following:

Law i

"Let every man walk in circumspection; let the tax farmer bring gifts."

That was all. But the sense of the law was clear, and the very next day the tax farmer showed up at the mayor's. A discussion followed. The tax farmer argued that he had been ready even before, to the extent of the possible; Benevolensky objected that he was unable to remain in the former uncertain state; that the expression "to the extent of the possible" spoke neither to the mind nor to the heart, and that only the law made it clear. They agreed on three thousand rubles a year and set this amount as lawful, till the time when "circumstances would bring about a change in the laws."

Having recounted this incident, the chronicler asks himself: "Was there any use in such a law?" and answers the question positively. "The inhabitants of Foolsburg," he says, "were not in the least troubled by the reminder about walking in circumspection, for even before then they were endowed, by their very nature, with a great ability for such walking and constantly exercised it. But the tax farmer truly felt the usefulness of this law, because, when Benevolensky's successor, Pustule, instead of the usual three thousand demanded twice as much, the tax farmer most boldly answered: 'I cannot, for by law I am not obliged to give more than three thousand.' Pustule then said: 'We will change this law.' And so he did."

Encouraged by the success of the first law, Benevolensky began to actively prepare for issuing a second one. The fruits were not slow to come, and soon a new and now more expanded law appeared in the streets of the town, in the same mysterious way, announcing this:

Regulations for the Respectable Baking of Pies

(1) Let everyone bake pies on feast days, and feel free to pursue the baking also on ordinary days.

(2) Let everyone use a filling according to circumstances. Thus, having caught a fish in the river, put it into a pie; having chopped up some meat, put it into a pie; having chopped cabbage—do the same. Poor people should make pies with tripe.

Note. To make pies out of mud, clay, and building materials is permanently forbidden.

(3) Once the filling is ready and a due amount of butter and eggs is added, let the pie be put in the heated oven and kept in it till it is golden and ready.

(4) Once the pie comes out of the oven, let the cook take a knife in hand, cut out the middle portion, and offer it as a gift.

(5) Let whoever does so then eat.

The Foolsburgers understood the meaning of this new legislation the more quickly since from time immemorial they had had the habit of cutting out a portion from their pies and offering it as a gift. Though of late, under the liberal rule of Mikaladze, this custom had been neglected and not followed, they did not murmur against its renewal, hoping that this would still better seal the amiable relations between them and the new mayor. Everyone hastened to gladden Benevolensky; they vied in offering the best portion, and some even offered a whole pie.

After that the lawmaking activity in Foolsburg was at a boil. No day passed without a new stealthily planted leaflet appearing to gladden the hearts of the Foolsburgers. There finally came a moment when Benevolensky even began to contemplate a constitution.

"A constitution, I must tell you, my esteemed Marfa Terentievna," he said to the merchant's widow Raspopova, "is not at all such a bogey as unthinking people suppose it to be. The meaning of every constitution is this: let everyone stay safely in his own home! What, may I ask, my good madam, is so terrible or shameful in that?"

And he began to ponder his intention, but the more he pondered, the more entangled he became in his thoughts. The most confusing was his inability to give a sufficiently firm definition of the word "rights." He had a very clear idea about the word "responsibilities," so much so that he could write whole reams of paper on the subject, but "rights"?—what are "rights"? Would it be enough to define them by saying, "Let everyone stay safely in his home"? Would it not be much too brief? On the other hand, if he starts explaining, will it not be too broad and burdensome for the Foolsburgers themselves?

These doubts were resolved by Benevolensky in the guise of a transitional measure, publishing "Regulations of Benevolence Proper to a Mayor," which, being extensive, is provided among the supporting documents.

"I know," he said to the merchant's widow Raspopova on that occasion, "that this document does not yet contain a real constitution, but I beg you, most esteemed lady, to take into consideration that no building, be it even a chicken coop, can be completed all at once! In due time we will accomplish the rest of this cause so dear to me, and meanwhile let us comfort ourselves by placing our hopes in God!"

Nevertheless there is no reason to doubt that sooner or later Benevolensky would have realized his intention, but just then there were clouds gathering over him. The fault lay with Bonaparte. This was the year 1811, and the relations of Russia and Napoleon became very strained.[11] However, the renown of this new "scourge of God" had not yet faded and even reached Foolsburg. There, among his many lady admirers (it is remarkable that it was the female sex that distinguished itself by a particular partiality for the enemy of the human race), the most ardent fanaticism was shown by the merchant's widow Raspopova.

"Ah, how I long for this Bonaparte!" she said to Benevolensky. "I would spare nothing, I think, just to catch a glimpse of him!"

At first Benevolensky was angry and even called Raspopova a "stupid woman," but since Marfa Terentievna would not calm down and pestered the mayor more and more—"Just go and present me with Bonaparte"—he finally gave in. He realized that it was impossible not to fulfill the demand of the "stupid woman" and gradually even came to see nothing reprehensible in it.

"Well, so! Let the stupid woman have some fun!" he said to comfort himself. "It won't do any harm!"

And he entered into secret contact with Napoleon . . .

God alone knows how this became known, but it seems that Napoleon himself spilled it out to Prince Kurakin at one of his *petits levers*.[12] And so, one fine morning, Foolsburg was astonished to find that it was governed not by a mayor, but by a traitor, and that a special committee was coming from the provincial capital to look into his treason.

Here everything was revealed: that Benevolensky secretly invited Napoleon to Foolsburg, and that he issued his own laws. He could only justify himself by saying that Foolsburgers had never been as prosperous as under him, but this was not accepted as vindication, or, better to say, the response was that "he would be more right if he had driven Foolsburgers to destitution, as long as he refrained from issuing his absurd writings, which he most brazenly referred to as laws."

It was a warm moonlit night when a kibitka drove up to the mayor's house. Benevolensky came out to the porch with firm steps and was about to bow to all four sides when he was perplexed to see that there was no one in the street except for two gendarmes. On this occasion the Foolsburgers, as usual, astonished the world by their ingratitude, and as soon as they learned that things were going badly for their mayor, they deprived him of their favor. However bitter this cup was, Benevolensky drained it in good cheer. "Do-nothings!" he pronounced in a distinct and clear voice, got into the kibitka, and successfully proceeded to the back of beyond.[13]

Thus ended the administrative career of a mayor in whom the passion for issuing laws was in perpetual conflict with the passion for savory pies. In our time, by the way, the laws he issued are no longer in force.

But apparently the good fortune of the Foolsburgers was not to end soon. Lieutenant-Colonel Pustule came to replace Benevolensky, bringing along a still more simplified system of administration.

Pustule was no longer young, but he was remarkably well-preserved. Broad-shouldered and heavyset, he seemed by his very figure to be saying: "Don't look at my gray whiskers: I'm still able! Still very much able!" He was ruddy, with red and full lips and a row of white teeth showing behind them; his gait was energetic and brisk, his gestures quick. All that was adorned with gleaming officer's epaulets, which flashed on his shoulders at the slightest movement.

Following the custom, he paid introductory visits to the town dignitaries and other members of the local nobility of both sexes, and during these visits developed his program before them.

"I'm a simple man," he said to some, "and I didn't come here to issue laws. My duty is to preserve them intact and see that they do not just lie about on desks. I certainly have a plan of campaign, but the plan is this: to repose!"

To others he said:

"My fortune, thank God, is substantial. I was a commander, so I didn't spend, but increased.[14] Consequently, whatever laws there are on this account—those I know, and I have no wish to issue any new ones. Of course, many in my place would rush into an attack or maybe even start bombarding, but I'm a simple man and see no comfort for myself in attacking!"

To still others he spoke thus:

"I'm not a liberal and have never been a liberal, gentlemen. My actions are always straightforward, and therefore I steer clear of the laws. In difficult cases I have some research done, but I request one thing: that the law should be old. I don't like new laws, gentlemen. In them much is omitted, and certain things are not mentioned at all. I've always spoken thus, and I spoke thus just now, before coming here. Spare me from new laws, and I hope to accomplish the rest in exactly the right way!"

He finally portrayed himself to a fourth group in these colors:

"About myself I can say one thing: I've never been in battles, but I am seasoned in parading, even beyond proportion. I don't understand new ideas. I don't even understand why they need to be understood."

Moreover, on the first Sunday he gathered a general assembly of the Foolsburgers and before it formally confirmed his views of administration.

"So, old boys," he said to the townsfolk, "let's live peacefully. You leave me alone, I leave you alone. Plant and sow, eat and drink, set up mills and factories—very well! It's all for your own good! As far as I'm concerned, you may even erect monuments—I won't hinder you in that, either! Only, for Christ's sake, be careful with fire, because in this you're not far from harm's way. You'll burn up your property, you'll burn up yourselves—what good is that!"

However much the Foolsburgers had been spoiled by the last two mayors, such boundless liberalism made them ponder: Isn't there a catch somewhere? Therefore they spent some time looking around, finding out, talking in whispers, and generally "being circumspect." It seemed a bit strange that the mayor not only renounced interference in people's affairs, but even asserted that such noninterference was precisely the whole essence of administration.

"And you won't issue any laws?" they asked him mistrustfully.

"I won't issue any laws—live and God help you!"

"Aha! Please don't! You know what the rascal"—that was how they called Benevolensky—"got for that! If you start doing the same, both you and we may have to answer for it!"

But Pustule was perfectly sincere in his statements and firmly resolved to follow the chosen path. Having put an end to all activity, he went around visiting, accepted invitations to dinners and balls, and even got himself a pack of hounds with which he hunted hares and foxes on the town common and once even hunted down a very pretty girl. About his predecessor, who was then languishing in exile, he spoke not without irony.

"It was mostly on paper," he said, "that Filat Irinarkhovich promised that during his rule people would supposedly be prosperous and peaceful, while I will provide the same in practice . . . yes, sirs!"

And so he did: although Pustule's first steps were met with mistrust by the Foolsburgers, before long they had twice and three times more of everything than before. Bees swarmed remarkably well, so that almost as much honey and wax was sent to Byzantium as under Prince Oleg.[15] Although there were no cattle plagues, there were a lot of hides, and since, despite that, the Foolsburgers paraded around more comfortably in bast shoes than in boots, the hides were packed off to Byzantium *in toto*, and were paid for in full with sterling banknotes. And as there was now freedom for everyone to produce dung, the harvest of grain was so huge that after the sale, there was even some left for their own use. "Not as in other towns," the chronicler remarks bitterly, "where railroads* are unable to transport the fruits of the earth meant for sale, while farmers starve for lack of food. That happy year in Foolsburg not only the owners but all the hired hands ate real bread, and hot cabbage soup was not a rarity."

Pustule rejoiced at the sight of such well-being. And he could not but rejoice, for this general abundance contributed to his prosperity. His barns were bursting from offerings in kind; his coffers were not large enough to contain the silver and gold, and the banknotes simply lay about on the floor.

Thus one more year passed, in the course of which the Foolsburgers acquired not two or three, now, but four times more of various goods than before. But as freedom developed, so also its primordial enemy—analysis—was springing up. The growth of material prosperity led to the acquisition

---

* There had been no thought of railroads at the time, but this is one of those harmless anachronisms that often occur in his chronicle.—*Publisher*

of leisure, and leisure led to the ability to examine and test the nature of things. This always happens, but the Foolsburgers employed this "newly sprung-up ability of theirs" not to secure their well-being, but to undermine it.

Not yet firm in self-governing, the Foolsburgers began to ascribe this phenomenon to the mediation of some unknown power. And since in their language "unknown power" was a name for devilry, they began to think that things were not quite right, and it followed that the devil's part in these matters could not be doubted. They began to keep an eye on Pustule and found something dubious in his behavior. It was said, for instance, that someone once found him sleeping on a couch with his body surrounded on all sides by mousetraps. Others went further and asserted that Pustule went to sleep every night in the ice cellar. All that pointed to something mysterious, and although no one asked himself who cares if the mayor sleeps in the ice cellar and not in an ordinary bedroom, everybody was alarmed. General suspicions grew still more when it was noticed that the local marshal of nobility had for some time been in an unnaturally excited state, and each time he met the mayor, he began to circle around him and perform strange capers.[16]

One could not say that the marshal had any special qualities of mind and heart; but he did have a stomach in which all sorts of morsels disappeared as in a grave. This none-too-sophisticated gift of nature turned for him into a source of most lively pleasure. Early every morning he set out on a journey over the town and sniffed the smells coming from people's kitchens. Before long his sense of smell became so refined that he could unerringly guess the composition of a most complicated stuffing.

Already during his first encounter with the mayor, the marshal sensed that there was something quite extraordinary concealed in this dignitary—namely, that he smelled of truffles. For a long time he fought his conjecture, taking it for a dream of his imagination inflamed by food products, but the more often he met the mayor, the more tormenting his doubts became. In the end, unable to stand it, he confessed his suspicions to Halfkin, the clerk of the board of trustees.

"He smells!" he said to his amazed confidant. "He does! Just like a delicatessen shop!"

"Maybe, sir, he applies truffle pomade to his hair?" suggested Halfkin.

"Ah, no, brother, fiddlesticks! In that case every suckling pig will lie in your face that he is not a suckling pig, but only sprays himself with suckling-pig scent!"

This initial conversation had no follow-up, but the notion of suckling-pig scent sank deeply into the marshal's soul. He fell into a gastronomic anguish and wandered around town as if enamored and, seeing Pustule somewhere, licked his chops most absurdly. Once during some general assembly that was supposed to organize enhanced gastronomic festivities during Meatfare Week,[17] the marshal, driven to a frenzy by the pungent smell coming from the mayor, jumped up wildly from his seat and shouted: "Fetch some mustard and vinegar!" And leaning toward the mayor's head, he began to sniff it.

The amazement of the persons who were present at this mysterious scene was boundless. Strange, too, was that the mayor said quite imprudently, though through his teeth:

"He's guessed it, the scoundrel!"

And then, catching himself, he added with an obviously sham casualness:

"It seems our most worthy marshal thinks I've got stuffing in my head . . . ha, ha!"

Alas! This indirect confession was the most bitter truth!

The marshal fainted, became delirious, but, having recovered, forgot nothing and learned nothing.[18] Several scenes took place, almost indecent ones. The marshal fidgeted, circled around, and at last, finding himself one-on-one with Pustule, boldly advanced.

"A tiny piece!" he moaned, standing before the mayor, watching keenly the expression in his chosen victim's eyes.

At the first sound of such a clearly formulated request, the mayor faltered. All at once his situation became outlined with that definitive clarity which renders any negotiation useless. He glanced timidly at his assailant and, meeting his gaze filled with resolution, suddenly lapsed into a state of boundless anguish.

Nevertheless, he still made a feeble attempt at resistance. A struggle ensued; but the marshal was already in a frenzy and beside himself. His eyes flashed, his stomach felt a delicious longing. He gasped, moaned, called the mayor "sweetie," "darling," and other names inappropriate to this rank; he licked him, sniffed him, etc. Finally, in unprecedented self-abandon, the marshal fell upon his victim, cut off a chunk of his head, and swallowed it at once . . .

A second chunk followed the first, then a third, until there was not a scrap left . . .

Then the mayor suddenly jumped up and began to paw those places of his body the marshal had sprinkled with vinegar. Then he spun in place and his whole body suddenly crashed to the floor.

The next day the Foolsburgers found out that their mayor had had a stuffed head . . .

But nobody guessed that this was precisely why the town had attained to such prosperity as had never been known in the chronicles from the time of its foundation.

The Worship of Mammon and Repentance

Man's life is a dream, spiritualist philosophers tell us, and if they were entirely logical they would add: history, too, is a dream. Of course, taken in an absolute sense, both of these comparisons are equally absurd; however, one cannot but admit that there are in history sinkholes, as it were, which make human thought stop not without perplexity. It is as if the stream of life ceases its natural course and forms a whirlpool, which spins, sprays, and gets covered with turbid foam, through which it is impossible to make out either clear typical features or even any specific phenomena. Confused and senseless events follow one another disconnectedly, and people apparently do not pursue any other goals than the safeguarding of the present day. They alternate between trembling and triumph, and the more strongly they feel humiliation, the more harsh and vengeful is the triumph. This anxiety proceeds from a source that is already turbid; the principles in the name of which the struggle began are effaced; what remains is struggle for struggle's sake, art for art's sake, which invents the rack, walking on nails, etc.

Of course, this anxiety is concentrated chiefly on the surface; however, it is hardly possible to maintain that at the same time things are well at the bottom. What is happening in those layers of the deep which are below the upper one and farther down to the very bottom? Is there peace and quiet in those layers, or are they, too, under the pressure of anxiety we find in the upper layer? This cannot be determined with full accuracy, since we generally have no habit of paying attention to what happens deep inside. But we will hardly be mistaken if we say that the pressure can be felt there as well. It shows partly in the form of material damages and losses, but most of all in the more or less prolonged delay of social development.[1] And although the results of these losses are manifested with particular grievousness only later, still one can guess that contemporaries do not especially enjoy the pressures that weigh on them.

During the time described by the chronicler, Foolsburg was probably going through one of these difficult historical periods. The town's own inner life hid at the bottom, and some sort of malignant emanations rose to the surface, which took total control of the arena of history. Artificial extraneous admixtures entangled Foolsburg from top to bottom, and while it may be said that in the general economy of its existence this artificiality was not utterly useless, it would be no less true to assert that people who live under such oppression are not altogether happy people. To endure Wartbeardin in order to learn about the usefulness of certain plants; to endure Urus-Kugush-Kildibaev in order to learn about true valor—like it or not, such a destiny cannot be called either truly normal or particularly flattering, although, on the other hand, it cannot be denied that some plants are indeed useful, and there is no harm in valor, if applied at the right time and place.

Under such circumstances it is impossible to expect people to commit any feats in the line of public amenities and order, or to be particularly successful in the line of learning and the arts. For them such historical epochs are years of formation, during which they test themselves in one thing: to what extent they are able to endure. This is precisely how the chronicler presents his compatriots to us. One can see from his account that the Foolsburgers unquestioningly submit to the caprices of history and do not present anything that would allow us to judge the degree of their maturity in the sense of self-governing; that, on the contrary, they rush about helter-skelter, without any plan, as if driven by unconscious fear.

No one will deny that the picture is not flattering, but it cannot be otherwise, because the material for it is a person whose head is being hammered with astounding persistence and who, naturally, cannot arrive at any other result than stupefaction. The chronicler reveals to us the history of these stupefactions with the artlessness and truth which always distinguish the accounts of chroniclers and archivists. In my opinion, this is all we have the right to demand of him. No deliberate mockery can be noticed in his accounts; on the contrary, in many places one can even discern a compassion for the poor, stupefied people. The fact alone that despite a mortal struggle, the Foolsburgers still go on living, is a sufficient testimony to their resilience, which deserves serious attention on the part of the historian.

Let us not forget that the chronicler tells mostly about the so-called mob, which even to this day is regarded as seemingly outside the limits of history.[2] On the one hand, his mental eye pictures a power that stole up from afar and managed to organize itself and grow strong; on the other—some little wretches and orphans scattered in nooks and crannies and always taken unawares. Can there be any doubt concerning the nature of the relations that are to emerge when such opposed elements are brought together?

That the power in question is not anything invented is proven by the fact that the notion of it even lay at the basis of a whole school of historical thinking. The representatives of this school preach quite sincerely that the more people are annihilated, the more prosperous they become and the more brilliant history itself will be. This, of course, is a none-too-intelligent opinion, but how are we to prove that to people who are so sure of themselves that they do not heed or accept any proofs? Before one starts proving anything, one has to make an opponent listen, and how can that be done if the complainer himself is not entirely convinced that he need not be exterminated?

"I told him: 'What reason, sir, do you have for beating me?' and he just punched me in the jaw: 'Here's the reason for you! Here's the reason!'"

This is the only clear formula of mutual relations possible under such conditions. There is no reason for beating, but there is also no reason for not beating: the obvious result is the grievous tautology in which a punch is explained by a punch. Of course, this tautology hangs by a thread, just a single thread, but how is one to break this thread? That is the whole question. And so an opinion emerges by itself: Would it not be better to put our hopes in the future? This opinion is none too intelligent, either, but what is to be done if no other opinions have been worked out yet? It is this opinion that was apparently held by the Foolsburgers.

Having likened themselves to eternal debtors who are in the power of eternal creditors, they decided that there were different creditors in the world: reasonable and unreasonable. A reasonable creditor helps his debtor to get out of constrained circumstances and receives his debt as a reward for being reasonable. The unreasonable creditor puts the debtor in jail or flogs him ceaselessly, and gets nothing as a reward. Having reflected in this way, the Foolsburgers began to wait to see if all the creditors would become reasonable. And they are waiting to this day.

Therefore I see nothing in the chronicler's account that would infringe upon the dignity of the townsfolk of Foolsburg. They are people like any other, with this one reservation: that their natural qualities are overgrown with a mass of alien particles, under which it is impossible to see anything. Therefore there is no talking about any actual qualities, but only about the alien particles. Would it be better or even more agreeable if the chronicler, instead of describing disorderly movements, portrayed Foolsburg as an ideal center of legality and rights? For instance, would the readers find it more agreeble if, at the moment when Wartbeardin demanded that mustard be used everywhere, the chronicler had made Foolsburgers not tremble before him, but successfully prove that his measure was untimely and inappropriate? In all sincerity I maintain that such a perversion of Foolsburgian customs would be not only useless, but even downright disagreeable. And the reason for that is very simple: it would render the chronicler's account *discordant with the truth*.

The unexpected beheading of Major Pustule had almost no effect on the well-being of the inhabitants. For a while, owing to the dearth of mayors, the town was governed by police officers; but since liberalism was still giving the tone to life, they did not attack the people, but politely strolled through the market, casting tender glances and trying to choose the fattest morsel. But even these modest promenades were not always successful, because the townsfolk became so bold that they readily presented them with nothing but offal.

The consequence of this well-being was that in the course of a whole year only one conspiracy took place in Foolsburg, and it was not by the townsfolk against the policemen (as usually happens) but, on the contrary, by the policemen against the townsfolk (as never happens). Namely: the starving policemen decided to poison all the dogs in the shopping arcade, so as to enter the shops unhindered during the night. Fortunately, the attempt was uncovered in good time, and the conspiracy was resolved by the participants being deprived for a time of their appointed portions of offal.

After that the state councillor Ivanov arrived in Foolsburg, but he turned out to be so short that he had no room inside to accommodate anything extensive. As if on purpose, this was precisely the time when a passion for lawmaking in our fatherland acquired all but dangerous dimensions; offices overflowed with decrees like fairy-tale rivers with milk and honey, and every decree weighed no less than a pound. It was this circumstance that caused the downfall of Ivanov, though the story of it exists in two totally different versions. According to one version, Ivanov died of fright, having received a vast senatorial regulation which he could not hope to comprehend. The other version maintains that Ivanov did not die, but was retired, because the condition of his head reverted to the rudimentary as a result of a gradual drying up of the brain (from constant disuse). After which he supposedly lived for a long time on his own estate, where he managed to produce a whole species of "short-headed" humans, the Microcephalae, who exist to this day.

Which of these two versions is more trustworthy is hard to tell; but it would be fair to say that the atrophy of such an important member as a head could hardly occur in such a short time. However, on the other hand, there is no doubt that Microcephalae really exist, and tradition traces their ancestry to the state councillor Ivanov. For us, however, this is a secondary matter; what is important is that during the time of Ivanov, the Foolsburgers continued in their prosperity and, consequently, his defect did not harm them but served to their advantage.

In 1815 Viscount Du Chariot, a Frenchman, came to take the place of Ivanov. Paris had been taken; the enemy of mankind had been forever installed on the island of Saint Helena;[3] the *Moscow Gazette* announced that the enemy's disgrace meant their task was over, and promised to cease to exist, but the next day it took back its promise and gave another one, pledging to cease to exist only when Paris was taken for a second time. There was general rejoicing, and Foolsburg rejoiced with everyone else. They recalled the merchant widow Raspopova and how she, together with Benevolensky, had intrigued in favor of Napoleon. They dragged her outside and allowed the street boys to make fun of her. The little scoundrels pursued the ill-fated widow for the whole day, called her "Bonapartovna," "Antichrist's concubine," and so on, until she finally got beside herself and began to prophesy. The meaning of her prophecies became clear only later, when Sullen-Grumble arrived in Foolsburg and left no stone upon stone.

Du Chariot was happy. First, his émigré heart was glad because Paris had been taken; second, he had not eaten properly for so long that Foolsburg's savory pies seemed like the food of paradise to him. Having eaten his fill, he requested that he immediately be shown a place where he could *passer son temps à faire des bêtises* ("spend his time fooling around"), and was mightily pleased on learning that there was in the Soldiers' suburb an establishment of exactly the sort he wished for. Then he began to babble and never stopped until the authorities ordered him to be sent out of Foolsburg and abroad. But since he was, after all, a child of the eighteenth century, the spirit of analysis occasionally burst from his babble. This could have produced very bitter fruit, had it not been considerably softened by the spirit of frivolity. Thus, for instance, he once started talking to the Foolsburgers about human rights, but fortunately ended by telling them about the rights of the Bourbons.[4] On another occasion he began by persuading the inhabitants to believe in the goddess of Reason, and ended by asking them to recognize the infallibility of the pope. All this, however, was nothing but various *façons de parler* ("manners of speaking"), and in fact the viscount was ready to take the side of any persuasion or dogma if he could hope that a bit of cash would come his way.

He made merry tirelessly, giving masked balls daily, dressing up as a woman, dancing the cancan, and had a particular liking for flirting with men.* He was an expert singer of frivolous songs, and maintained that his teacher had been the comte d'Artois (the future king of France Charles X), when they were both in Riga. At first he ate anything, but once he had eaten enough, he started choosing mostly the so-called unclean stuff, with a marked preference for offal and frogs. He did not perform any deeds, nor did he interfere in the administration.

This last circumstance promised to prolong the well-being of the Foolsburgers endlessly, except that they themselves wore out under the burden of their happiness. They forgot themselves. Spoiled by five consecutive mayorships, driven almost to brutishness by the crude flattering of police

---

* In which there was nothing astonishing, since the chronicler himself tells us that this Du Chariot had been investigated at some point and found to be a woman.—*Publisher*

officers, they imagined that happiness belonged to them by right and that no one could take it away from them. Victory over Napoleon confirmed them still more in this opinion, and it was probably in that period that the famous saying "We'll walk all over them!" was first used, which served for a long time afterwards as a motto for the victories of the Foolsburgers on the battlefield.

And so a whole series of woeful events followed, which the chronicler calls "a shameless Foolsburgian frenzy," but which it would be much more suitable to call "short-lived Foolsburgian antics."

They began by throwing bread under the table and making a frenzied sign of the cross. The accusations of the time are filled with the most bitter mentions of this woeful fact. "Once upon a time," roared the accusers, "Foolsburgian piety could put to shame the ancient Platos and Socrateses; nowadays not only have they themselves turned into Platos, but worse than that, for one would think that even Plato put bread into his mouth instead of throwing it on the floor, as the fashion of the day enjoins us to do." But the Foolsburgers did not heed these accusations and brazenly objected: "Let swine eat bread, and we'll eat swine—that'll be the same bread!" And Du Chariot not only did not forbid such responses, but even saw in them the emerging spirit of some sort of analysis.

Feeling themselves free, the Foolsburgers rushed somehow frenziedly down the slippery slope that now lay at their feet. They immediately decided to build a tower, in such a way that its top would be sure to reach up to heaven. But since they had no architects, and their carpenters were uneducated and not always sober, they raised the tower halfway and abandoned it, and probably only for that reason avoided the confusion of tongues.[5]

But even this did not seem enough. The Foolsburgers forgot the one true God and clung to idols. They recalled that already under Vladimir the Fair Sun, some obsolete gods had been put on the shelf. They rushed to the shelves and produced two idols: Perun and Volos.[6] Having had no renovation for several centuries, the idols were in a terrible state, and Perun even had a mustache drawn on him with a piece of coal. Nevertheless, the Foolsburgers found them very attractive. They called an assembly at once and decided: upper-class persons of both sexes were to worship Perun, and commoners were to offer sacrifices to Volos. They summoned some clergy and demanded that they become sorcerers. But the clergy did not respond and only trembled in their cassocks. Then it was recalled that there was in the Musketeers' suburb someone called "Defrocked Kuzma" (the old priest who, if the reader remembers, in the time of Wartbeardin, intended to join the schismatics), and they sent for him. By then Kuzma was already completely deaf and blind, but the moment they gave him a ruble coin to smell, he agreed to everything and began to shout something incomprehensible in verses from Averkiev's opera *Rogneda*.[7]

Du Chariot watched this whole ceremony from the window, rolled with laughter, and cried: *"Sont-ils bêtes! Dieux des dieux! Sont-ils bêtes, ces moujiks de Foolsberg!"* ("How stupid they are! By God! How stupid these Foolsburg muzhiks are!")

The corruption of morals progressed by the hour. Cocottes and coquettes appeared; men began to wear waistcoats cut so low that their chests were completely open; women constructed elevations in the rear that had a transformative meaning and aroused free thoughts in passersby. A new language was formed, half human half ape, and unsuited to expressing any abstract thoughts whatever. Persons of distinction walked in the streets singing "A moi le pompon" or "La Vénus aux carottes";[8] the rabble loitered around pothouses bawling folk songs. The understanding was that while they were carousing, bread would grow by itself, and so they stopped cultivating the land. Respect for older people vanished; the question was raised: Should people, on reaching a certain age, be removed from life? But mercenary instinct prevailed, and it was decided to sell the old men and women into slavery. To top it all off, they cleared out some arena and produced *La Belle Hélène* in it, inviting Mademoiselle Blanche Gandon to sing the main role.[9]

And, with all that, they continued to regard themselves as the wisest people in the world.

Such was the situation in Foolsburg when State Councillor Erast Andreevich Melancholin arrived. He was a sensitive man, and blushed when he talked about relationships between the sexes. Just prior to that, he had written a novella entitled *Saturn Stopping His Course in the Arms of Venus*, in which, as critics of the time put it, the tenderness of Apuleius happily combined with the playfulness of Parny.[10] Under the name of Saturn he portrayed himself, under the name of Venus the famous beauty of the time Natalia Kirillovna de Pompadour.[11] "Saturn," he wrote, "was stooped and burdened by years, but was still capable of certain things. It came to pass that Venus, observing this particularity of his, rested her favorable gaze on him . . ."

But his melancholy appearance (the forerunner of his future mysticism) concealed many inclinations that were undoubtedly depraved. Thus, for instance, it was known that while serving as a quartermaster in the active army, he quite freely managed the government funds and relieved himself from the reproaches of his own conscience only by the abundant tears he shed at the sight of the soldiers eating moldy bread. It was also known that he got into Madame de Pompadour's favor not owing to a certain "particularity," but simply by way of monetary offerings, and that it was through her mediation that he evaded a trial and was even appointed to a higher post. And when this Pompadour woman, "having been lax in keeping a certain secret," was exiled to a convent and tonsured under the name of the nun Nimphodora, he was the first to cast a stone at her and wrote "The Story of a Certain Exceedingly Amorous Woman," which contained very clear allusions to his former benefactress. On top of that, although he was timid and blushed in the presence of women, this timidity was a cover for that greater sensuality which first likes to exacerbate itself and after that unswervingly presses for the set goal. There were many examples of his hidden but burning sensuality. Thus he once dressed as a swan and swam up to a bathing girl,[12] the daughter of noble parents, whose only dowry was her beauty, and, while she was stroking his head, ruined her for life. In short, his knowledge of mythology was thorough, and although he liked to pretend to be pious, he was in fact an inveterate idolater.

The dissoluteness of the Foolsburgers was to his liking. The moment he rode into the town, he met a procession which immediately interested him. Six girls dressed in transparent tunics were carrying the idol of Perun on a litter; at the head, in a state of ecstasy, leaped the wife of the marshal of nobility, covered in nothing but ostrich feathers; behind followed a crowd of noble men and women, among whom some more prominent representatives of the Foolsburg merchantry could be glimpsed (the peasants, tradesmen, and shopkeepers of a poorer sort were worshipping Volos at the time). On reaching the square, the crowd stopped. The Perun was set on a podium, the leader knelt and began in a loud voice to recite *An Evening Sacrifice* by Mr. Boborykin.[13]

"What's this?" asked Melancholin, peeking out of the carriage and looking from the corner of his eye at the marshal's wife's outfit.

"They're celebrating Perun's nameday, Your Honor!" the policemen responded with one accord.

"And girls . . . are there . . . any girls?" Melancholin asked somehow languidly.

"A whole synod of them, sir!" the policemen answered, exchanging sympathetic glances with each other.

Melancholin sighed and gave the order to drive on.

Stopping at the mayor's house and learning from the chief clerk that there were no arrears, that trade was flourishing and agriculture was developing from year to year, he paused for a moment, then hesitated slightly, as if unable to utter a cherished thought, and finally asked in a sort of uncertain voice:

"And do you have any wood grouse?"

"Yes, we do, Your Honor!"

"You know, my good man, I like sometimes . . . It's sometimes nice to watch . . . when there's this exultation in nature . . ."[14]

And he blushed. The clerk was also at a loss for a moment, then at once found what to say.

"What could be better, sir!" he replied. "Only, if I may venture to tell Your Honor: in this line there are even better spectacles here!"

"Hmm . . . really?"

"In our town, Your Honor, cocottes appeared under your predecessor, and in their popular theater they have a real mating ground, sir. They get together every evening, they whistle, they move their feet up and down . . ."

"That I'd like to see!" said Melancholin, and he lapsed into sweet reverie.

There was an opinion at the time that a mayor was the host of the town, and the inhabitants were as if his guests. The difference between "host" in the general sense of the word and "host of the town" was only that the latter had the right to flog his guests, something that common decency did not allow to an ordinary host. Melancholin recalled this right and fell into a still sweeter reverie.

"Do you have frequent floggings?" he asked the clerk, without raising his eyes to him.

"We have abandoned that fashion, Your Honor. No instance can be found since the time of Onufry Ivanych, Mr. Blaggardov. Everything is gentleness, sir."

"Well, but I will flog . . . the girls!" said Melancholin, suddenly blushing.

Thus the character of internal policy was clearly defined. It was supposed to continue the activity of the last five mayors, but increasing the element of frivolity introduced by the Viscount Du Chariot, and enriching it, for the sake of appearance, with a certain nuance of sentimentality. The influence of the short-termed stay in Paris was showing everywhere. The victors, having in their haste taken the hydra of despotism for the hydra of revolution and vanquished it, were in turn vanquished by those they had defeated. The majestic savagery of former times vanished without a trace; instead of giants who bent horseshoes and broke ruble coins, effeminate people appeared who had nothing but sweet indecencies on their mind. These indecencies had their own language. The amorous tryst of a man with a woman was called "a voyage to the isle of love"; the crude terminology of anatomy was replaced by a more refined one, as in "a playful misanthrope," "a sweet recluse," and so on.[15]

Nevertheless, life was easy, comparatively speaking, and this ease was particularly to the taste of the so-called commoners. Representatives of the Foolsburg intelligentsia, having thrown themselves into a polytheism complicated by frivolity, became indifferent to anything that occurred outside the closed sphere of "voyages to the isle of love." They felt happy and content and, being so, did not wish to prevent the happiness and contentment of others. In the times of Wartbeardin, Blaggardov, and others, it seemed, for instance, unforgivably brazen if a muzhik poured oil on his kasha. It was brazen not because it harmed anyone, but because people like Blaggardov are always desperate theoreticians and presume one ability in a muzhik: to be firm in adversity. Therefore they took the kasha from the muzhik and threw it to the dogs. Now this attitude changed considerably, to which, of course, the then-fashionable disease the softening of the brain contributed not a little. Muzhiks took advantage of this and filled their stomachs with heavy kasha to the utmost. They were still ignorant of the truth that man does not live by kasha alone, and therefore they thought that if their stomachs were full, it meant that things were well with them.[16] For the same reason they so willingly embraced polytheism: it seemed more convenient to them than monotheism. They more willingly worshipped Volos or Yarilo, all the while considering that if it does not rain for a long time, or rains for far too long, they could flog their beloved gods, smear them with dung, and generally vent their vexation on them. And although it is obvious that such crude materialism could not nourish society for long, still, as a novelty, it was pleasing and even intoxicating.

Everyone hastened to live and enjoy, and so did Melancholin. He completely abandoned his function as mayor and limited his administrative activity to doubling the taxes set up by his predecessors, and demanded that they be paid at the appointed time without delay. He devoted the rest of the time to the worship of Venus in the unprecedentedly diverse forms developed by the civilization of the time. This careless attitude toward the duties of his office was, however, a big mistake on Melancholin's part.

Even though Melancholin, while serving as quarter-master, had quite deftly concealed government money, his administrative experience was neither deep nor versatile. Many think that if a man knows how to surreptitiously steal a handkerchief from his neighbor's pocket, it is already enough to consolidate his reputation as a politician or reader of human hearts. This, however, is a mistake. Thieves who can read human hearts occur very rarely; more often it happens that even the most grandiose crook is a remarkable figure only in this sphere, and does not show any ability outside it. To steal successfully, one needs only deftness and greed. Greed in particular is necessary, because one can wind up in court even for a small theft. But with whatever names robbery covers itself, still the sphere of robbery is altogether different from the sphere of the reader of hearts, for the latter is a fisher of men, while the former fishes out only the wallets and handkerchiefs that belong to them. Consequently, if a man appropriates a sum of several million rubles, and afterwards becomes a Maecenas and builds a marble palace in which he collects all the wonders of science and art, even so he cannot be called a skillful public figure, but merely a skillful crook.

But at the time, these truths were still unknown, and Melancholin's reputation as a knower of human hearts was established without hindrance. In fact, however, this was not so. If Melancholin had indeed been equal to the occasion, he would have realized that his predecessors, who had raised

parasitism to an administrative principle, were bitterly de-
luded, and that parasitism can be a life-giving principle and
regard itself as achieving useful goals only if it is contained
within certain limits. Granted that parasitism exists, it goes
without saying that alongside it industry also exists—that is
the foundation of the whole science of political economy. Industry nourishes parasitism, parasitism fertilizes industry—
this is the sole formula that, from a scientific point of view,
can be freely applied to all the phenomena of life. Melancholin did not understand any of that. He thought that everyone
to a man could be a parasite, and that the productive powers
of the land not only would not be exhausted by it, but would
even increase. This was his first bad delusion.

The second consisted in his being too carried away by
the brilliance of his predecessors' internal politics. Hearing about the well-meaning inactivity of Major Pustule, he
was seduced by the picture of the general rejoicing that was
the result of this inactivity. But he failed to see, first, that
even quite mature nations cannot enjoy prosperity for very
long without the risk of falling into crude materialism, and,
second, that in Foolsburg itself, owing to the spirit of free-
thinking imported from Paris, prosperity was considerably
entangled with mischief. There is no arguing that people may
and even must be given an opportunity to taste the fruit of
the knowledge of good and evil, but this fruit should be held
in a firm hand, so that at any time it can be taken away from
much-too-relishing mouths.

The consequences of these delusions manifested themselves very soon. Already in 1815 there was a painfully poor
harvest, and the next year nothing grew at all, because the
townsfolk, corrupted by constant carousing, had relied so
firmly on their good fortune that they simply scattered seeds
without having tilled the soil.

"The rascal will produce anyway!" they said, befuddled by their own pride.

But their hopes did not come true, and when the fields in spring were free of snow, the Foolsburgers were amazed to see that they were completely bare. As usual, this was ascribed to the action of hostile powers, and the gods were accused of not giving people sufficient protection. They flogged Volos, who endured the punishment stoically, then started on Yarilo, and fancied that tears appeared in his eyes. The Foolsburgers scattered in terror, ran to the taverns, and began to wait for what would happen. But nothing special took place. There was rain, then fair weather, but no useful growth appeared on the unsown fields.

Melancholin was present at a masked ball (that year the Foolsburgers celebrated Shrovetide every day) when the news of the disaster threatening Foolsburg reached him. Apparently he had suspected nothing. He was bantering with the marshal's wife, telling her that he expected there would soon be such design in ladies' dresses as would allow one to look down in a straight line to the parquet on which the woman stood. Then he turned the conversation to the delights of solitary life, and mentioned in passing that he himself hoped to find repose someday within the walls of a monastery.

"You mean a convent, of course?" the marshal's wife asked with a coy smile.

"If you are the mother superior, I'm ready to take my vows even this very minute," Melancholin replied gallantly.

But that evening was destined to draw a deep demarcation line in Melancholin's internal politics. The ball was at its height; the dancers whirled furiously; in the flurry of flying dresses and locks flashed white, bare, fragrant shoulders. Gradually warming up, Melancholin's fantasy finally raced off to a world beyond the stars, where he transported himself and all these half-naked goddesses, whose breasts wounded his heart so much. Soon, however, he felt stifled even in that world beyond the stars; then he withdrew to a remote room, settled among the greenery of orange and myrtle plants, and sank into oblivion.

At that very moment a mask appeared before him and a hand was placed on his shoulder. He understood at once that it was *she*. She approached him so quietly, as if it were not a woman but a sylph concealed under a satin domino, which, however, quite distinctly outlined her airy forms. Blond, almost ash-blond curls tumbled down on her shoulders, blue eyes looked through the mask, and the bare chin showed a dimple in which it seemed Amor himself had made his nest. Everything in her was filled with some modest and at the same time not uncalculated gracefulness, beginning with the perfume Violettes de Parme, with which her handkerchief was scented, and ending with an elegant glove tightly covering her small, aristocratic hand. It was obvious, however, that she was agitated, because her chest heaved and her voice, resembling the music of paradise, trembled slightly.

"Awake, my fallen brother!" she said to Melancholin.

Melancholin did not understand; she seemed to think that he was asleep, and to prove that this was a mistake he began to reach out with his hands.

"I speak not of the body, but of the soul!" the mask continued sorrowfully. "It is not the body but the soul that is asleep . . . deeply asleep!"

Only now did Melancholin understand what it was about, but since his soul was steeped in idolatry, the word of truth could not penetrate it at once. First he even suspected that it was the holy fool Anisyushka hiding behind the mask, the one who, already in the time of Ferdyshchenko, had foretold the great fire in Foolsburg, and who, when the Foolsburgers fell into idolatry, alone remained faithful to the true God.

"No, I am not the one you suspect me of being," the mysterious stranger continued, as if guessing his thoughts. "I am not Anisyushka, for I am not worthy to kiss even the dust under her feet. I am a simple sinner, just as you are!"

So saying, she took the mask from her face.

Melancholin was stunned. Before him was the loveliest woman's face he had ever seen. True, he had happened to meet one like that in the free city of Hamburg, but that was so long ago that the past seemed as if covered with a veil.[17] Yes, those were precisely the same ash-blond curls, the same matte whiteness of the face, the same blue eyes, the same full and tremulous bust; but how transformed it all was in the new setting, how prominent were its best, most interesting sides! But Melancholin was still more astounded that the stranger had so shrewdly divined his surmise about Anisyushka.

"I am your inner word! I have been sent to proclaim to you the light of Tabor, which you seek unknowingly!" the stranger meanwhile continued. "But do not ask who sent me, because I myself do not know how to speak of it."

"But who are you?" Melancholin cried in alarm.

"I am that foolish maiden whom you saw with her lamp extinguished in the free city of Hamburg![18] For a long time I went about in a state of anguish, for a long time I unsuccessfully strove toward the light, but the Prince of Darkness is too artful to let his victim escape his clutches so quickly! *There*, however, my path had already been marked out! The local apothecary Pfeiffer appeared and, having married me, brought me to Foolsburg; here I became acquainted with

Anisyushka, and the task of enlightenment appeared before me with such clarity that my whole being was filled with ecstasy. But if you only knew what a cruel struggle it was!"

She stopped, oppressed by woeful memories; his hands greedily reached out for her, as if wishing to touch this inconceivable being.

"Take your hands away!" she said meekly. "You should touch me not with your hands, but with your thought, so as to hear out what I am to reveal to you!"

"Won't it be better if we withdraw to a more solitary room?" he asked timidly, as if himself doubting the decency of his question.

She accepted, however, and they withdrew into one of those charming retreats which, from the time of Mikaladze, had been set up for the mayors in every even slightly respectable house in Foolsburg. What happened between them remained a mystery; but he left the retreat upset and with tear-stained eyes. The *inner word* had such a strong effect that he did not grant the dancers a single glance and went straight home.

This incident made a strong impression on the Foolsburgers. They began to inquire where this Pfeiffer woman came from. Some said she was nothing more than an intriguer, who, with her husband's knowledge, had decided to take possession of Melancholin in order to drive out of town the apothecary Salzfisch, who was a strong competitor to Pfeiffer. Others maintained that the Pfeiffer woman had fallen in love with Melancholin already in the free city of Hamburg, owing to his sorrowful appearance, and she had married Pfeiffer for the sole purpose of being united with Melancholin, so as to focus on herself the sensitivity he so uselessly wasted on cocottes and such empty spectacles as mating wood grouse.

Be that as it may, it cannot be denied that she was a far from ordinary woman. The correspondence left behind her shows that she was in touch with all the famous mystics and pietists of the time, and that Labzin, for instance, dedicated to her his selected writings, which were not meant for publication.[19] On top of that, she wrote several novels, in one of which, entitled *Dorothea the Wanderer*, she portrayed herself in the best light. "She was of attractive appearance," she wrote of the heroine of this novel, "but, though many men desired her caresses, she remained cold and as if mysterious. Nevertheless, there was yearning in her soul, and when, in the course of her search, she met with a famous chemist (as she called Pfeiffer), she clung to him eternally. But with the first earthly feeling, she realized that her thirst was not satisfied . . ." and so on.[20]

On returning home, Melancholin spent a whole night weeping. His imagination drew the abyss of sinfulness, at the bottom of which devils milled about. There were cocottes of all sorts in it and even wood grouse, and all of them were fiery. One of the devils got out of the abyss and offered him his favorite food, but the moment he touched it with his lips, a stench filled the room. What horrified him most was the bitter certainty that not only he had sunk, but in his person the whole of Foolsburg had sunk as well.

"Answer for all or save all!" he cried, numb with fear, and of course he decided to save.

The next day, early in the morning, the Foolsburgers were astonished to hear the measured ringing of the bell calling townsfolk to the morning liturgy. They had not heard this ringing for a very long time, and had even forgotten about it. Many thought there was a fire somewhere; but instead of a fire, they saw a touching spectacle. Hatless, in a torn uniform, his head bent down and beating himself on the chest, Melancholin came leading a procession that consisted, however, only of teams of policemen and firemen. Behind the procession walked the Pfeiffer woman, without crinoline; she was flanked on one side by Anisyushka, on the other by the famous holy fool Paramosha, who replaced in the hearts of the Foolsburgers the no less famous Arkhipushko, who had burned so tragically during the great fire (see the chapter "The Straw Town").

After the liturgy Melancholin came out of the church cheered up and, pointing to the firemen and policemen standing at attention ("who," the chronicler adds, "even during the Foolsburg dissipation, had secretly remained faithful to the true God"), said to the Pfeiffer woman:

"Seeing the unexpected zeal of these people, I now know for certain how quickly this thing works which you, my lady, rightly call the inner word."

And then, turning to the police chiefs, he added:

"Give them ten kopecks each for their zeal!"

"At your service, Your Honor!" the policemen barked with one voice and quickly marched off to a pothouse.

This was Melancholin's first action after his sudden revival. Then he went to Anisyushka, since without her moral support it was impossible to expect any success in the further course of things. Anisyushka lived at the very edge of the town, in some sort of dugout, which was more like a mole's burrow than a human dwelling. With her, in moral cohabitation, lived the blessed Paramosha. Accompanied by the Pfeiffer woman, Melancholin gropingly descended the dark staircase and was barely able to feel the door. The spectacle that met his eyes was astonishing. On the dirty bare floor lay two half-naked human bodies (these were the blessed people who had already come back from church), muttering and crying out some incoherent words, and all the while quaking, grimacing, and writhing as if in a fever. Dim light penetrated into the burrow through a single tiny window covered with a layer of dust and cobwebs; the damp walls were all moldy. The smell was so repulsive that Melancholin at first became embarrassed and held his nose. The clairvoyant old woman noticed it.

"Perfume of the kings! Perfume of paradise!" she sang in a shrill voice. "Doesn't anyone want perfume?"

And she made a gesture that would have sent Melancholin reeling if the Pfeiffer woman had not been there to support him.

"Your soul's asleep . . . fast asleep!" she said sternly. "And just now you boasted of your good cheer!"

"Your little soul sleeps on a pillow . . . it sleeps on a featherbed . . . and goddy-god knock-knocks! on your head he knock-knocks! on your pate he knock-knocks!" the blessed woman shrieked, throwing wood chips, dirt, and litter at Melancholin.

Paramosha barked like a dog and crowed like a cock.

"Satan, scram! The cock is crowing!" he muttered in between.

"You of little faith! Remember the inner word!" the Pfeiffer woman repeated for her part.

Melancholin took heart.

"Mother Aksinya Egorovna, kindly grant me absolution!" he said in a firm voice.

"I'm Egorovna, and I'm Taratorovna! Yarilo tratatilo! Volos is lolos! Perun's an old pr . . k! Paramon does the trick!" the blessed woman shrieked, squirmed, and fell silent.

Melancholin looked around in perplexity.

"This means you have to bow to Paramon Melentyich!" the Pfeiffer woman prompted.

"Father Paramon Melentyich, kindly grant me absolution!" Melancholin bowed.

But Paramosha went on squirming and hiccupping.

"Lower! Bow lower!" the blessed woman commanded. "Don't spare your back! It's God's back, not yours!"

"Kindly grant me absolution, Father!" Melancholin repeated, bowing lower.

"No pain, no gain!"[21] the blessed man muttered in a wild voice, and suddenly leaped to his feet.

Following him, Anisyushka also leaped up, and they began to turn. At first they turned slowly, softly sobbing; then they began to turn more and more quickly, until their turning became a perfect whirl. They guffawed, shrieked, trilled, and spluttered, similar to what one can hear in spring from a pond inhabited by myriads of frogs.

Melancholin and the Pfeiffer woman stood horrified for a time, but finally could not help themselves. At first they shuddered and crouched, then gradually began to turn, and suddenly started whirling and guffawing.[22] This meant that inspiration had come and the requested absolution had been received.

Melancholin came home weary to the point of exhaustion; however, he found enough strength in himself to sign the order for the most urgent expulsion from the town of the apothecary Salzfisch. The faithful rejoiced, and the lower clergy, who for many years had subsisted only on worthless cereals, slaughtered a lamb and not only ate the whole of it, not sparing even the hooves, but spent a long time scraping a knife over the table on which the meat had lain and greedily eating the shavings, as if fearing to lose even an atom of nourishment. That same day Melancholin put on chains (later, however, it turned out that they were simply suspenders, which had not been in use previously in Foolsburg), and subjected his body to flagellation.[23]

"Today for the first time I understood," he wrote on the

occasion to the Pfeiffer woman, "the meaning of the words 'sweetly hath He wounded me,' of which you told me at our first meeting, my dear sister in spirit. At first I whipped myself with some reluctance, but, gradually becoming inflamed, I summoned my valet and told him: 'Flog away!' What then? Even that turned out to be insufficient, so I found it necessary to pick open a wound in an inconspicuous place, yet that caused me not suffering but ecstasy. It wasn't painful at all! This astonished me so much that I am still asking myself: Come, now, is this suffering? Does it not conceal some form of fleshly pleasure and self-indulgence? I await your arrival, my dear sister in spirit, in order to resolve this question by considering it conjointly."

It may seem strange that Melancholin, from being one of the most frivolous worshippers of Mammon, so quickly turned into an ascetic. To this I can say one thing: whoever does not believe in magic transformations should not read the chronicles of Foolsburg. One can find in them even more such miracles than necessary. Thus, for instance, one superior spat in his subordinate's eyes, and the subordinate began to see clearly.[24] Another superior began to flog a man for nonpayment of taxes, pursuing on this occasion only an educational goal, and quite unexpectedly discovered that there was a treasure hidden in the backside of the flogged man.* If such outlandish facts do not arouse mistrust in anyone, should we be astonished by such an ordinary transformation as the one that took place in Melancholin?

But, on the other hand, this same fact could be explained in another, more natural way. There are indications which make us think that Melancholin's asceticism was not as

---

* This is corroborated by the fact that flogging has been regarded ever since as the best method of collecting arrears.—*Publisher*

strict as it would appear at first sight. We already saw that his so-called chains were nothing but suspenders; we see from the further clarifications of the chronicler that Melancholin very much exaggerated his other feats and that they were considerably spiced by spiritual love. The whip with which he flogged himself was made of velvet (it is still preserved in the Foolsburg archive); his fasting consisted in adding to his other dishes the fish turbot which he ordered from Paris at the expense of the townsfolk. Is it surprising that flogging drove him into ecstasy and the very wounds seemed delightful?

Meanwhile, the bell continued the call to prayer at the appointed time, and the number of the faithful increased every day. First only policemen came; then, watching them, others began to come. Melancholin, for his part, set an example of true piety by spitting at the temple of Perun each time he passed by it. Perhaps the whole matter would have resolved itself peacefully if this had not been prevented by the plottings of some ambitious troublemakers, who already at that time were known under the name of "the extremists."

At the head of the party stood the same Anisyushka and Paramosha, who were the leaders of a whole crowd of beggars and cripples. For the beggars the only source of subsistence was begging for alms at church porches; but since in Foolsburg the ancient piety had ceased for a time, this source had naturally declined significantly. The reforms undertaken by Melancholin were met by them with loud approval; a dense crowd of cripples filled the courtyard of the mayor's house; some hobbled on crutches, others crawled on all fours. Everyone was singing hymns, but at the same time they all demanded in one voice that the renewal be carried out at once and that they be entrusted with supervising the process. Here, as usual, hunger turned out to be a poor counsellor, and the slow but firm and farsighted actions of the mayor were perversely interpreted. In vain did Melancholin cater to the passions of the cripples, sending them the leftovers of his abundant meals; in vain did he explain to the select representatives of these beggars that gradualness is not indulgence, but merely the consolidation of the undertaken project. They did not want to hear any of it. They angrily shook their crutches and loudly threatened to raise the banners of rebellion.

The danger was a serious one, because in order to control crippled beggars one needs a greater supply of courage than to shoot at people with no defects. Melancholin was aware of it. Besides that, he already felt himself defenseless before the demagogues, because they regarded him, so to speak, as their creature and in this sense acted extremely adroitly. First, they surrounded themselves with a whole network of informers, through whom Melancholin received all the rumors that had to do with disgracing his honor; second, they lured the Pfeiffer woman to their side, promising her a share of the socalled bag tax (this tax was imposed on every beggar's bag; later it laid the basis for the whole financial system of the town of Foolsburg).

The Pfeiffer woman pestered Melancholin day and night, pursuing him especially in her correspondence, which in a short time amounted to a whole big volume. The basis for her letters was her visions, the contents of which changed depending on whether she was pleased or displeased with her "spiritual brother." In one letter she saw him "walking on a cloud" and insisted that not only she but Pfeiffer also had seen it; in another she observed him in fiery Gehenna, in the company of devils of all possible denominations. In one of her letters she develops the notion that in general mayors have the right to unconditional bliss in the afterlife, for the sole reason that they are mayors; in another she maintains that mayors should pay particular attention to their behavior, because in the afterlife they are subject to two or three times as much torture as others. The same as popes or princes.

In such cases her letters had a menacing character. "I hasten to inform you," she wrote in one of them, "of what I saw in a dream last night. You were standing in a dark and stinking place tied to a post, and the ties were made of snakes, and on your chest was a plaque with the inscription: 'This one is the known patron of the impious and the Hagarenes [sic!].'[25] And the demons gathered around are rejoicing, and the righteous, standing at a distance and looking at us, shed tears. Kindly consider for yourself whether there is in it some portent that is not quite beneficial for you?"

Reading these letters, Melancholin became extraordinarily troubled. On the one hand there was his natural inclination toward apathy, on the other the fear of devils. It all produced an unprecedented turmoil in his head, a tangle of the most contradictory suggestions and schemes. One thing seemed clear: his own well-being would be secured only when all the Foolsburgers to a man started going to the all-night vigils and when Paramosha was named the inspector and auditor of all the schools in Foolsburg.

This last condition was particularly important, and the beggars set it forth very insistently. Moral corruption reached such a point that the Foolsburgers ventured to probe the mystery of the structure of the universe and openly applauded the teacher of calligraphy who, overstepping the bounds of his profession, preached from the podium that the world could not have been created in six days. The beggars reasoned very judiciously that if this opinion became firmly established, then along with that, generally, the whole worldview of Foolsburg would collapse.[26] All the parts of this worldview were so closely interconnected that it was impossible to dislodge one without destroying the rest. It was not the question of the order of creation of the world that was important, but that along with this question some completely new principle could invade people's life, which was sure to make a mess of everything. All the travelers of the time unanimously testify that the life of the Foolsburgers struck them by its integrity, and they rightly ascribe this to the happy absence of the spirit of inquiry. If the Foolsburgers firmly endured the most terrible adversities and went on living after that, they owed it only to the fact that they saw any adversity in general as something totally independent of them and therefore unavoidable. The most that was allowed in view of an approaching disaster was to press yourself somewhere to the side, hold your breath, and vanish all the while the calamity rollicked and frolicked. But even this was regarded as obstinacy; while to fight or openly go against the disaster—God forbid! Therefore, if the Foolsburgers had been allowed to reason, they might, perhaps, have gone so far as to question whether, for instance, there indeed exists a predestination that makes it necessary for them to suffer such an adversity as, for instance, the brief but totally senseless mayorship of Shagmug (see the chapter "Music Box" above)? But since the question was a long one, and their arms were short, it was obvious that the existence of the question would only undermine their firmness in adversity, but would not make a significant improvement in their situation.

But while Melancholin hesitated, the beggarly folk decided to act on their own. They burst into the lodgings of the teacher of calligraphy, Linkin, searched them, and found the book *Means of Extermination of Fleas, Bedbugs, and Other Insects.*[27] They triumphantly drove Linkin outside and, rending the air with their joyful cries, led him to the mayor's courtyard. At first Melancholin was at a loss and, taking a look at the book, tried to explain that it contained nothing against religion or morality, or even against public order. But the beggarly folk no longer listened to anything.

"You haven't read it right!" they shouted brazenly at the mayor, and raised such a tumult that Melancholin became frightened and decided that good sense dictated yielding to the demands of public opinion.

"Did you write this malignant book yourself? And if not, who is the indubitable thief and veritable robber who performed this villainy? And how did you make his acquaintance? And is it from him that you obtained this wretched book? And if from him, then why did you not inform the right persons about it, but instead, forgetting all shame, connive in his profligacy and imitate it?" Thus Melancholin began his interrogation of Linkin.

"I did not write this book, nor did I ever see its author, and it was printed in the capital city of Moscow by the university printing house, funded by the booksellers Manukhin," Linkin answered firmly.

The crowd did not like his response, and generally this was not what they had expected. They thought that the moment they brought in Linkin, Melancholin would tear him to pieces, and that would be the end of it. But instead he was talking! Thus the mayor had only just opened his mouth to ask a second question when the crowd began to drone:

"Why do you go on chewing the fat with him! He doesn't believe in God!" Then the horrified Melancholin tore his uniform.

"Is it true you don't believe in God?" He threw himself at Linkin and, the accusation being serious, did not wait for an answer, but slapped him lightly on the cheek by way of down payment.

"I've never said so to anyone," said Linkin, avoiding a direct answer.

"There are witnesses! Witnesses!" roared the crowd.

Two witnesses stepped forward: the retired soldier Karapuzov and the blind beggar woman Maremyanushka. "And each of those witnesses received five kopecks in silver for their false evidence," says the chronicler, who on this occasion clearly takes the side of the downtrodden Linkin.

"The other day, I don't remember exactly when," said the witness Karapuzov, "I was sitting in a pothouse drinking vodka, and not far from me sat this same teacher, also drinking vodka. And having drunk a good dose of vodka, he said: 'All of us, men and dumb brutes—we're all the same; we'll all die and go to the devil's dam!'"

"But when—" Linkin tried to begin.

"Wait! Don't open your maw! Let the witness speak first!" the crowd yelled at him.

"And I, being tempted by his words," Karapuzov went on, "meekly said to him: 'How's that, Your Honor? Can it be that men and dumb brutes are all the same? And why do you besmear us the way you do, not even finding another place for us than with the devil? The priests, our spiritual fathers, taught us something else—so there!' Then he looked at me sort of askance: 'You one-legged devil,' he says (and it's true, Your Honor, that my leg got blown off at Ochakov),[28] 'so you must be in with the police?' And he grabbed his hat and left the pothouse."

Linkin opened his mouth, but this inflamed the crowd still more.

"Shut his maw!" they shouted to Melancholin. "What a babbler we've got here!"

Karapuzov was replaced by Maremyanushka.

"The other day I was sitting in a pothouse," she testified,

"and I felt sick at heart, poor blind woman that I am; so I sit and think: how much prouder people have grown nowadays compared to the old times! They've forgotten God, eat meat on fasting days, don't give alms; look, pretty soon they'll start looking straight at the sun! Really. So then this fine fellow comes up to me: 'You're blind, Granny?' he says. 'I am, Your Honor,' I say. 'And how come you're blind?' he says. 'It was God's will, Your Honor.' 'God nothing, it must've been smallpox.' That's him still talking. 'And who sends smallpox?' I say. 'Oh, yeah, God's will, my foot! You poke around in dampness and foulness all your life, and it's God's fault!'"

Maremyanushka stopped and burst into tears.

"And that offended me so much," she went on, sobbing, "I can't tell you how much! 'Why do you offend God?' I say to him. And he just up and spits right in my eyes. 'Wipe them,' he says, 'then maybe you'll see again'—and off he goes."[29]

The circumstances of the case were fully clarified; but since Linkin insisted that his defense be heard out, Melancholin grudgingly had to fulfill his demand. In fact, some retired clerk stepped from the crowd and began to speak. At first he spoke incoherently, but he gradually entered into the subject and, to everyone's surprise, instead of defending began to accuse. This affected Linkin so much that he immediately not only confessed everything, but even added many things that had never happened.

"Once I was watching frogs in a pond," he said, "and was tempted by the devil. And I began idly wondering whether it's true that humans alone possess a soul, or whether reptiles, too, have one! And, taking a frog, I did some research. And on finishing the research, I discovered it's true, frogs also have a soul, only it's small and not immortal."[30]

Then Melancholin turned to the beggars and, saying "See

for yourselves!" ordered them to take Linkin to the police station.

Unfortunately, the chronicler does not report further details of this story. In the correspondence of the Pfeiffer woman only the following lines about this case are preserved: "You men are very lucky; you are able to be firm; but I was so affected by yesterday's spectacle that Pfeiffer was seriously worried and quickly gave me some calming drops." That is all.

The event was important in this respect: that if previously Melancholin still had doubts about the course of action before him, from that moment on they disappeared completely. In the evening of that same day he appointed Paramosha inspector of the Foolsburg schools, and to another holy fool, Yashenka, he offered the chair of philosophy, which had been created for him on purpose in the local high school. He himself began assiduously to write the treatise "On the Ecstasies of a Pious Soul."

In a very short time the physiognomy of the town changed beyond recognition. Instead of the former reveling and dancing, there was a sepulchral silence interrupted only by bells ringing in every manner: all at once, and singly, and in a carillon. The pagan temples became empty; the idols were drowned in the river; and the arena where Mademoiselle Gandon had given performances was burned down. After that all the streets were filled with the smoke of myrrh and incense, and only then was there hope that the power of the enemy had finally been put to shame.

But that did not add any corn to the fields, for from happily riotous idleness the Foolsburgers went over to gloomy idleness. In vain did they raise their hands to heaven; in vain did they impose prostrations on themselves, make vows, keep fasts, hold processions—God did not heed their prayers. Someone tried to drop a hint that "like it or not, we'll have to go and plow the fields," but they almost stoned the brazen fellow, and in response to his suggestion tripled their zeal.

Meanwhile, Paramosha and Yashenka were at work in the schools.[31] Paramosha was unrecognizable. He brushed his hair, acquired a velvet coat, used scent, washed his hands thoroughly with soap, and, dressed up like that, went around the schools fulminating against those who put their trust in the prince of this world. He bitterly mocked the vain, the ambitious, the high-minded, who concern themselves with bodily food and neglect the spiritual, and he invited everyone to withdraw to the desert. Yashenka, for his part, taught that this world, which we think we see with our eyes, is a sort of dream vision sent upon us by the enemy of mankind, and that we ourselves are no more than visitors from the bosom coming and to the same bosom returning. In his opinion, human souls, like spiritual grain, are kept in a certain granary and from there descend into the world as needed, so as to quickly see this dream vision and shortly afterwards fly up swiftly to this longed-for granary. The essential conclusions of this teaching were the following: (1) there is no need to work; (2) there is still less need to foresee, be concerned, and take care; and (3) there is a need to hope and to contemplate—nothing more. Paramosha even taught how to contemplate. "For this," he said, "withdraw to the farthest corner of the room, sit down, cross your arms on your chest, and fix your gaze on your navel."[32]

Anisyushka also did not lag behind, but tirelessly twiddled her thumbs. She went around the houses telling how the devil once dragged her through the torments, and how at first she took him for a pilgrim, but then figured him out and fought him.[33] The basic principles of her teaching were the same as Paramosha's and Yashenka's—that is, there is no need to work, there is a need to contemplate. "And, above all, to give alms to the poor, because the poor don't care about Mammon, but about saving their souls," she added, and held out her hand. This preaching was so successful that Foolsburg kopecks poured into her pockets, and very soon she managed to accumulate a considerable capital. It was impossible not to give her alms, because she unceremoniously spat in the face of anyone who did not, and instead of apologizing merely said: "No offense intended!"

But even this austere atmosphere no longer satisfied the representatives of the local intelligentsia. It satisfied them only externally, but did not provide any real sting. Of course they did not say so publicly, and they even followed with precision the ritualistic side of life, but those were the externals they used to flatter the passions of the people. Walking the streets with their eyes lowered, reverently approaching church porches, they seemed to be saying to the muzhiks: "See! We don't scorn to keep your company!"—but in fact their thoughts wandered far away. Spoiled by the recent bacchanalia of polytheism and satiated by the spices of civilization, they were not content with simple faith, but sought some "ravishments." Unfortunately, Melancholin was the first to set foot upon this pernicious path, and he drew everyone else with him. Having noticed at the exit from town a decrepit building where military veterans once were stationed, he arranged nightly gatherings in it, where all the so-called *beau monde* of Foolsburg assembled. They began by reading the critical articles of Mr. N. Strakhov, but since the articles were stupid, they would quickly pass on to other occupations. The chairman rose and began to twist about; others followed his example; then little by little everyone began to leap, spin, sing, and shout, and continued in this frenzy until they fell down in total exhaustion. This moment proper was called a "ravishment."[34]

Could such a way of life continue? And for how long? It is quite difficult to give a clear answer to this question. The main obstacle to its going on indefinitely was, of course, a lack of food, which was the direct consequence of the reigning asceticism. But, on the other hand, the history of Foolsburg has positive examples demonstrating that food is not as necessary for people's happiness as it seems at first sight. If a man has beef at hand, he certainly eats it more willingly than other less nourishing substances; but if there is no meat, he eats bread as willingly, and if there is not enough bread, he will eat goosefoot. So here we have a point of controversy. Be that as it may, this outrageous Foolsburg diversion was resolved in a very unexpected way and not at all from the causes that one would suppose were most natural.

The thing was that there lived in Foolsburg a certain staff officer with no special occupation, who was accidentally slighted. Namely, still in the times of polytheism, at Melancholin's birthday party, all the best guests were served fish soup with sterlet, while this staff officer—unbeknownst to the host, of course—got soup with perch. The guest swallowed the insult ("though the spoon in his hand trembled," says the chronicler), but in his soul he vowed revenge. Disputes began; initially the struggle was low-key, but the longer it went on, the more it flared up. The question of the fish soup was forgotten and replaced by other questions of a political and theological sort, so that when, out of politeness, the staff officer was invited to take part in the "ravishments," he flatly refused.

And this staff officer was an informer . . .

Although he was not personally present at the gatherings, he kept a close eye on everything that was happening there. The leaping, the spinning, the reading of Strakhov's articles—nothing escaped his grasp. But neither by word nor by deed did he express either disapproval or approval of all these actions, but waited coolly until the abscess ripened. And then this desired moment finally came: a copy of Melancholin's book *On the Ravishments of a Pious Soul* fell into his hands . . .

One night the Foolsburg ladies and gentlemen gathered as usual in the former house of the military veterans. The reading of Strakhov's articles was already over, and the guests were beginning to quake slightly; Melancholin, as chairman of the gathering, had just begun to squat and generally perform the preliminary movements of the soul's ravishments, when noise came from outside. Terrified, the sectarians rushed for all the exits, forgetting even to put out the lights and remove material evidence . . . But it was too late.

At the main exit stood Sullen-Grumble, his mesmerizing gaze fixed on the crowd . . .

What a gaze it was! . . . Oh Lord, what a gaze! . . .

Repentance Confirmed. Conclusion

It was terrible.

But he was scarcely aware of it, and with a sort of severe modesty let slip: "After me comes someone who will be still more terrible than I."[1]

He was terrible; but, on top of that, he was curt, and with his amazing narrow-mindedness he combined an intransigence that bordered almost on idiocy. No one could accuse him of aggressive enterprise, as they did, for instance, Wartbeardin, or of impulses of insane fury, something that Shagmug, Blaggardov, and many others were given to. Passion was crossed off from the number of elements that made up his nature, and was replaced by a steadfastness that worked with the regularity of a most precise mechanism. He did not gesticulate, did not raise his voice, did not grind his teeth, did not guffaw, did not stamp his feet, did not dissolve in authoritatively sarcastic laughter; it seemed he did not even suspect the need for administrative manifestations of that sort. In a perfectly soundless voice, he expressed his demands and confirmed the necessity of fulfilling them by his glaring gaze, which expressed a sort of ineffable shamelessness. One on whom this gaze was fixed could not bear it. A certain quite special feeling was born in him, in which primacy belonged not so much to the instinct of self-preservation as to a fear for human nature in general. All possible anticipations of mysterious and insuperable dangers drowned in this vague fear. One began to think of the sky falling, of the earth opening under one's feet, of a tornado rushing from somewhere and swallowing up everything all at once ... It was a gaze bright as steel, totally devoid of thought, and therefore inaccessible to any nuances or hesitations. A naked resolution—nothing more.

As a narrow-minded man, he did not pursue anything except a regularity of formation. Straight lines, absence of variety, simplicity reduced to bareness—these were the ideals he knew and strove for. His notion of "duty" did not go beyond a general equality before the rod; his idea of "simplicity" went no further than the simplicity of an animal, exposing the perfect nakedness of its needs. He did not recognize reason at all, and even regarded it as the worst enemy, which entangles man in a net of temptations and dangerous fastidiousness. He stopped in perplexity before anything that smacked of gaiety or mere leisure. This is not to say that these natural manifestations of human nature drove him to indignation: no, he quite simply did not understand them. He never was enraged, did not seethe, did not seek revenge, did not persecute, but, like any other unconsciously active force of nature, went ahead, sweeping from the face of the earth everything that had no time to step out of his way. "What for?" was the only phrase with which he expressed the impulses of his soul.

Step aside in time—that was all that was needed. The space within the horizon of this idiot was very narrow. Outside that space you could wave your arms, talk loudly, breathe, even cast off all restraint—he noticed nothing. Within that space

you could only march. If the Foolsburgers had understood
this in good time, they would simply have had to step aside
and wait. But they were slow to figure it out, and initially,
like all authority-loving people, they purposely kept trying to
catch his eye. Hence the countless number of freewheeling
tortures that spread over the existence of the townsfolk like a
net; hence, too, the far-from-merited name of "Satan," which
popular rumor conferred upon Sullen-Grumble.[2] When the
Foolsburgers were asked what occasioned such an unusual
epithet, they did not say anything sensible by way of explanation, but only trembled. They silently pointed at their houses
stretched out in a straight line, at the broken-down palings
in front of them, at the same uniform coats in which all the
inhabitants to a man were dressed—and their trembling lips
whispered: "Satan!"

The chronicler himself, generally quite well disposed
toward mayors, is unable to conceal a vague sense of fear
when he begins to describe the actions of Sullen-Grumble.
"There was at the time," so he begins his story, "in one of the
town churches, a painting depicting the sufferings of sinners
in the presence of the enemy of the human race. Satan is
portrayed in Hell, standing on the upper step of the throne,
his hand imperiously stretched forward and his dull gaze directed into space. Neither the figure nor even the face of the
enemy of mankind shows any particular desire for torture;
all you see is a deliberate abolition of nature. This abolition
produced only one distinct action: the imperious gesture—
and then, having concentrated on itself, it turned into a pet-
rification. But what deserves notice is this: no matter how
terrible the tortures and torments abundantly scattered all
over the painting, no matter how soul-chilling the grimaces
and convulsions of the villains for whom these torments
are prepared, every beholder is bound to imagine that even

these sufferings are less intense than the sufferings of this true monster, who has overcome all that is natural in himself to such an extent that he is able to contemplate these unprecedented sufferings with a cool and uncomprehending gaze." Such is the beginning of the chronicler's account, and, although the story breaks off at this point and the chronicler never comes back to this recollection of the painting, one cannot help thinking that it is thrown in here for a reason.

A portrait of Sullen-Grumble is preserved in the town archive to this day.[3] He is a man of medium height, with a wooden face, apparently never lit up by a smile. Thick, pitch-black, closely cropped hair covers the conical skull and frames the narrow and receding forehead tightly like a skullcap. The eyes are gray, sunken, with slightly puffy lids; their gaze is clear, unhesitating; the nose is dry, descending almost straight down from the forehead; thin, pale lips, with a trimmed, bristly mustache above them; jaws well-developed, though without any special carnivorousness in them, but armed with an inexplicable readiness to crush or bite in two. The whole figure is lean, with narrow, slightly raised shoulders, with the chest artificially thrust forward, and with long, muscular arms. He is dressed in a fully buttoned frock coat of military cut, and in his right hand he holds Wartbeardin's *Regulations of Relentless Flogging*, but evidently he is not reading it, as if astonished that there could be people on earth who regard this relentlessness as needing to be furnished with some sort of regulations. Around him a landscape depicting a desert, in the middle of which stands a jailhouse; above, instead of the sky, hovers a gray army trench coat . . .

This portrait makes a very dismal impression. Before the eyes of the beholder rises the pure type of an idiot, who has made some dark decision and sworn in his heart to accomplish it. Idiots in general are very dangerous, not even because they are necessarily wicked (wickedness and goodness in an idiot are totally indifferent qualities), but because they are strangers to any reasoning and always push straight ahead, as if the path they are on belongs only to them. From a distance it may seem that they are people of strict but well-established convictions, who consciously strive toward a firmly fixed goal. That, however, is an optical illusion, which one ought not to fall for. They are simply beings tightly sealed off on all sides, who barge ahead because they have no way of knowing they are connected with any order of things . . .

Usually certain measures are taken against idiots, so that in their mindless precipitousness they do not overturn everything that stands in their way. But these measures almost always deal only with simple idiots. When on top of idiocy there is authority, the task of protecting society becomes significantly more complicated. In this case the threatening danger is increased by the sum total of the exposure for the sake of which, in certain historical moments, one seems to give one's life . . . Where a simple idiot smashes his head or throws himself onto the stake, the authoritative idiot breaks all possible stakes and commits his, so to speak, unconscious evildoings quite unhindered. He does not draw any lesson even from the very fruitlessness or obvious harmfulness of these evildoings. He does not care about any results, because these results have no effect on him (he is too frozen for anything to affect him), but on something else with which he has no organic connection. If the whole world turned into a desert owing to his idiotic activity, even this result would not frighten the idiot. Who knows, maybe it is precisely the desert that in his eyes represents the ideal setting for the common life of mankind?

It is this stonelike and perfectly complacent idiocy that strikes the beholder in the portrait of Sullen-Grumble. No questions can be seen in his face; on the contrary, there is in all his features a soldier's imperturbable assurance that all questions were answered long ago. What are these questions? How have they been answered? This riddle is so tormenting that one risks thinking of all possible questions and answers without hitting on those that are to the point. Maybe it is the answered question about universal destruction, or maybe only that all men should have their chests thrust out in a wheel-like fashion. Nothing is known. All we know is that this unknown question will be brought into action at all costs. And since a preternatural link between the known and the unknown causes a still greater confusion, there can be only one consequence of such a situation: general panic fear.

Sullen-Grumble's very way of life was such as to increase the terror evoked by his appearance. He slept on the bare ground, and only when it was freezing cold allowed himself to hide in the firemen's hayloft; he lay his head on a stone instead of a pillow; he got up at dawn, put on his uniform, and then began to beat the drum; he smoked cheap tobacco, which made such a stench that even the policemen blushed when its smell reached them; he ate horseflesh and readily chewed up ox sinews.[4] To complete the picture, he marched three hours a day in the courtyard of the mayor's house, alone, without any comrades, giving commands to himself and subjecting himself to disciplinary penalties and even to flogging ("flogging himself," adds the chronicler, "not in pretense, like his predecessor Melancholin, but according to the precise meaning of the regulations").

He did have a family, but during his term as mayor no one saw either his wife or his children. Rumor had it that they were languishing somewhere in the basement of the mayor's house and that he personally gave them bread and water once a day through an iron grate. And, in fact, when his administrative disappearance took place, some naked and completely wild creatures were found in the basement, who were biting, shrieking, clawing each other and snapping at people around them. They were led out to the fresh air and given hot cabbage soup; seeing the steam, they first snorted and showed superstitious fear, but then became more tame and fell on the food with such beastly greed that they immediately overate and gave up the ghost.

The story went that Sullen-Grumble owed his ascent to a very particular occasion. There supposedly lived in the world some superior who suddenly began to worry that none of his subordinates loved him.

"We do love you, Y'r'xellency!" assured his subordinates.

"So you all say when nothing's happening," the superior insisted, "but if it comes to a real matter, not a one of you will sacrifice a little finger for me!"

Gradually, despite the protestations, this idea settled so firmly in the zealous superior's head, that he decided to test his subordinates and sent out a call:

"Whoever wants to prove that he loves me," he announced, "let him chop off the index finger of his right hand!"

No one hastened to the call, however. Some, the sybarites, turned away, knowing that chopping off a finger is attended by pain; others held back out of misunderstanding: they thought the superior was asking whether they were pleased with everything and, fearing to be taken for rebels, bawled, as was their wont: "We do our best, Y'r'xcellency!"

"Who wants to prove it? Step forward! Don't be afraid!" the zealous superior repeated his call.

This time, again, the answer was silence, or the same shouts, which by no means settled the question. The superior's face first turned purple, then somehow drooped mournfully.

"Scoun—"

But before he finished, a simple latrine scrubber,[5] exhausted by rod beating, stepped from the ranks and cried in a loud voice:

"I'll prove it!"

With these words, he put his finger on a plank and chopped it off with a dull cutlass.

Having done that, he smiled. This was the only time in his much-flogged life when there was a glimpse of something human in his face.

Many thought that he had performed this feat only to deliver his back from the rods; but no, some sort of idea had ripened in the latrine scrubber's head . . .

Seeing the crushed finger that fell at his feet, the superior was amazed at first, but then lapsed into a sweet tenderness.

"You've loved me," he exclaimed, "and I will love you a hundredfold!"

And he sent him to Foolsburg.

At the time nothing was known for certain about communists, or socialists, or so-called nivellators in general.[6] Nevertheless nivellating did exist, and on quite a vast scale. There were nivellators of "toeing the line," nivellators of "putting the screws to," nivellators of "hedgehog mittens," et cetera, et cetera. But no one saw in it anything threatening to society or undermining its foundations. It seemed that if for the sake of equalizing him with his peers, a person is deprived of life, that will not be of any great benefit to the person, but will be beneficial and even necessary for the preservation of social harmony. The nivellators themselves did not have the least suspicion that they were nivellators, but called themselves good custodians and caretakers, who were zealous for the happiness of their subordinates and others subject to them . . .

Such was the simplicity of morals at the time that for us, who have witnessed later epochs, it is difficult even to imagine those still recent times when every squadron commander, without calling himself a communist, regarded it as his honor and duty to be one from top to bottom.

Sullen-Grumble belonged among the most fanatical nivellators of that school.[7] Having drawn a straight line, he intended to force onto it the whole visible and invisible world, and to make sure that it would be impossible to turn either back, or forward, or right, or left. Was this supposed to make him a benefactor of mankind? It is hard to answer this question positively. It is, rather, possible to think that there were no suppositions of any kind in his head. Only in recent times (almost before our eyes) was the notion of combining the idea of a straight line with the idea of universal happiness elevated into a very complex administrative theory not devoid of ideological subterfuge; but nivellators of the old school, like Sullen-Grumble, acted in the simplicity of their hearts, solely out of an instinctive aversion to curved lines and all zigzags and meanders. Sullen-Grumble was a latrine scrubber in the fullest sense of the word. Not only because he had occupied this post in the regiment, but a latrine scrubber in his whole being, in his whole way of thinking. The straight line seduced him not because it was the shortest—shortness meant nothing to him—but rather because one could march and march along it for ages without ever getting anywhere. The virtuosity of the straight line, like the wooden stake, lodged itself in his lamentable head and there sprouted a whole impenetrable web of roots and ramifications. It was a sort of mysterious forest, filled with magical dreams. Mysterious shadows followed each other in single file, buttoned up, hair cropped, in uniform step, in uniform dress, on and on . . . They were all fitted out with the same face, they were all silent in the same way, and they all disappeared in the same way. Where? It seemed that beyond this dreamily fantastic world there existed a still more fantastic chasm, which resolved all difficulties, because they all disappeared into it—all without a trace. When this fantastic chasm had swallowed up enough fantastic shadows, Sullen-Grumble turned, if we may put it so, on his other side and began another identical dream. Again the shadows walked in single file, one after another, on and on . . .

Long before arriving in Foolsburg he had already composed in his head a whole systematic delirium, in which all the details of this ill-fated future municipality were regulated down to the last dot. In this delirium the approximate form of the town, which he intended to present as exemplary, was the following.

In the middle—a square, from which streets, or "companies," as he mentally called them, radiate outwards. At some distance from the center, the companies are intersected by boulevards, which form a double circle around the town and at the same time serve as a defense against external enemies. Then there are the suburbs, earthworks—and a dark curtain, which is the end of the world. No river, no brook, no ravine, no hill—in short, nothing that could serve as an obstacle to free marching has been envisaged. Each company is forty feet wide, neither less nor more. Each house has three windows that give onto a front garden where grow meadow campions, Turk's-cap lilies, beetroot, and scarlet lychnis. All the houses are painted a light gray, and though in nature one side is always turned to the north or east, and the other to the south or west, that has been ignored, because it is supposed that all sides are lit by the sun and the moon in the same way and at the same time of day and night.

In each house there live two elderly persons, two adults,

two adolescents, and two children, difference of sex being no embarrassment to them. Sameness of age is matched with sameness of height. In some companies live only tall ones, in others only short ones, or skirmishers. Children who at birth give little promise of being firm in adversity are put to death; the old or unfit for work may also be put to death, but only when, in view of the local police chief, there is a surplus of workforce in the general economy of the town. In every house there is one representative of each useful animal, male and female, whose duty is, first, to do the work proper to them and, second, to multiply. The square is surrounded by stone buildings, which house various public offices, namely: administrative quarters and all sorts of arenas, for teaching gymnastics, fencing, and infantry formation, for eating, for general genuflection, and so on. Public places are called headquarters, and those serving in them, scribes. There are no schools, and literacy is not mandatory; the knowledge of numbers is taught on the fingers. There is no past or future, and therefore chronology is abolished. There are two feasts: the one in spring, just after the snow melts, is called the Feast of Steadfastness, and serves as preparation for future adversities; the other, in the fall, is called the Feast of the Powers That Be, and is dedicated to the memory of already experienced adversities. These feasts differ from ordinary days only in a more intense exercise of marching.

Such was the external organization of this delirium. Then he had to regulate the internal arrangement of the living beings caught up in it. In this respect Sullen-Grumble's fantasy reached a truly amazing precision.

Each house was none other than a *residential unit*, which had its commander and its spy (he insisted particularly on spies) and belonged to the group of ten that was called a *platoon*. The platoon, in turn, had a commander and a spy;

five platoons made a company; five companies, a regiment. There were four regiments, which formed, first, two brigades and, second, a division; each of these formations had a commander and a spy. Then followed the town proper, which was renamed and now called not Foolsburg, but the town of Steadfastia, "to the eternally illustrious memory of Grand Prince Sviatoslav Igorevich."[8] Over the town, in a cloud, hovers the mayor, which is to say the commander-in-chief of the land and sea forces of the town of Steadfastia, who disputes with everybody and lets them all feel his power. Beside him . . . a spy!!

In each residential unit time is allocated most strictly.[9] Everyone in the house gets up with the rising of the sun; adults and adolescents put on the same clothes (after special designs certified by the mayor), straighten themselves and tighten their belts. The babies hastily suck at their mothers' breasts; the elderly utter a brief homily that always ends with an unprintable word; the spies hasten with their reports. Within half an hour only the elderly and the babies remain in the house, all the rest having already gone to do the duties that have been laid on them. First they go to the "arena for genuflection," where they quickly recite a prayer; then they direct their steps to the "arena for bodily exercise," where they strengthen their bodies by fencing and gymnastics; finally they go to the "arena for taking meals," where they get a piece of dark bread sprinkled with salt. After the meal they form up on the square by platoons, and from there, led by their commanders, they march to the public works. The work is done on command. The townsfolk bend down and straighten up in unison; the blades of the scythes gleam, the rakes swing up and down, the spades pound, the plows furrow the earth—all on command. The plows trace monograms—the first letters of the names of historic figures who were most famous for their steadfastness. Next to each working platoon a soldier with a rifle marches up and down and every five minutes shoots at the sun. Amid these swingings, bendings, and unbendings, Sullen-Grumble promenades along a straight line, all sweaty, all filled with barrack stench, and strikes up:

One-two, one-two!

And the workmen all join in:

Heave-ho!
Swing it! Heave-ho!

But now the sun reaches its zenith, and Sullen-Grumble shouts: "Knock off!" Again the people line up by platoons and return to town, where they proceed in a ceremonial march through the "arena for taking meals" and they each get a piece of black bread with salt. After a brief rest, which consists of marching, the people line up again and, as in the morning, are taken to work until sunset. At sunset everyone gets one more piece of bread and hurries home to sleep. During the night the spirit of Sullen-Grumble hovers over Steadfastia and vigilantly keeps watch on the sleep of the townsfolk . . .

No God, no idols—nothing . . .

In this fantastic world there are no passions, no interests, no attachments. They all live together every minute, and each one feels alone. Never for a moment does life digress from fulfilling a countless number of idiotic duties, which are devised beforehand and weigh on every one of them like fate. Women have the right to bear children only in winter, because the violation of this rule may disrupt the smooth course of summer work. Young people are associated with each other only according to height and build, so that they correspond to the demands of a regular and attractive front. Nivellation, simplified to a strict ration of black bread—that is the essence of this soldierly fantasy . . .

Nevertheless, when Sullen-Grumble expounded his delirium to his superiors, not only were they not alarmed, but they looked with astonishment, amounting almost to awe, at the obscure latrine scrubber, who had made a project of ensnaring the universe. The formidable mass of efficiency, acting as one person, struck the imagination. The whole world was pictured as covered with black dots, on which people move to a drumbeat along a straight line, and go on and on. Those settlement units, those platoons, companies, regiments—all this taken together, does it not imply the existence of some radiant horizon, which is covered in fog for now, but in time, when the fog lifts and the horizon is revealed . . . ? What, however, is this horizon? What is concealed in it?

"Bar-r-racks!" the imagination, aroused to the point of heroism, responded quite definitely.

"Bar-r-racks!" the sullen latrine scrubber repeated in his turn, like an echo, accompanying this word with such an outlandish oath that the superiors felt as if they had been scorched by some mysterious fire . . .

Having dealt with Melancholin and dispersed the insane gathering, Sullen-Grumble immediately set about realizing his delirium.

But as Foolsburg presented itself to his eyes, the town was far from corresponding to his ideals. It was more a disorderly pile of huts than a town. There was no clear central point; the streets went every which way; the houses were disposed

anyhow, without symmetry, sometimes close together, sometimes leaving huge vacant lots in between. Consequently, he
was faced not with improving, but with creating anew. But
what was the meaning of the word "create" in the mind of a
person who, from early youth, had been seasoned in the duties of a latrine scrubber? To "create" meant to imagine that
you are in a thick forest; it meant to take an axe and, waving
this instrument of creativity right and left, to go steadfastly
wherever your feet carry you. This was exactly what Sullen-
Grumble did.

The day after his arrival he went around the whole town.
Neither the crooked streets, nor the great number of little
nooks, nor the way the townsfolks' huts were scattered—
nothing stopped him. One thing was clear to him: before
his eyes was a thick forest, and he had to deal with this forest. Having encountered some irregularity, Sullen-Grumble
fixed his puzzled gaze on it for a moment, then at once came
out of his stupor and silently gestured forward, as if projecting a straight line. He walked like that for a long time, his
arm stretched forward and projecting, and only when a river
appeared before his eyes did he sense that something extraordinary had taken place in him.

He had forgotten . . . he had never anticipated anything
like that . . . Up to then his fantasy kept going straight, on a
level surface. It removed, dissected, and raised up instantly,
knowing no obstacles and nourished only by its own content.
And suddenly . . . a meandering strip of liquid steel flashed
in his eyes—flashed and not only did not disappear, but did
not even stop under the gaze of this administrative basilisk.
It went on moving, heaving, and producing some special but
unquestionably living sounds. It was alive.

"Who's there?" he asked in horror.

But the river went on murmuring, and in its murmuring could be heard something seductive, even sinister. These sounds seemed to be saying: "Clever is your delirium, latrine scrubber, but there is another delirium which may be more clever than yours." Yes, this too was a delirium, or, better, here two deliriums stood face-to-face: one created personally by Sullen-Grumble, and the other which burst from somewhere and declared its total independence from the first one.

"What for?" Sullen-Grumble, his eyes directed at the river, asked the accompanying policemen, once the first moment of stupefaction had passed.

The policemen did not understand; but there was in the mayor's eyes something which so completely precluded any possibility of avoiding an explanation that they decided to respond even without understanding the question.

"The river, sir ... the dung, sir ..." they mumbled at random.

"What for?" he repeated in dismay, and suddenly, as if afraid of going more deeply into the question, did an abrupt about-face and went back.

With fitful steps he returned home, muttering under his nose:

"Subdue it, I'll subdue it!"

At home it took him only a minute to resolve the matter in principle. He had before him two equally great feats: to destroy the town and to remove the river. The means for accomplishing the first feat had been thought over beforehand; the means for accomplishing the second still seemed unclear and confused. But since there was no power in nature that could persuade the latrine scrubber of his ignorance of anything whatsoever, the ignorance in this case was not only tantamount to knowledge, but was in a certain sense more solid.

He was neither a technician nor an engineer; but he had

the firm soul of a latrine scrubber, and that was also strength of a sort, which could enable him to conquer the world. He knew nothing either about the origin of rivers or about the laws of their flowing down and not up, but he was sure that he needed only to point out from here to here, and in the allotted space a continent would certainly emerge, and then the river would continue to flow as before, to the right and to the left.

Having arrived at this thought, he began to prepare.

Immersed in some sort of wild reverie, he wandered the streets, his hands behind his back, muttering incoherent words under his nose. On his way he was met by townsfolk dressed in rags of all sorts, who bowed very low to him. He stopped before some of them, fixed an uncomprehending gaze on the rags, and uttered:

"What for?"

And, again lapsing into reverie, he continued on his way.

The moments of this reverie were most oppressive for the Foolsburgers. They froze before him as if transfixed, unable to tear their eyes from his bright steely gaze. There was concealed in this gaze some inscrutable mystery, and this mystery hung over the whole town like a heavy, almost leaden canopy.

The town wilted; the air felt stale and stuffy.

He had not yet given any orders, had not uttered any thoughts, had not informed anyone of his plans, but everyone already understood that *the end* had come. They were convinced of it by the constant flitting about of the idiot who carried the mystery in him; convinced of it by the soft growling coming from inside him. Unperceived by anyone, a vague terror crept among the townsfolk and took absolute possession of them all. All mental powers were concentrated on the mysterious idiot, and in tormenting anxiety they turned in one and the same magic circle of which *he* was the center. People forgot the past and gave no thought to the future. They reluctantly did necessary everyday chores, reluctantly came together, reluctantly lived from day to day. Why so?— that was the one question clearly rising before everyone at the sight of the idiot appearing in the distance. Why live, if life is forever poisoned by the notion of the idiot? Why live, if there is no means of shielding one's eyes from his terrible ubiquitousness? The Foolsburgers even forgot their mutual disagreements and hid in the corners in anxious expectation . . .

It seemed he himself realized that the end had come. He was not taken up with any current affairs and never even stopped by the office. He decided once and for all that the old life had irrevocably sunk into oblivion, and therefore there was no need to mess with this trash that had no relation to the future. The policemen suffered morally and physically; with bated breath, they stood at attention on the line along which he walked and waited to receive orders; but there were no orders. He silently passed by without even deigning to glance at them. There was no justice in Foolsburg, either merciful or unmerciful, either speedy or slow. At first the Foolsburgers, from an old habit, began to address him with their old claims and complaints against each other; but he did not even understand them.

"What for?" he said, looking the plaintiff up and down with some sort of wild amazement.

The Foolsburgers, dismayed, looked back and were horrified to see that indeed there was nothing there.

Finally the terrible moment came. After a brief hesitation, he decided thus: first to destroy the town, and then accost the river. Obviously, he still hoped that the river would come to its senses on its own.

A week before Saint Peter's Day he announced an order: everyone was to fast and pray. Although the Foolsburgers were always ready to fast and pray, still, hearing Sullen-Grumble's sudden order, they were perplexed. Did it really mean that they were facing something decisive, if such preparations were necessary in order to be ready for it? This question wrung all their hearts with anguish. They first thought he would start shooting; but peeking into the mayor's courtyard, where the cannons stood with which the shooting of townsfolk was usually done, they ascertained that the cannons stood unloaded. Then they arrived at the thought that there would be an all-around "perquisition" and began to get ready: hid books, letters, scraps of paper, money, and even icons—in short, everything that could be considered as some sort of "evidence."

"Who knows what his faith is?" the Foolsburgers whispered among themselves. "Maybe he's even a Freemason."[10]

But *he* kept marching along the straight line, his hands behind his back, and did not reveal his secret to anyone.

On Saint Peter's Day everyone took communion and many even took the last sacraments. When they sang the communion hymn, sobbing broke out in the church, "and loudest of all howled the headman and the marshal of nobility, as they feared for their great possessions." Then, going past the mayor after communion, they bowed and congratulated him, but he stood brazenly and did not even nod to anyone. The day went by unimaginably quietly. People broke their fast, but the food stuck in their throats, and again everyone wept. But when they passed by the mayor (he did accelerated marching that day), they quickly wiped their tears and tried to give their faces a carefree and trustful expression. They still had some hope. They kept thinking: the superiors will see our innocence and forgive us . . .

But Sullen-Grumble did not see anything and did not forgive anything.

"On June 30," narrates the chronicler, "the day after the feast of the holy and laudable apostles Peter and Paul, there was a first venture at breaking up the town." The mayor, axe in hand, was the first to run out of his house and, as if fired up, assaulted the municipal office building. The townsfolk followed suit. Divided into groups (in each group a special sergeant and a special spy had been appointed the evening before), they immediately began the work of destruction at all points. There was the thudding of axes and the shrieking of saws; the air was filled with the shouts of the workmen and the noise of the beams that were falling to the ground; dust hung over the town in a thick cloud, obscuring the light of the sun. Everybody was there to a man: the strong adults cut and broke; the young and weak piled up the litter and took it to the river. From morning till evening people tirelessly pursued the task of the destruction of their own dwellings, and for the night they took shelter in barracks set up on the common, where their possessions were also taken. They themselves did not understand what they were doing, and they did not even ask each other whether it was all really happening. They knew only one thing: that the end had come, and that the uncomprehending gaze of the sullen idiot followed them everywhere, everywhere. Glancingly, as if in sleep, some old men recalled examples from history, especially from the epoch of the mayor Wartbeardin, who had filled the town with tin soldiers and once, in a moment of insane audacity, commanded: "Knock it down!" But that was during the war, while now . . . without any reason . . . in the midst of a deep peace in the country . . .

Sullen-Grumble walked in a measured step amid the general devastation, and the same smile played on his lips which had shone on his face at the moment when, in a burst of subservience, he chopped off the index finger of his right hand.

He was pleased; he even dreamed. Mentally he already went beyond mere destruction. He sorted people by height and build; he divorced husbands from their lawful wives and united them with other men's wives; he distributed children to various families, depending on the given family situation; he appointed platoon and company sergeants and other commanders, selected spies, and so on. The vow made to his superior was already half fulfilled. Everything was on the alert, everything was at the boil, everything was ready to emerge fully armed; what was left were mere details, but even they had long been foreseen and resolved. Some sweet rapture pervaded the whole being of the sullen latrine scrubber and carried him off far, far away.

Drunk with pride, he peered into the sky, looked at the heavenly luminaries, and the sight seemed to perplex him.

"What for?" he muttered barely audibly, and for a long, long time thought about something and figured something out. What, precisely?

In a month and a half or two months there was no stone left upon stone. But as the work of devastation approached the bank of the river, the brow of Sullen-Grumble grew darker. The last house, the one closest to the river, collapsed; the blow of the axe rang out for the last time, but the river would not calm down. As before, it flowed, breathed, burbled, and meandered; as before, its one bank was steep and the other was a low meadow flooded far and wide in spring. The delirium went on.

Enormous heaps of garbage, dung, and straw already lay on the banks and only waited for a signal to disappear into the depths of the river. The frowning idiot wandered among the heaps and counted them, as if fearing that someone might steal the precious material.

Every once in a while he muttered with confidence:

"Subdue it! I'll subdue it!"

And then the longed-for moment came. One bright morning, he summoned the policemen, brought them to the bank of the river, paced out an area, indicated the current with his eyes, and said in a clear voice:

"From here—to here!"

However downtrodden the townsfolk were, even they felt something. Up to then only the works of men's hands had been destroyed, but now it came the turn of things perennial, not man-made. Many opened their mouths to protest, but he did not even notice this hesitation, and only seemed surprised that people were tarrying.

"On with it!" he commanded the policemen, glancing up at the swarming crowd.

The war with nature had begun.[11]

The masses that with secret sighing had demolished their own houses, with the same secret sighing began mulling about in the water. It seemed that the workforce of Foolsburg became inexhaustible, and the more pronounced the shamelessness of the demands, the more expandable became the number of tools to be employed.

There were many mayors who had come to Foolsburg and caused destruction, some as a joke, others in a moment of melancholy, impetuousity, or passion; but Sullen-Grumble was the only one who decided to destroy it seriously. From morning to night people swarmed in the water, driving piles into the river bottom and filling the gap that looked bottomless with garbage and dung. But the blind element effortlessly tore apart and dispersed the trash piled up at the price of inhuman efforts, and each time made its bed deeper and deeper. Wood chips, dung, straw, litter—it was all carried off by the swift current into the unknown distance, and Sullen-Grumble, with an astonishment bordering on fright, watched with uncomprehending eyes this almost magical disappearance of his hopes and intentions.

Finally the people became weary and ill. Sullen-Grumble sternly listened to the daily reports of the foremen about the number of workers who had dropped out and, not batting an eye, commanded:

"On with it!"

New parties of workers appeared who, like fern flowers, had mysteriously grown somewhere, only to disappear at once into the depth of the whirlpool.[12] Finally they brought the marshal of the nobility, who alone in the whole town considered himself free from work, and started pushing him into the river. However, the marshal did not go in at once, but protested, referring to some sort of rights.

"On with it!" commanded Sullen-Grumble.

The crowd guffawed. Seeing how the marshal, blushing and embarrassed, rolled up his trousers, the people felt cheered and redoubled their efforts.

Now a new difficulty emerged: the heaps of garbage were diminishing before everyone's eyes, so that soon there would be nothing left to dump into the river. They started on the last heap, in which Sullen-Grumble placed his firmest hopes. The river paused as if pondering, churned down to the bottom, but a moment later flowed on more merrily than before.

At one point, however, luck smiled on him. Gathering their last strength, and having exhausted the entire stock of garbage, the townsfolk started on the building material and moved the whole mass of it into the river at once. Then the crowds, hooting, rushed into the water and began sinking it to the bottom. The whole mass of the river's water streamed against this new obstacle and suddenly went into a whirl at one spot. There was crashing, swooshing, and some enormous gurgling, as if millions of mysterious vipers were simultaneously sending their hissing from the watery abyss. After that everything became quiet; the river stopped for a moment and then slowly, slowly began to spread over the meadow bank.

By evening the flooding was so great that its boundaries could not be seen, and still the water kept rising more and more. Noise could be heard from somewhere; it seemed as if whole villages were being destroyed, and screams, moans, and curses came from them. Haystacks floated on the water, beams, rafts, pieces of cottages; reaching the dam, they crashed into each other, went under, came up again, and crowded together in one place. Of course, Sullen-Grumble had not foreseen any of it; but looking at the enormous watery mass, he brightened up so much that he even regained the gift of speech and began to boast:

"Let the people behold this!" he said, thinking to fall into the Fotievo-Arakcheev tone that held sway at the time;[13] but then, recalling that he was no more than a latrine scrubber, he turned to the sentinels and ordered the town priests to be rounded up:

"On with it!"

Nothing is more dangerous than the imagination of a latrine scrubber not harnessed by anything and not threatened by the constant image of possible bodily punishment. Once aroused, it throws off the whole yoke of reality and begins to picture to its owner the most grandiose exploits. To extinguish the sun, to drill a hole in the ground in order to watch through it what happens in hell—those are the only goals that a true latrine scrubber acknowledges as worthy of his efforts. His head is like a wild desert, in all the corners of which emerge images of a most whimsical demonology. It is all rioting, whistling, hooting, and it rushes off into some dark, dawnless distance flapping invisible wings . . .

That is what happened with Sullen-Grumble. No sooner did he see the mass of water than the thought already lodged itself in his head that he would have his own sea. And since no one threatened him with rods for having this thought, he began to develop it further and further. There is the sea—that means there are fleets: first, of course, warships, then merchants. The warships bombard all the time; the merchant fleet transports valuable cargoes. But since Foolsburg abounds in everything and consumes nothing except flogging materials and administrative undertakings, while other places, like the village of Naughttoeat, the hamlet of Starveton, and so on, go completely hungry and are extraordinarily greedy besides, the trade balance, naturally, will always tend to favor Foolsburg. This will lead to a great abundance of hard cash, which, however, the Foolsburgers scorn and throw into the dung, but the Jews secretly dig up and use to buy railroad concessions.[14]

And what then! All these dreams crumbled the very next morning. No matter how assiduously the Foolsburgers pounded down the newly created dam, no matter how they watched over its safety in the course of the whole night, treason managed to penetrate their ranks.

Barely opening his eyes, Sullen-Grumble hastened to admire the work of his genius, but, approaching the river, he stood as if rooted to the spot. A new delirium had taken place. The meadows stood bare; the remnants of the monumental dam floated down the current in disorder, and the river burbled and flowed within its banks exactly as the day before.

For some time Sullen-Grumble remained silent. With a

sort of strange curiosity, he watched wave follow wave, first one, then another, and another, and another ... And it all rushes somewhere, and must disappear somewhere ...

Suddenly he bellowed piercingly and turned sharply on his heel.

"Abo-o-o-out-face! Follow me!" came the command.

He had made up his mind. The river did not want to go away from him—then he would go away from it. The place where the old Foolsburg stood was hateful to him. The elements there did not obey, ravines and gullies obstructed a speedy course at every step; miracles took place in broad daylight, of which nothing was noted either in statutes or in individual regulations by the authorities. He must flee!

He left the town at a quick pace, and the townsfolk, their heads down, followed him, barely able to keep up. Finally, toward evening, he arrived. Before his eyes spread a perfectly level plain with not even a single hummock, not a single gully on its surface. Wherever you looked, there was a smooth, level cover, on which you could march endlessly. This was also a delirium, but it coincided exactly with the delirium that nested in his head ...

"Here!" he cried in a level, toneless voice.

A new town was being built in a new place, but at the same time something else was creeping out into the world, something for which no name had been thought up at the time, and which only later became known under the highly precise names of "evil passions" and "untrustworthy elements." It would not be right, however, to assume that this "something else" appeared then for the first time; no, it already had its history ...

Back in the time of Wartbeardin, the chronicler mentions a certain Iona Trump, who, after prolonged wanderings amid warm seas and custard isles, returned to his native town bringing along a book of his own writings entitled *Letters to a Friend on Establishing Virtue upon Earth*. Since the biography of this Iona contains precious material for the history of Russian liberalism, the reader will certainly not begrudge its being retold here in some detail.

Iona's father, Semyon Trump, was a simple ragpicker, who, taking advantage of the time of troubles, had amassed a considerable fortune for himself.[15] In the brief period of anarchy (cf. "The Tale of the Six Mayoresses"), when, in the course of seven days, six mayoresses were wresting the helm of government from each other, he, with an adroitness astonishing in a Foolsburger, had turned coats from one party to another, at the same time covering his tracks so skillfully that each lawful government never doubted for a moment that Trump had always been its best and most reliable supporter. Taking advantage of this blindness, he first provisioned the troops of Iraidka, then the troops of Klemantinka, Amalka, Nelka, and finally fed peasant treats to Dunka Fatheels and Matrenka Nostril. For all that he was paid the list price which he himself had set, and since for Amalka, Nelka, and the rest of them those were hot times and they could not be bothered with counting money, the accounting ended by Trump digging his hand into the bag and hauling out fistfuls.

Neither the deputy mayor nor the dauntless staff-officer—no one knew anything about Trump's intrigues, so that when the genuine mayor, Epikurov, arrived in Foolsburg and the scrutiny of "this preposterous and laughable kerfuffle of the Foolsburgers" began, not only was Semyon Trump found not guilty in the least, but, on the contrary, it turned out that he had been "truly the worthiest citizen, who greatly contributed to the suppression of the revolution."

Epikurov liked Semyon Trump for many reasons. First, for his wife, Anna, who baked excellent pies; second, because

Semyon, sympathizing with the mayor's deeds of enlightenment, built a beer brewery in Foolsburg and donated a hundred rubles for establishing a town academy; third, finally,
because Semyon not only never forgot Saint Simeon the
God-receiver or the virgin Glyceria (the name days of the
mayor and his wife), but even celebrated them twice a year.

Long remembered was the decree in which Epikurov informed the townsfolk about the opening of the brewery and
explained the harmfulness of vodka and the benefits of beer.
"Vodka," said the decree, "not only does not instill mirthful-
ness, as many suppose, but, consumed in sufficient quantity,
even deflects from it and generates a passion for murder. As
for beer, one can consume as much as one likes without any
danger, for it does not inspire sorrowful thoughts, but only
good and mirthful ones. And therefore we advise and order
that vodka be drunk only before dinner and in a small glass;
at all other times it is safe to drink beer, which is now produced, in excellent quality and at a not very high price, by
the brewery of Semyon Trump, a merchant of the 1st guild."
The consequences of this decree for Trump were incalculable.
After a short period of time, he flourished so much that he
began to think that Foolsburg was not big enough for him
and that "I, Trump, must soon get to Petersburg, and there
present myself to the court."

During the mayorship of Ferdyshchenko, Trump was
even more lucky, thanks to the influence of Alenka, the cabbie's wife, who was his grandniece. At the beginning of 1766
he foresaw a famine and started buying up grain in advance.
At his bidding, Ferdyshchenko posted policemen at all the
gates to stop the carts with grain and drive them straight to
the dealer's yard. There Trump announced that he had paid
"the tax price" for the grain, and if any of the farmers had
doubts, the doubters were sent to the police station.

But as this fabulous wealth came, so it also evaporated. First, Trump did not get along with the musketeer woman Domashka, who replaced Alenka. Second, after visiting Petersburg, Trump began to boast: he called Prince Orlov "Grishka," said of Mamonov and Ermolov that they were none too smart, that he, Trump, "explained a lot to them about state politics, but they understood little."[16]

One fine morning, out of the blue, Ferdyshchenko summoned Trump and addressed him as follows:

"Is it true," he said, "that you, Semyon, referred to His Serene Highness Grigory Grigorievich Orlov, prince of the Roman Empire, as 'Grishka' and, hanging around in pothouses, passed him off as your friend before all sorts of people?"

Trump faltered.

"And I have witnesses to confirm it," Ferdyshchenko continued in a tone that allowed no doubts about his real knowledge of what he was saying.

Trump turned pale.

"And I, out of the goodness of my heart, forgive you these trivial doings!" Ferdyshchenko went on. "And as for the fortune you've acquired by robbery, I, the brigadier, write it over to myself. Go and pray to God."

And just so: that same day the brigadier wrote over to himself Trump's property, movable and immovable, though he gave the guilty man a hut at the edge of the town, where he could save his soul and provide for himself.

Sick, embittered, forgotten by everybody, Trump was living out his life, and in the twilight of his years he suddenly felt the onrush of "evil passions" and "untrustworthy elements." He began to preach that property was a dream, that only beggars and ascetics will enter the kingdom of heaven, and the rich and the drunkards will lick red-hot frying pans and boil in pitch. And, addressing Ferdyshchenko (things then were simple in this respect: people robbed, but listened to the truth in good humor), he added:

"And so you, too, devil's friend, will feast on burning coals with your brother Satan in hell, while I, Semyon, will rest in the bosom of Abraham."

Such was the first Foolsburg demagogue.

Iona Trump was not in Foolsburg when the terrible catastrophe befell his father. When he returned home, everyone expected that Ferdyshchenko's doings would at least make him indignant; but he listened to the bad news calmly, expressing neither dismay nor even surprise. He was of a rather cultivated but totally dreamy nature, completely indifferent to the facts of reality, and he supplemented this indifference with a big dose of utopianism. In his head flickered some sort of paradise, in which virtuous people lived, who performed virtuous deeds and achieved virtuous results. But in fact it all merely flickered, without assuming any definite forms and going no farther than simple and not entirely clear aphorisms. His book *On Establishing Virtue upon Earth* was nothing but a collection of such aphorisms, which did not point or even aspire to point to any practical application. Iona liked to consider himself virtuous, and he would have liked it even better if others, too, considered themselves virtuous. This was the need of his mild, dreamy nature; this also underlay his need for propaganda. The virtuous living with the virtuous; the absence of envy, troubles, and cares; gentle conversation, serenity, moderation—those were the ideals he preached, knowing nothing of the means for attaining them.

In spite of its vagueness, Trump's teaching acquired so many followers in Foolsburg that the mayor, Wartbeardin, thought it not superfluous to be concerned about it. First he ordered the book *On Establishing Virtue upon Earth* and examined it; then he summoned the author for examination.

"I read this book of yours, Iona," he said, "and was driven to revulsion by the many villainies written in it."

Iona seemed amazed. Wartbeardin went on:

"You think to make all people virtuous, but you forget that virtue comes not from you, but from God, and it is from God that each man receives his proper place."

Iona was more and more amazed by this assault, and waited, not so much with fear as with curiosity, for what conclusions Wartbeardin would come to.

"If there are slanderers, thieves, villains, and murderers in this world (something that is constantly present in reports)," the mayor went on, "why on earth, Iona, has it come into your head that they should not exist? And who gave you the power to remove all these people from their natural calling and insert them, along with virtuous people, in some place worthy of ridicule which you brazenly call 'paradise'?"

Iona opened his mouth to give some explanation, but Wartbeardin interrupted him:

"Wait. And if all the people 'in paradise' spend their time singing and dancing, who then, in your, Iona's, reasoning, will plow the earth? And, having plowed it, sow? And, having sown, reap? And, having gathered the fruits, provide and nourish with them the nobility and people of other ranks?"

Again Iona opened his mouth, and again Wartbeardin restrained his impulse.

"Wait. And for those shameless utterances I have judged you, Iona, with a quick judgment, and decided thus: your book is to be torn up and trampled upon" (so saying, Wartbeardin tore it up and trampled upon it), "and you yourself, as a corrupter of good morals, will first be put in the pillory, and then be dealt with as I, the mayor, deem fit."

Thus Iona Trump initiated the martyrology of Foolsburgian liberalism.

This conversation occurred on a Sunday morning, and at noon Iona was taken to the marketplace and, to make him look more repulsive, was clothed in a sarafan (since among his followers there were many women), and on his chest a plaque was hung with the inscription "Womanizer and Adulterer." To complete it all, the policemen invited the market people to spit on the criminal, which they did. Toward evening Iona was no more.

Such was the debut of Foolsburgian liberalism. However, in spite of the failure, the "evil passions" did not die, but formed a tradition, which passed in succession from generation to generation under all the subsequent mayors. Unfortunately, the chroniclers did not foresee the terrible spread of this evil in the future, and therefore, paying no due attention to the facts that took place in front of them, set them down in their notebooks with regrettable brevity. Thus, for instance, under Blaggardov there is mention of a certain nobleman's son, Ivashka Farafontiev, who was put in chains for speaking blasphemous words, and the content of these words was that "all people have the same need of food, and he who eats a lot, let him share with the one who eats little." "And sitting in chains, Ivashka died," adds the chronicler. Another example occurred in the time of Mikaladze, who, though a liberal himself, being a passionate man and also new to his duties, was not always able to refrain from boxing people's ears. During his time as mayor thirty-three philosophers were scattered over the face of the earth for having "the absurd habit of saying: let the one who works eat; let the one who works not taste the fruit of his idleness." There was a third example in the time of Benevolensky, when a young man of noble origin, Aleshka Bespiatov, was "subjected to interrogatory procedure" for maintaining, in reproach of the mayor's fondness for issuing laws, that "bad are the laws that need to be written, but good are the laws that are written not-by-hand in every man's nature." And he, too, "following that interrogatory procedure, died of fear and pain."

After Bespiatov the liberal martyrology stopped for a time. Pustule and Ivanov were stupid; Du Chariot was both stupid and also himself infected with liberalism. Melancholin, in the first half of his mayorship, not only did not hinder but even patronized liberalism, because he confused it with free behavior, to which he had an insuperable disposition. Only later, when blessed Paramosha and the holy fool Aksinyushka took the reins of government in their hands, was the liberal martyrology reinitiated in the person of the teacher of calligraphy Linkin, whose doctrine, as we know, was that "all of us, men and brutes, will die and go to the devil's dam." Along with Linkin, two very famous philosophers of the time, Funich and Marasmitsky, all but got themselves into a scrape, but thought better of it just in time and began, together with Melancholin, to be present at the "ravishments" (see "The Worship of Mammon and Repentance").[17] Melancholin's turnabout gave liberalism a new direction, which can be called the centripetally-centrifugally-inscrutably nonsensical. But all the same this was liberalism, and therefore it could not succeed, because the moment had come when there was no need of any liberalism. No need at all, not in any way, not in any form, not even in the form of absurdity, nor even in the form of the ravishment of the authorities.

The ravishment of the authorities! What does that mean? It means such ravishment as, at the same time, allows for the possibility of nonravishment! And from that to revolution is—one step!

Once the mayor Sullen-Grumble came into office, liberalism in Foolsburg ceased entirely, and the martyrology was never renewed. "Being burdened with bodily exertions beyond measure," says the chronicler, "the Foolsburgers were so tired that they could think of nothing except how to straighten their toil-bent bodies." Thus it went on all the while Sullen-Grumble was destroying the old town and struggling with the river. But as the new town neared completion, the bodily exertions diminished, and along with leisure the flame of treason began to smolder under the ashes . . .

The thing was that the final completion of the town was followed by a series of celebrations. First, a celebration was held on the occasion of changing the town's name from Foolsburg to Steadfastia; second, there followed a celebration in remembrance of the victories won by former mayors over the townsfolk; and third, on the occasion of the coming of autumn, there was the Feast of the Powers That Be. Although the initial plan of Sullen-Grumble was that the feast days should differ from all other days only in that, instead of working, the people took up more intense marching, this time the vigilant mayor committed a blunder. Sleepless tramping in a straight line had so destroyed his iron nerves that when the last sound of an axe died in the air, he had just time enough to shout "Knock off!" and straightaway collapsed on the ground and began to snore, before even giving the order to appoint new spies.

The exhausted, maligned, and annihilated Foolsburgers, after a long interval, breathed freely for the first time. They looked at each other—and suddenly felt ashamed. They did not understand what precisely had happened around them, but they felt that the air was filled with foul language, and it was no longer possible to breathe this air. Did they have a history? Were there moments in this history when they had been able to manifest their independence? They did not remember any. They remembered only that they had had Urus-Kugush-Kildibaevs, Blaggardovs, Wartbeardins, and, to crown their disgrace, this terrible, this ignominious latrine scrubber! And they had all throttled them, gnawed them, torn them with their teeth—in the name of what? Blood rose in their chests, their breath stopped, their faces were distorted with wrath on remembering the ignominious idiot who came to them with an axe in his hand, no one knew from where, and with inscrutable impudence uttered a death sentence on the past, the present, and the future . . .

And meanwhile, he lay motionless right in the hot sun and snored loudly. He was now in everyone's view; everyone could freely look at him and ascertain that he was a genuine idiot and nothing else.

While he destroyed, fought with elements, commited everything to fire and the sword, it could seem that in him something enormous was embodied, some all-vanquishing force which, regardless of its content, could strike one's imagination; now, when he lay prostrate and exhausted, when his shameless gaze did not weigh on anybody, it was clear that this "enormous," this "all-vanquishing force" was nothing but a boundless idiocy.

No matter how intimidated their minds were, the need to free their souls from the obligation of penetrating the mysterious meaning of the phrase "son of a gun" was so strong that it changed the very view of Sullen-Grumble's significance. This was already a significant step forward in the cause of "untrustworthy elements." The latrine scrubber woke up, but his gaze no longer produced the same impression. He annoyed, but he did not frighten. The conviction that he was not a villain, but a simple idiot, who marched straight ahead and did not see anything that was going on around him, gained more and more authority every day. This caused still greater annoyance. The thought that his marching was perpetual, that there was some power hidden in the idiot that froze people's minds, became unbearable. No one tried to suggest that the idiot could calm down or turn to better feelings, and that such a turn would make life possible and, perhaps, even peaceful. Not only peace but even happiness itself seemed offensive and humiliating in view of this latrine scrubber, who had single-handedly destroyed a whole mass of thinking beings.

"He" will give them some happiness! "He" will tell them: "I devastated you and stupefied you, and now I will allow you to be happy!" And they will listen to that talk imperturbably! They will avail themselves of his permission and be happy! Shame!!!

But Sullen-Grumble kept marching and kept looking straight ahead, not at all suspecting that evil passions were swarming under his very nose and untrusworthy elements were surfacing almost before his eyes. On the example of all benevolent benefactors, he saw only one thing: that the thought that had been ripening for so long in his calloused head had finally been realized, that he truly owned a straight line and could march along it as much as he liked. And whether in the path of that line there was anything living, and whether that living thing was able to feel, to think, to rejoice, to suffer, whether it was, finally, capable of turning from "the trustworthy" into "the untrustworthy"—all that was not even a question for him . . .

The vexation was growing stronger, because the Foolsburgers were still obliged to execute all the tangled formalities introduced by Sullen-Grumble. They cleaned themselves up, tightened their belts, went through all the arenas, formed into squares, went off to various works, and so on. Every moment seemed suited to becoming free, and every moment seemed premature. There were constant night discussions; here and there occurred isolated cases of violated discipline; but it was all somehow so uncoordinated that it could, in the very slowness of the process, arouse suspicion even in such a confirmed idiot as Sullen-Grumble.

And in fact he began to suspect something. He was struck by the silence during the day and the rustling during the night.

As darkness began to fall, he saw some shadows moving about the town and vanishing no one knew where, and at daybreak the same shadows reappearing in the town and running to their homes. This phenomenon was repeated several days in a row, and each time he was about to run out of the house to personally investigate the cause of the night's turmoil, but held back out of superstitious fear. As a true latrine scrubber, he was afraid of devils and witches.

And then one day an order appeared in all the settlement units announcing the appointment of spies. This was the drop that made the cup overflow . . .

But here I must confess that the notebooks containing the details of this affair have been lost, no one knows where. Therefore I must limit myself to telling the denouement of this history, and that only owing to the accidental survival of one page where it is described.

"A week later" (after what?), writes the chronicler, "the Foolsburgers were astonished by an unprecedented spectacle. The north turned dark and was covered with storm clouds; something was rushing at the town from there: a torrential rain, or a tornado. Filled with wrath, *it* came rushing, furrowing the ground, rumbling, howling and moaning, and from time to time belching out some dull, croaking sounds. Though *it* was not yet near, the air in the town shook, the bells began to ring of themselves, the trees ruffled up, the cattle went mad and rushed about the fields, unable to find the road back to town. *It* was drawing near, and as it drew near, time was stopping its course. Finally the earth trembled, the sun grew dark ... the Foolsburgers fell prostrate. Inconceivable terror appeared on all faces, seized all hearts.

"*It* came ...

"At that solemn moment Sullen-Grumble suddenly turned his whole body toward the stunned crowd and said in a clear voice:

"'There will come ...'

"But before he finished, there was a loud snap, and the former latrine scrubber instantly disappeared, as if melting in air.

"History ceased its course."

The End

1. Thoughts about the Like-Mindedness of Mayors, and also about the Absolute Power of Mayors and Other Things

*Written by the Mayor of Foolsburg Basilisk Wartbeardin**

It is necessary that there be like-mindedness among mayors. So that they speak, as it were, with "like mouths" everywhere in the world. On the harmfulness of a many-mindedness of mayors I will be brief. What are the rights and duties of a mayor? The rights are: that villains should tremble and the

---

* The text is written in a child's notebook in quarto. The reading of it is difficult, because the orthography is nothing short of barbaric. For instance, he writes the word "stupid" as "stoopid," and the word "when" as "hoowen." But this makes the manuscript all the more valuable, for it proves that it was penned, undoubtedly and directly, by a thoughtful administrator and was not even reviewed by his secretary. This also proves that in older times mayors were expected not so much to be brilliantly educated as to be profound thinkers naturally inclined to philosophical exercise. —*Publisher*

rest should obey. The duties are: to apply measures of leniency, but not neglect measures of strictness. And along with that to encourage learning. These brief terms contain the simple but not easy science of being a mayor. Let us reflect briefly on what may come of that.

"Villains should tremble"—wonderful! But who are those villains? Obviously, if there is many-mindedness on the subject, it may lead to great confusion. A thief is a villain, but he is, so to speak, a third-rate villain; a murderer is also a villain, but he, too, is only a second-rate villain; finally, a freethinker may be a villain—but this time a real villain, an inveterate and unrepentant villain. Of these three sorts of villains, each, of course, should tremble, but should they tremble to the same degree? No, not the same. A thief may be allowed to tremble less than a murderer; a murderer less than a godless freethinker. This latter must always have before him a piercing mayoral gaze, which should make him tremble incessantly. Now, if we allow many-mindedness on this subject among mayors, many things will wind up in reverse: the godless freethinkers will tremble moderately, thieves and murderers constantly and most terribly. And thus a sound administrative economy will disappear and a majestic administrative harmony will be broken!

But let us go further. It was said above: "the rest should obey"—but who are "the rest"? Obviously what is meant here is the townsfolk in general. However, it is necessary to make distinctions in this general appellation: first, high-born nobility; second, respectable merchants; and third, farmers and other low-born folk. Though it is unquestionable that each of these three sorts of townsfolk should obey, it is also impossible to deny that each can do it in his own special way. For instance, a gentleman obeys nobly and offers reasons casually; a merchant obeys readily and offers bread and salt;[1]

finally, low-born folk obey simply and, feeling guilty, repent and ask forgiveness. What will happen if a mayor does not enter into these nuances, particularly if he allows low-born folk to offer reasons? It is terrible to say, but I fear that the many-mindedness of mayors might have consequences that would be not only harmful, but also difficult to set right!

I have heard the following story. A preoccupied mayor went into a café, asked for a glass of vodka, and on receiving his order along with some copper change, swallowed the coins and poured the vodka into his pocket. I fully believe the story, because, given a mayor's preoccupations, such calamitous confusions are quite possible. But for all that I cannot help saying: thus mayors must be very careful in regard to their own actions!

Let us go further still. I mentioned above that besides rights mayors also have duties. "Duties!"—oh, what a bitter word this is for many mayors. But let us not be too hasty, my dear colleagues! Let us reflect maturely, and perhaps we will see that judicious employment can make even bitter things sweet! It has been said that a mayor's duties consist in applying measures of leniency, without, however, neglecting measures of strictness. What are measures of leniency? They mostly are expressed in greetings and kind regards. Townsfolk, particularly of low birth, have a great fondness for that; but it is necessary that a mayor wear a uniform, have an open expression and a benevolent gaze. A smile playing on his lips is also not out of place. It has happened more than once that, wearing such a triumphant look, I came out to the crowds of inhabitants, and when I cried in a sonorous and pleasant voice: "Greetings, lads!"—my word of honor, there would be few among them who, at my first affable gesture, were not ready to throw themselves into the water and drown, as long as it would earn them my benevolent approval. Of course,

I never asked for that, but I confess, to see such readiness on all faces always made me happy. Such are the measures of leniency. As for the measures of strictness, they are quite well-known to everyone, even if they have not been in the cadet corps. Therefore I will not enlarge upon them, but will proceed directly to the way of applying both measures.

First of all I will observe that a mayor should never act otherwise than by way of measures. His every action is not an action but a measure. His affable look, his benevolent gaze are as much measures of inner politics as is flogging. The townsfolk are *always* guilty of something, and so there is *always* a need to influence their corrupt will. In this sense, the first measure of influencing should be a measure of leniency. For if a mayor, on coming out of his house, immediately starts shooting, he achieves nothing more than the destruction of all the people and, like Marius of old, will be left on the ruins alone with his clerk.[2] Thus, having first applied a measure of leniency, the mayor should note well whether it has borne the proper fruit, and when he has made sure that it has, he may go home; if he sees that there is no fruit, he must apply further measures without delay. The first action in this sense should be a stern look, which would instantly make the people fall on their knees. Then, too, his speech should be abrupt, his gaze should promise further orders, his gait should be uneven, as if spasmodic. But if the crowd remains stubborn even despite that, he must suddenly make a rush at them, snatch one or two persons who are designated as instigators, and, stepping away from the rioters, immediately deal with them. If even that should prove insufficient, he must separate every tenth man from the crowd, recognize them as instigators, and deal with them like the first ones. On most occasions these measures (especially if they are taken in good time and quickly) should be sufficient; however, it may happen that the crowd, inveterate and as if hardened in its coarseness, is also hardened in its violence. Then it is time to shoot.

Such is the variety of existing measures, and the sort of wisdom necessary for perceiving all their nuances. Now let us imagine what may happen if there should be a harmful many-mindedness among the mayors on this subject. Here is what: in one town the mayor will be content with sensible orders, while in another neighboring town another mayor, under the same circumstances, will start shooting. And since we learn everything by word of mouth, this absence of like-mindedness may instill a justified perplexity and even many-mindedness in the townsfolk. Of course, people should always be ready to endure all sorts of measures, but even so they are not to be deprived of their right to gradualness. In an extreme case they can even demand that they should first be given orders and only then be shot at. For, as I have already said, if a mayor starts shooting without calculation, in time he will have no one left to give orders to . . . And thus administrative economy will again cease to exist, and the majestic administrative harmony will again be disrupted.

I also said that a mayor should encourage learning. That is so. But here, too, it is necessary to consider: What sort of learning? There are various kinds of learning: some deal with fertilizing the fields, with building human and animal dwellings, with military valor and insuperable firmness— this is useful learning; others, on the contrary, deal with the harmful freethinking of Freemasons and Jacobins, with certain notions and rights supposedly natural for human beings, including even the structure of the universe—those are all harmful.[3] What will happen if one mayor starts promoting the first kind and another the second? First, the latter will be put on trial and thereby be deprived of his pension; second, there will be harm and not benefit from it for the people. For if they should meet somewhere between two towns, the inhabitant of one would ask about fertilizing the fields, and the inhabitant of the other would respond by talking about the natural organization of the world. And thus, having talked to each other, they would go their separate ways.

Consequently, the necessity and benefit of mayoral like-mindedness is obvious. Having developed this matter in a suitable fullness, let us begin to discuss the means of its realization.

To this end I propose briefly:

(1) To set up a special institute for educating mayors.[4] Mayors, having a special destiny, should also receive a special education. Mayors ought to be weaned from their mothers' breasts and brought up not on ordinary mother's milk, but on the milk of the governing senate's decrees and the regulations of the authorities. This is true mayoral milk, and he who is nourished on it will be firm in like-mindedness and will perform his mayoral duties zealously and strictly. Meanwhile, other food should be taken in moderation, with an unconditional abstention from drink, and, with respect to morals, there should be a constant reminder that the exacting of arrears is the first mayoral duty and responsibility. To satisfy the imagination, pictures will be permitted. They might portray, for instance, a finance minister sitting on an empty chest and howling loudly. Or they might portray the figure of a loyal cadet, with the inscription "A Candidate for Mayor, or Dying of Love." Of subjects, three should be taught: (a) arithmetic, as the necessary tool for exacting arrears; (b) instruc-

tions for clearing the streets of dung; and (c) the science of the gradual application of measures. Leisure time should be occupied by the reading of government regulations and stories from the lives of valorous administrators. It may be predicted that such a system will assure: (a) that the mayors will be firm; and (b) that they will not flinch.

(2) To publish pertinent guidebooks. This is necessary in view of eliminating certain vile weaknesses. Though nurtured on strict mayoral milk, a mayor is nevertheless organized as a human being and, consequently, has some natural needs. One of these needs—and the principal one—is for the enticing female sex. It is impossible to exaggerate how pressing it is and what great harm comes from it for the treasury. There exist mayors who lust every moment and, being in this pitiful state, leave government orders unconfirmed for whole months. It is imperative in such cases that guidebooks forewarn the mayors on the subject of this pernicious need and urge them to keep their marital bed in good order. The second quite pernicious weakness is the penchant of mayors for refined food and excellent wines. There are mayors who eat such a quantity of the sterlets supplied by the merchants that in a short time they grow fat and become quite indifferent to the prescriptions of their superiors. On these occasions, too, it is imperative to refresh the mayors with guiding articles— and in extreme cases, even to threaten them with strict mayoral milk. Finally, the third and most vile weakn— [Here several lines of the manuscript are missing, because the author, intending to pour sand

on the written part, mistakenly used ink.[5] There is a note in the margin: "This place is covered with ink by mistake."]

(3) To organize from time to time secret assemblies of mayors in provincial capitals. At these assemblies to entertain them by reading the guidelines for mayors and refreshing their memory in regard to mayoral learning. To admonish them to be firm and unheeding. And

(4) To introduce a universal system of mayoral rewards. But this is such a vast subject that I hope to speak of it separately.

Having been thus established in the very center, mayoral like-mindedness will inevitably lead to general like-mindedness. Every townsperson, seeing that mayors (a) give orders like-mindedly, (b) also shoot like-mindedly, will thus prepare like-mindedly for these measures. For there will be nowhere to escape from such like-mindedness. Consequently, there will be neither quarreling nor discord, but only orders and shooting everywhere.

In conclusion, I will say a few words about mayoral autocracy and other things. This is also necessary, because without mayoral autocracy, mayoral like-mindedness is also impossible. On this account opinions vary. Some, for instance, say that mayoral autocracy consists in subduing the elements. One mayor said to me personally: "What sort of mayors are we, brother! The sun rises every day in the east, and I am unable to give an order that it should rise in the west!" Although these words belong to a truly exemplary mayor, even so I cannot praise them. For one should wish only for something that can be attained; if you wish for something unattainable, as, for instance, the taming of the elements, the suspension of the course of time, and the like, you thereby not only do not exalt mayoral power, but embarrass it still more. Therefore a mayor's autocratic rule should be regarded not from the viewpoint of sunrise or some other hostile elements, but from the viewpoint of the assessors, councillors, and secretaries of various state departments, executive boards, and courts. In my opinion, all those persons are harmful, for they hinder a mayor in his, so to speak, unceasing administrative course . . .

[Here this extraordinary piece of writing breaks off. Further follow only brief notes, such as: "Testing the pen," "Polly want a cracker," "report," "report," "report," etc.]

II. On the Seemly Appearance of All Mayors

Written by the Mayor,
Prince Xavery Georgievich Mikaladze*

It is imperative that a mayor have a seemly appearance. That he should be neither fat nor skinny, not enormously tall, but also not too short, proportionate in all the parts of his body, and have a clear face, not disfigured by warts or (God forbid!) malignant rashes. His eyes should be gray, capable of expressing both mercy and severity according to circumstances. A suitable nose. Above all he must wear a uniform.

---

* This manuscript is several pages long in quarto; the orthography is quite good, but it must be mentioned that the author used lined paper.—*Publisher*

Excessive corpulence, just as excessive leanness, may have equally unpleasant consequences. I knew a mayor who, though he had excellent knowledge of the laws, was not a success, because the quantity of fat accumulated inside him suffocated him. I knew another mayor, a very skinny one, who also had no success, because as soon as he appeared in his town, the townsfolk immediately nicknamed him "Pharaoh's Lean Kine,"[6] and after that not one of his orders could have any effective force. On the other hand, a mayor who is neither fat nor skinny, even if ignorant in matters of law, will always be successful. For he is brisk, fresh, quick, and always ready.

What is said above about fatness and leanness can also be applied to a mayor's height. This height should be between five and a half and six feet. Remarkable are the examples of noncompliance with this rule, so negligible at first sight. I personally know of three such examples. In one of the Volga provinces, the mayor was over seven feet tall—and what then? An inspector of small stature arrived in that city, became indignant, started intriguing, with the result that this quite worthy man was taken to court. In another province, a mayor of the same height suffered from a tapeworm of an extraordinary size. Finally, the third mayor was so short that there was no room in him for extensive laws and he died of strain. Thus all three suffered on account of inordinate height.

To keep the parts of the body in good proportion is also important, for harmony is the foremost law of nature. Many mayors have very long arms, and for that are eventually dismissed from their posts; many are distinguished by an unusual development of their extremities or their unsightly smallness, which may seem ridiculous or shameful. This should be avoided at all costs, for nothing undermines authority so much as some unusual or conspicuous ugliness.

A clear face adorns not only a mayor but any man. Besides, it renders manifold services, of which the first is the trust of superiors. Smooth skin without effeminacy, a brave look without insolence, an open physiognomy without conceit—all this charms superiors, especially if the mayor stands with his body thrust forward as if striving ahead. Here the slightest blemish may disrupt the harmony and give the mayor an impudent look. The second service rendered by a clear face is the love of subordinates. When the face is clean and refreshed by ablutions, the skin shines so much that it even becomes capable of reflecting the rays of the sun. This gives the mayor a look that is very agreeable for his subordinates.

A mayor must have a clear voice that can be heard from afar; he should remember that mayoral lungs are created for giving orders. I knew a mayor who, while preparing for this post, settled specially on the seashore and there shouted at the top of his lungs. Later on this mayor subdued eleven big rebellions, twenty-nine medium-size disturbances, and over fifty small misunderstandings. All this with the help of his afar-heard voice.

Now about the uniform. Of course, freethinkers may (at their personal responsibility) suppose that in the face of natural laws it makes no difference whether a superior is clad in a metal chain vest or a short coachman's coat, but in the eyes of experienced and serious people this matter will always be of particular importance in comparison with all else. Why so? Because, gentlemen freethinkers, for someone performing official duties, it is the uniform, so to speak, that precedes the man, and not the other way round. Of course, I do not mean to say that the uniform can act and give orders independently of the man contained in it, but it seems one can boldly maintain that once there is a splendid uniform, even puny mayors can be tolerated in service. And therefore, finding that all presently existing uniforms fulfill this important purpose only to a slight degree, I would deem it necessary to organize a special committee on this matter, and charge it with making a design for a mayoral uniform. I, for my part, foresee the possibility of offering this idea: a short jacket of silver brocade with ostrich feathers in the back, gold armor plate in front, trousers also of brocade, and on the head a solid gold helmet crowned with feathers.[7] It seems to me that, dressed like this, any mayor will put his affairs in order in the shortest possible time.

All that has been said above about the seemliness of mayors will be of still greater importance if we recall how often they are obliged to be in secret communications with the female sex. Everyone knows the benefit that proceeds from it, but that is all far from exhausting the subject. If I say that through the female sex an experienced administrator is able at any time to know all the hidden actions of his subordinates, that alone is enough to prove how important this administrative method is. By it more than one diplomat has discovered the plans and designs of the enemy, thus making them useless; more than one general, by this same method, has won battles or been able to beat a timely retreat. I, for my part, having tried this method in practice, can testify that just the other day, owing to it, I exposed the weak tactics of a police captain, who, as a result, was relieved of his duties.

It seems it will also not be superfluous to say that while captivating the frail female sex, a mayor should seek solitude, and by no means subject his victim to publicity and orality. In such pleasant retirement, under the guise of the tenderness of jocular behavior, he can find out many things that are not always available even to the most efficient sleuth. Thus, for instance, if the person in question is a scientist's wife, it should be possible to find out what her husband's ideas are concerning the structure of the universe or the powers that be, and so on. In general, the inevitable consequence of such curiosity is that the mayor in a short time acquires the reputation of a reader of hearts . . .

Having expounded all of the above, I feel that I have done my duty conscientiously. The elements of the mayoral nature are so many that it is, of course, impossible for one man to embrace them all. Therefore I do not boast of having embraced and explained everything. Let some write about mayoral strictness, others about mayoral like-mindedness, still others about mayoral first-everywhere presence. I, having told what I know about mayoral seemliness, comfort myself with this:

That here, too, is a small drop of my honey . . . [8]

III. Decree Concerning a Mayor's Kindheartedness

Written by Mayor Benevolensky

(1) Let every mayor be kindhearted.

(2) Let every mayor remember that strictness alone, however severe it may be, cannot satisfy people's hunger or clothe people's nakedness.

(3) Let every mayor hear out the person who comes to him; the one who without listening begins to shout or, worse still, to flog—will shout and flog in vain.

(4)   Let every mayor, seeing a person pursuing his business, leave him to pursue it without hindrance.

(5)   Let each of them bear in mind that if at some point a person transgresses, the same one may still be able to accomplish useful things.

(6)   Therefore: if any person transgresses, do not subject him to flogging at once, but consider diligently whether the effect and protection of Russian laws extend to him.

(7)   Let a mayor remember that the glory of the Russian Empire is adorned and the gains of its treasury are increased through none other than the person.

(8)   Therefore: the punishing, dispersing, or in any other way destroying of persons should be done with prudence, lest this action harm the Russian Empire and incur losses to the treasury.

(9)   Should any person fail to offer gifts, there should be a thorough investigation of the reason for such non-offering, and if it turns out to be poverty, it should be forgiven, and if it is laziness or stubbornness, there should be reminders and admonishments, until he mends his ways.

(10) Every person should work and, having worked, taste of repose. Therefore: a person who is strolling or walking by should not be seized by the collar and put in jail.

(11)   Laws should be passed that are good and conform
        to human nature; do not promulgate laws that are
        contrary to nature, still less those that are incompre-
        hensible and difficult to realize.

(12)   Do not crush people at festivities and popular gath-
        erings; on the contrary, keep a benevolent smile on
        your face, so as not to frighten the merrymakers.

(13)   Do not hinder anyone's eating and drinking.

(14)   Education should be instilled in good measure,
        avoiding bloodshed as far as possible.

(15)   In all the rest follow your own will.

Translators' Notes

From the Publisher

The "Publisher" in question is, of course, the author himself. By taking this distance, Saltykov gives himself freedom to make all sorts of satirical comments, connecting the history of fantastic Foolsburg to the history of very real Russia. His satire looks not only into the past, but to his present, and to the future, not only his but ours as well.

All the dates are given according to the Gregorian calendar.

1. **tax farmers:** In Imperial Russia, private persons who bought from the government the right to collect taxes, including taxes on the sale of alcohol. This was a complicated but lucrative occupation.

2. **Biron . . . Potemkin . . . Razumovsky:** Duke Ernst Johan von Biron (1690–1772), a German nobleman in service of the Russian throne, the favorite of the empress Anna Ivanovna; in 1740 served briefly as regent of the Russian Em-

pire. Prince Grigory Alexandrovich Potemkin (1739–1791), Russian courtier, field marshal of the Russian army; from a family of minor nobility, he came to power as a favorite and the morganatic husband of the empress Catherine the Great. Count Alexei Grigorievich Razumovsky (1709–1771), of obscure Cossack origin, rose to be a field marshal and the favorite of the empress Elizaveta Petrovna.

3. **They all flog the inhabitants:** Flogging as a basic method of "education" was practiced in Russia not only in the time of serfdom, but in the more or less liberal 1860s. In 1890, in one of the local regional governments, "it was deemed necessary to reintroduce bodily punishment with the aim of improving people's morality." All Russian historians mention the total absence of peasants' rights under Catherine the Great and later, the boundless power of owners over them, and their right to punish them in all possible ways: with flogging, with rods, whipping, putting in chains, keeping on bread and water for weeks—these were all quite ordinary practices, even the norm.

4. **rose to the trembling filled with trust:** "There is in the souls of your subjects a nuance of a panic fear—probably the consequence of a long series of upheavals and prolonged despotic rule. It seems as if they live in constant fear of an earthquake and do not believe that the earth beneath them is not going to tremble" (Denis Diderot in a letter to the empress Catherine the Great).

5. **The chronicle . . . covers the period from 1731 to 1825:** This means that formally the chronology of the chronicle covers the period from the beginning of the rule of the em-

press Anna Ioannovna (1730) to the death of the emperor Alexander I and the Decembrist uprising (1825). However, the content of the events and processes described goes beyond this period and, as a rule, cannot be tied to any specific time. They satirically combine certain features of different epochs in the history of the Russian autocratic state. This explains the presence of what the Publisher calls anachronisms, the mixture of certain "historic evidences," the diversity of Foolsburg mayors, and so on. **literary activity ceased to be admissible even for archivists:**This is an allusion to the very strict reactionary times after the Decembrist uprising and the ascent to the throne of Nicholas I, who created, in 1826, the Third Section of the Imperial Office (often referred to as the Special Section) to conduct police investigations.

6. **Pogodin's depository:** Mikhail Petrovich Pogodin (1800–1875) was a major Russian historian, journalist, writer, and publisher. He loved Russia and thought that it had a special role in history. A convinced monarchist, he was an adherer to the formula "Orthodoxy, Autocracy, Nationality," the imperial ideological doctrine of the emperor Nicholas I. His underlying thought was that an autocratic ruler in Russia was God on earth, that his people should trust him and be devoted to him. This, in his opinion, was the basis of Russian power. His *depository* was a collection of Russian antiquities: written documents, and objects.

7. **One can just see some Pimen:** The Foolsburg chronicler is here likened to Pushkin's chronicler Pimen in the play *Boris Godunov*, who describes "quite simply everything he witnessed in his life." **Messrs. Shubinsky, Mordovtsev, and Melnikov:** Saltykov lists three prominent Russian

"journalist-historians" of his own time, who, as he writes ironically in a letter to his friend and publisher A. N. Pypin, "rummage in historical dung seriously taking it for gold."

ADDRESS TO THE READER
FROM THE LAST CHRONICLER

In this chapter the Publisher/author, using the ornate and archaic style of the last Foolsburg chronicler, reveals to the reader the basic theme of his unusual work: to probe, in an allegorical form, one of the most important questions of Russian social life of the eighteenth and nineteenth centuries—the question of the relations between the people and unlimited despotic power.

1. we Christians, who have received the light from Byzantium: The light is, of course the light of wisdom. Christianity came to Kievan Russia from Byzantium in the tenth century. According to semilegendary accounts in the twelfth-century *Russian Primary Chronicle,* the prince of Kiev, Vladimir, facing the choice between Judaism, Islam, and Christianity, sent his envoys to Constantinople, and they came back under a deep impression of the beauty they had seen. That determined Prince Vladimir's decision to embrace Orthodox Christianity.

2. Neros of great glory and Caligulas of shining valor: Nero and Caligula were Roman emperors of the first century AD. The quotation about Caligula's horse comes from the poem "The Courtier" (1794) by G. R. Derzhavin (1743–1816). The episode with Caligula's horse Incitatus, whom the mad emperor wanted to make a consul, is reported in Suetonius's *The Twelve Caesars*. Historians of our time tell us that Caligula only intended to bring his horse into the Senate, but never actually did it.

3. **vineyard:** Vineyard here is a poetic reference to the people in general, or readers, or listeners. The author is the vintner.

4. **Mishka Triapichkin . . . and another Mishka Triapichkin:** Triapichkin (a plausible last name, formed from the Russian *triapka,* a rag), is the last name of Khlestakov's friend, a Moscow journalist, in Gogol's *Inspector.* The coincidence is hardly accidental.

5. **Mr. Bartenev and he publishes them in his *Archives:*** In 1863 the Moscow journalist P. I. Bartenev began to publish an historical and literary magazine, *The Russian Archive.* The reference is ironic: the magazine used to publish mostly uninteresting, randomly chosen, or simply anecdotal materials.

On the Roots of the Foolsburgers' Origins

The basis for the story is the semilegendary account in the *Russian Primary Chronicle* about the people of Novgorod "inviting" three Varangian princes, Riurik, Sineus, and Truvor, in the mid-ninth century, to rule their princedom, on the advice of the ancient wise man Gostomysl, thus voluntarily renouncing their freedom and transforming themselves from Headwhackers into Foolsburgers. The following history of Foolsburg is assimilated to the official history of Russia. The

Riurik dynasty of princes of Kievan Rus and then tsars of Russia, with the capital moved to Moscow, lasted till the end of the sixteenth century.

1. **Nikolai Kostomarov:** (1817–1885) was an eminent Russian-Ukrainian historian and poet, founder of the populist movement. Vladimir Solovyov (1853–1900) was a philosopher with a vision combining the historical and the religious/mystical. For Pypin, see note 7 on page 249.

2. *The Song of Igor's Campaign:* (dated to 1185–1187) is an anonymous old Russian narrative poem, considered the first masterpiece of Russian literature. Boyan, a bard of the tenth or eleventh century, is mentioned in the *Song*.

3. **a great many independent tribes:** In response to criticism, Saltykov, in his letter to the editor of *The European Messenger*, maintained that none of the following outlandish nominations were of his invention and that before the consolidation of Russia under a Moscow tsar, disunited small groups around various not-yet-Russian towns actually referred to one another by these amusing nicknames, which we have conveyed in English to the best of our ability.

4. **Dregs-eaters, Whitefish-eaters, and Skewbellies:** These nicknames correspond to the Novgorod republic and the Tver and Riazan princedoms—the longest to preserve their independence before joining the centralized Russian state.

5. **gave themselves up:** This story is an actual legend about the battle between these two tribes, collected by the lover of

Russian antiquity Ivan Petrovich Sakharov (1807–1863), in his book *Legends of the Russian People*.

6. **but cites only some episodes:** What follows are the actual sayings and phrases cited by Sakharov and also by the lexicographer Vladimir Dal (1801–1872) in his book *Sayings of the Russian People*. Dal is best known for his *Explanatory Dictionary of the Great Russian Language*, still very much in use by linguists, writers, and translators.

7. **Chukhloma:** An ancient town in the Kostroma region.

8. **the stealer-dealer:** *vor-novotor* in Russian, a rhyming nomination, meaning a thief from the town Novy Torzhok, apparently famous for its thievery.

9. **"Rustle not, dear mother green grove!":** A popular Russian so-called thieves' song, already widely known in the eighteenth century.

10. **greeted . . . with bread and salt:** A traditional symbolic sign of hospitality in Russia.

11. **Kaliazin:** Town in the Tver region.

THE REGISTER OF MAYORS APPOINTED TO
THE TOWN OF FOOLSBURG BY THE HIGHER
AUTHORITIES AT VARIOUS TIMES (1731–1826)

In this register Saltykov gives the reader an idea of what was common to the activity of most of these mayors ("went on a campaign against tax defaulters," "laid a tax upon the inhabitants," "took the town of Foolsburg by storm," and so on). These particularities lay the foundation for the further narrative. In the very title of the chapter, the connection of the "Register" with "Higher Authorities" gives the whole story of Foolsburg a "historical foundation."

1. **"Higher Authorities":** may refer to the higher administration or even to the tsar. A tsar, as "God's anointed," had his power come directly from God. The Russian word used by Saltykov may ironically refer to the divine origin of power in Russia. Thus he suggests that the first twenty-one successors of the first prince of Foolsburg were autocratic rulers.

2. **Biron, the Duke of Courland:** See note 2 on page 247.

3. **Ferapontov, Foty Petrovich, brigadier. Former barber for the same Duke of Courland:** An allusion to Ivan Pavlovich Kutaisov. Captured as a boy of ten, of Turkish or Georgian origin, he was given as a present to the then grand duke Pavel Petrovich, the future emperor Paul I, and raised at the Russian court. He became the favorite and the personal valet and barber of the emperor Paul, made a dizzying career at the court, acquiring wealth and political influence under the name of Kutaisov (after the name of the town where he was taken captive).

4. **In 1740, during the reign of the meek Elizabeth, was caught having a love affair with Avdotia Lopukhina:** Despite her reputation for being merciful and good-natured (she abolished capital punishment), the empress Elizaveta Petrovna was, in fact, suspicious, jealous, and could be vi-

ciously cruel, especially when jealous of her female rivals. Avdotia Lopukhina here is a collective character. Elizaveta dealt very cruelly with her lady-in-waiting Natalia Lopukhina, suspected of conspiracy against the throne.

5. **Leib Company:** A grenadier company (364 men) of the lifeguards of the Preobrazhensky Regiment, which contributed to the ascent to the throne of Elizaveta Petrovna. All the participants of her coup were afterwards generously rewarded with land and serfs.

6. **a native of Holstein . . . replaced in 1762 for ignorance:** The reference here is to the future emperor Peter III, who was born Duke of Holstein-Gottorp. He was killed after a successful palace coup by his wife, Catherine, who ascended the throne as Catherine II (known as Catherine the Great).

7. **performed in Isler's garden at the mineral waters:** An "amusement garden" with artificial mineral waters was founded by the enterprising Swiss Ivan Ivanovich Isler in the middle of the nineteenth century.

8. **this is certainly a mistake:** This is the first anachronism marked by the "Publisher" of the *Chronicle*.

9. **Ferdyshchenko, Pyotr Petrovich, brigadier. Former orderly of Prince Potemkin:** Saltykov has in mind Alexander Danilovich Menshikov, of whom there was a story that he had sold pies in the street as a boy. He later became the orderly to Prince Potemkin, before rising to distinction at the Russian court and becoming the right hand of Peter the Great. Played a huge role in Russian politics of his time, as a general-in-chief fought and was victorious

in several battles, but then fell out of favor, was exiled, and died in neglect and poverty. According to Pushkin, his low origin was invented by ill-wishers, and in fact Menshikov belonged to the minor gentry. The name Ferdyshchenko is a plausible but very ugly Russian family name. For a Russian reader the name is immediately recognized as that of a character in Dostoevsky's *The Idiot*, a clowning, vulgar, and immoral young man who hangs around the heroine, Nastasya Filippovna.

10. **Wartbeardin, Basilisk Semyonovich:** Basilisk, a rare and extraordinary name. In European bestiaries and in Russian folklore, the basilisk is a legendary reptile said to kill everyone with his gaze.

11. **Blaggardov, Onufry Ivanovich, former stoker in Gatchina Palace:** The allusion here is to Alexei Miliutin, a stoker in the apartments of the empress Anna Ioannovna, who rose to power under Biron, the favorite of the empress. Gatchina Palace, near Saint Petersburg, built under Catherine the Great for her favorite Grigory Orlov in the late eighteenth century, later the residence of several emperors, now a museum.

12. **Novosiltsev, Czartorysky, and Stroganov:** Novosiltsev, Count Nikolai Nikolaevich (1761–1838), was a Russian statesman and close aide of the emperor Alexander I. He served as the imperial commissioner for the Polish Kingdom, which was then a constitutional monarchy. Czartoryski, Prince Adam Jerzy (1770–1861), Polish statesman, diplomat, and writer, was minister to the Russian emperor after Poland was partitioned between Russia, Prussia, and Austria. Later a leader of the Polish government in exile and a fierce

proponent of Polish independence. Stroganov, Count Pavel Alexandrovich (1774–1817), was a Russian military commander and statesman. The three were prominent members of the privy committee that worked in 1801–1803, under the young emperor Alexander I, preparing liberal reforms of the government.

13. **Mikaladze . . . the sensuous princess Tamara:** The Circassians are a Caucasian tribe and, as with other Caucasian ethnic groups (Georgians, Abkhasians, Chechens, etc.) have always had the reputation of being great lovers of the female sex. Princess Tamara was a Georgian princess, then queen (1166–1213). Of her sensuosness we know precisely nothing.

14. **Speransky at the seminary:** The character of Benevolensky is based mainly on Speransky. The reader will find detailed notes on Speransky in the chapter on the mayorship of Benevolensky ("The Epoch of Relief from Wars").

15. **open courts and the zemstvo:** Open courts were introduced in Russia in 1864, following the reforms of Alexander II, as was the institution of the zemstvo, an elected local government with its own assembly and officials from the gentry.

16. **marshal of the nobility:** An elected function, the "second person" of a province, the marshal of nobility was the head of the elected offices of the nobility of a province and an intermediary between the local noblemen's community and the administration.

17. **Karamzin's friend:** Nikolai Mikhailovich Karamzin (1766–1826) was a novelist, poet, and historian. He became

friends with Alexander I, who appointed him court historian. The result was his monumental twelve-volume *History of the Russian State*, as much literary as it was scholarly.

18. **Hijack-Swashbucklin, Archistratig Stratilatovich**: A military-sounding first name and patronymic. In Greek both have the meaning of "general in chief," "leader of the army."

Music Box

1. **Khotyn Fortress:** A Turkish fortress on the bank of the Dnestr that had been repeatedly attacked, taken, lost, and retaken by the Russian and Polish armies in the course of the seventeenth and eighteenth centuries. It finally surrendered and became Russian in 1807. It is now Ukrainian.

2. **policemen on duty:** In Russian *budochniki*, from *budka*, a booth. The lowest-ranking policemen, who stood in striped black-and-white booths at intersections and whose duty was to look after public order.

3. **Tushino "little tsar":** That is, the impostor the false Dimitry II (1582–1610), who set up his residence in the village of Tushino near Moscow and from there made sorties, attacking the nearby towns and villages. *Biron.* The favorite of the empress Anna Ioannovna (see note 11 on page 256).

4. **the shepherd of this vineyard:** A mixed metaphor: in the New Testament "shepherd" is a term for Christ, "vineyard" for the people.

5. **recalling the London agitators:** That is, A. I. Herzen and N. P. Ogarev, who published in London the radical magazine *Kolokol* (The Bell). They were referred to as "London agitators" in contemporary journalism. A. I. Herzen (1812–1870), writer and thinker, is considered a precursor of socialism in Russia and also of agrarian populism. He exiled himself from Russia in 1847. N. P. Ogarev (1813–1877), Herzen's friend and fellow publisher in exile, was a poet, historian, and social activist.

6. **Charles the Simple:** "The Simple" or "the Straight-forward"—a king of the Carolingian dynasty (879–929), who ruled over what is now France.

7. **sent Winterhalter an urgent telegram:** Another of the chronicler's anachronisms: the first experimental telegraphic device was installed in Russia in 1836.

8. **the staff-officer:** That is, a representative of the political police, the Third Section.

THE TALE OF THE SIX MAYORESSES

In this chapter Saltykov satirically portrays the real history of several palace coups that succeeded in raising to the throne empresses who had little or no right to it. The chapter also contains elements of parody of contemporary Russian journalists, who based their historical research on dubious anecdotal material. This kind of journalism abounded in the 1860s. One of the favorite topics was the allusions to the vicious anti-Polish campaign that explained all the disorders in Russia by "secret intrigues" of the Poles.

1. **the Frenchwoman, Miss de Sans-Culotte:** Sans-Culotte, literally "without pants," a mocking nickname given by French aristocrats, who wore short pants (*culottes*) and stockings, to low-class people, who wore long pants; later the word's pejorative meaning became the proud title of revolutionaries. Saltykov uses the word in its literal meaning, in indication of what sort of "fashionable establishment" was kept by Miss de Sans-Culotte.

2. **Marat:** Jean-Paul Marat (1743–1793), physician, journalist, and politician of the time, one of the leaders of the French Revolution.

3. **Iraida Lukinishna Paleologova, a childless widow of unbending character, of masculine build, with a face of dark brown color:** Here Saltykov alludes to the empress Anna Ioannovna, the niece of Peter the Great, who ruled Russia from 1730 to 1740. In part these features are also shared by Klemantinka de Bourbon, who replaced Iraida Lukinishna.

4. **she saw a mysterious sign in her name being Paleologova:** Paleologos was the name of the last ruling dynasty of Byzantine emperors (1261–1453).

5. **wine clerk:** A low-ranking government official, whose duty was to watch over local trading in wine, its quality, the state of wine shops, and the organization of wholesale wine.

6. **a Reval-born woman, Amalia Karlovna Stockfisch:** Reval, now Tallinn, the capital of Estonia, an ancient European town, in the past was one of the major towns of the Hanseatic League, a military and trade alliance of German

princedoms. Amalia Stockfisch represents the Russian empress Catherine the Great. She was a Prussian-born princess, married to her cousin, the future Peter III of Russia in 1745. She ascended the Russian throne by overthrowing her husband (1762) and later probably murdering him.

7. **bowing in all directions:** There was a Russian custom for a condemned criminal, at the moment of being taken to the place of exile or punishment, to bow to people surrounding him (to four sides or in all directions), asking forgiveness in case he had offended anyone.

8. **Miss Stockfisch was a stout blond German woman, with full breasts. . . . and plump cherry lips:** This perfectly fits the description of Catherine the Great by her contemporaries and also her portraits of the time.

9. **The ease with which the fat-fleshed German Stockfisch prevailed:** In one of her letters Catherine wrote that the revolution that had put her on the throne resembled a miracle and the unanimity of the people in supporting her was unbelievable.

NEWS ABOUT EPIKUROV

The image of the state councillor Epikurov may have been prompted by the image of the emperor Alexander I in the initial, more liberal years of his reign. Hence the mention of "constitutional principle" and also the allusion to "the horror" once experienced by Epikurov—that is, the horror after the murder of Alexander's father, Paul I, which all the memoirs of the time mention and in which he was probably involved, and the melancholy caused by the remembrance of it. But of course, it is also a collective image of an administrator, especially in his attitude toward learning (that is, seeing the "scrutiny" of learning as the main hindrance to its "spreading").

1. **a tempting pretext for looking for liberalism where, in fact, there was nothing but the principle of liberal flogging:** This is an allusion to some "constitutional impulses" of Catherine the Great, who, while being interested in the ideas of the French philosophers of the Enlightenment (she corresponded with Denis Diderot), also published decrees that allowed landowners to send their peasants to hard labor, and forbade peasants to complain—under threat of punishment and exile—about their masters.

2. **fought wars in the name of potatoes:** The so-called potato riots were mass rebellions of the imperial peasants (peasants on properties owned by the Russian imperial house) in 1834, and of state peasants in 1840–1844. The reason for the protests was the forced introduction of the cultivation of potatoes.

The Hungry Town

There is not much direct historical reference in this chapter. Nevertheless it should be noticed that in its history Russia repeatedly experienced hunger, and the year 1868 remained in the memory of contemporaries as "the hungry year."

1. **"This new Jezebel," the chronicler says of Alenka," brought drought upon our town":** In the Old Testament, Jezebel is the wife of Ahab, King of Israel—a pagan woman who prompted him to do "what was wrong in God's eyes" and

to worship the pagan god Baal. Because of that, the angry God of Israel sends drought and hunger upon the people. Ahab dies and Jezebel is thrown out the window and dogs eat her remains (1 and 2 Kings). Saint Nicholas's Day (here the spring Saint Nicholas) is May 9; Saint Elijah's Day is July 20.

2. **Nothing is more dangerous than roots and threads:** An ironic reference to the underground intrigues that the police try to unravel; a cliché of contemporary journalism.

The Straw Town

Like "The Hungry Town," this chapter tells of more calamities that kept befalling "wooden" and "straw" Russia, this time in the form of fires that began to be reported quite frequently in the 1860s. Saltykov looks at it as being part of the essentially absurd course of Russian history, the generally abnormal organization of Foolsburg "reality," which created a fertile ground for all sorts of disasters.

1. **the accursed musketeer girl Domashka:** Musketeers, in Russian *streltsy*, a tsar's private infantry company (like today's *siloviki*), created by Ivan the Terrible and abolished in 1698 by Peter the Great. Though professional soldiers, they were unruly and unreliable. Domashka is a casual name for Domna.

2. **around Saint Peter's Day:** That is, June 29.

3. **the holy fool:** "Holy foolishness" or "foolishness for God's sake" or "blessed foolishness" is an accepted form of holiness in the Orthodox Church. A holy fool may be a truly saintly person, but an ordinary local madman may also fall into this

category, as we will see later in the story. The line between the two is fine and cannot be formally drawn.

4. **began to sing "By the waters of Babylon":** The first line of Psalm 137, composed during the Babylonian captivity of the Jews, who were weeping for their lost motherland, Israel. This psalm is sung every year in Orthodox churches before the beginning of the Great Lent.

5. **soldiers' wives who practiced a shameful trade:** Once their husbands were conscripted, most women were left without resources and were reduced to the necessity of "practicing a shameful trade." In the eighteenth century the term of army service was for life. In 1793 it was reduced to twenty-five years, although exemptions and arbitrary changes were common. In 1825 this term was reduced to twenty-two years, then to twenty, but only for certain units of the army. In 1856 the tsar Alexander II approved a regulation that made conscription theoretically compulsory for all males under the age of twenty. The terms, however, were reduced and made more flexible.

6. **that he could not argue with God:** This may be a tongue-in-cheek reference to Alexander I as portrayed in Pushkin's poem *The Bronze Horseman*, where he says, watching from the balcony of his palace as the Neva floods Petersburg: "Tsars cannot master God's elements."

A FANTASTIC TRAVELER

This chapter deals with yet another aspect of Russian historical reality—the traditional solemn journeys of the authorities around their domains. These journeys occasioned almost the same kind of turmoil as natural disasters. Especially spectacular in this respect was the journey of Catherine the Great to Crimea in 1787, organized by Grigory Potemkin (the "patron" of Ferdyshchenko, as the chronicler attests him). Thousands of people were forcibly sent to "Little Russia" (present-day Ukraine) to build decorative villages and "enliven" the landscape. Everything was done to make things look picturesque, to conceal the flaws, to misrepresent it all, to create an artificial, fake, embellished impression of a reality that was far from beautiful. This event gave rise to the expression "Potemkin village."

1. **"You should've gotten yourselves ships to carry coffee and sugar," he said. "Where are they?":** The question of creating a merchant navy was the subject of lively discussion in Russia of 1860–1870.

2. **even the priests would have been envious:** In Russia, as elsewhere, there existed a popular notion of clergy being notoriously gluttonous.

3. **Marfa the Mayoress:** Marfa Boretskaya, one of the leaders of the Novgorod opposition to the tsar Ivan III. She fought for the independence of Novgorod from Moscow. In the war of 1477–1478 she lost all her lands and money, was taken prisoner, and ended her days in a convent. Some sources say she was executed. "Mayoress" was her nickname; her husband had been a mayor, but outside of Foolsburg there were no mayoresses at that time.

4. **there were no comets, and people had money enough to burn. Which would have been easy to do since it was all paper money:** Comets were regarded as a bad omen. Paper

money first appeared in Russia in 1769. Initially it could be easily exchanged for silver or gold, but already by the end of the century this free exchange had ceased and the course of banknotes sharply fell.

The Wars for Enlightenment

The subject of this chapter is yet another aspect of the actions of the Russian authorities: spreading "enlightenment" in Russia, as well as outside its borders. These wars were repeatedly conducted in the course of the eighteenth and nineteenth centuries, and Saltykov uses this material for his "biography" of Wartbeardin. One of these wars was against the so-called "potato riots" (see note 2 on page 262), conducted by the goverments of Catherine the Great and Nicholas I, who both tried to introduce potatoes, and eventually succeeded. There were also wars for the abolition of serfdom, on terms that provoked repeated rebellions of the peasants, who were liberated not on the best conditions. Generally, people resisted the politics of the tsarist government of the forcible imposition of "progress." External wars for "enlightenment" were with Turkey—with the ambition of subjecting Constaninople ("Byzantium"—that is, Istanbul) and acquiring access from the Black Sea to the ancient Propontis (the Sea of Marmara)—the secret dream of Wartbeardin. There were wars to subject the Caucasus, and also wars for the Middle East, in which military conquest was supposed to be followed by the peaceful conquest of the countries by Russian religion and culture. The story of introducing mustard in Foolsburg is a vicious satire of the general "civilizing" policy of the Russian government, based on force, intimidation, and flogging.

1. so as thereby hopefully to achieve the return (*sic!*) of the ancient Byzantium under the sway of the Russian state: Taking Byzantium had been a dream of Russian rulers from time immemorial. Byzantium had been the Eastern Rome. Russians call Byzantium "Tsargrad," the Tsar City. Russian religion came from there, the Russian double-headed eagle came from there, along with the dowry of Sophia Paleologina, a Byzantine princess, who became the second wife of Ivan III, the first Moscow tsar. Peter the Great and all his successors dreamed of conquering Constantinople. *To the Drava, to the Morava, to the distant Sava:* Three rivers flowing through the territories of Slovenia, Croatia, Bosnia and Herzegovina, and what is now the Czech Republic, before flowing into the Danube. The lines are slightly misquoted from a poem by A. S. Khomiakov (1804–1860).

2. addressed to our famous geographer K. I. Arseniev: Konstantin Arseniev (1789–1865), Russian historian and geographer (yet another deliberate anachronism). This is Saltykov's first allusion to Russian imperial ambitions.

3. the first place belonged, of course, to civilization: Clearly here and further the words "civilization" and "enlightenment" are used by Saltykov ironically. Hence Wartbeardin's absurd definition of the word "civilization." This is the first time that "firmness in adversity" is mentioned as the most important quality of every "valiant son of the fatherland."

4. It was some sort of wild energy deprived of all content: "We have had cruel governments," wrote Catherine the Great in one of her letters, "but we always had trouble enduring weak tsars. Our way of governing calls for energy; . . . if there is no energy, there is immediate general discontent."

5. **flourished like a lily of the field:** An image from the Gospels, used by Christ (Matthew 6:28–30).

6. **Most of all he was concerned with the Musketeers' suburb:** The musketeers had always been riotous and unruly, and took part in many political and social disturbances, which explains Wartbeardin's seeing in them "the source of all evil."

7. **A preacher appeared who transposed the name Wartbeardin into numbers and proved that if you omit the letter *r* you will get 666, which is the number of the Prince of Darkness:** In the New Testament Book of Revelation, the number 666 signifies "the beast from the abyss," that is, the Antichrist. This interpretation is possible because Greek letters, like the letters of the Hebrew and Slavonic alphabets, correspond to numbers. Such numerical interpretations (gematria) were very common. Pierre Bezukhov in Tolstoy's *War and Peace* tries to interpret his own name as the savior of Russia from Napoleon, whose name was also interpreted as Antichrist.

8. **"If you feel that a law hinders you, take it from your desk and put it underneath you. Thus the law is made invisible, and you will acquire great freedom of action":** This cavalier treatment of the law is confirmed by a true story which circulated at the time about a governor who, in the course of an argument, when someone pointed at the Code of Law, took the book and sat on it, saying: "Well, where is your law now?"

9. **later it turned out that he had fled to Petersburg, where he instantly succeeded in obtaining a railroad concession:**

Another anachronism. The first railroad connecting Petersburg and Tsarskoe Selo was built in 1837.

10. Only when day broke did they see that they had been fighting against their own . . . rollicking singing and dancing: V. I. Dal (see note 6 on page 253), reports this as an actual episode: "Born-blind" was the nickname of the Vyatka people. The Ustiug people came to their aid, but the Vyatka people thought they were the enemy and began to fight with them.

11. similar to what is usually presented in the third act of *Ruslan and Ludmila*, when frightened Farlaf rushes onstage: M. I. Glinka's opera *Ruslan and Ludmila* (1842) was based on Pushkin's poem of the same title. Farlaf, one of the heroes, is a cowardly knight; Naïna is a sorceress who wants to destroy the hero Ruslan and his bride, Ludmila, out of spite for the rival sorcerer Finn. One more anachronism.

12. Wartbeardin remembered that the prince Sviatoslav Igorevich . . . with the same greeting: We know about Sviatoslav's custom of announcing a war to the enemy from the *Russian Primary Chronicle*. Present-day rulers of Russia are not as chivalrous. They do not even call war a war, but "a special military operation." Of course, Wartbeardin, announcing a "war" on the Foolsburgers, could be certain of victory whether he warned them or not.

13. possibility of joining the schismatics: The schismatics, or Old Believers, were a group of Russian Orthodox Christians who split off from the Orthodox Church in the seventeenth century because of the reforms of the patriarch

Nikon. They insisted on retaining old customs and rites, and finally formed an alternative church that did not recognize the main one.

14. **Since among them were some officers and other persons of the first three ranks:** According to the Table of Ranks introduced by Peter the Great in 1722, official posts in the army, navy, and state administration were divided into fourteen ranks, the attribution of the higher ranks being carried out on personal orders of the emperor. The first three in the civil table were chancellor, active privy councillor, and privy councillor. There could be no persons of the first three ranks in the Dung settlement, but in Wartbeardin's imagination a little village grew to the size of a whole country.

15. **Baba Yaga . . . "I'll roll about, and I'll loll about, having had my fill of Ivanushka's sweet flesh!":** Baba Yaga, a wicked witch of Russian folklore, mutters these words as she prepares to roast and eat the little boy Ivanushka. In the folk tale Ivanushka outwits Baba Yaga and gets her roasted in his stead.

16. **the refusal of the townsfolk to cultivate Persian chamomile:** Dried and ground Persian chamomile was used to eliminate bedbugs. Another satirical reference to peasant riots.

17. **for having set up a phalanstery:** The phalanstery was invented in the early eighteenth century by Charles Fourier (1772–1837), French philosopher, a founder of utopian socialism. It is a standard building designed to house from five hundred to two thousand persons living together and working for mutual benefit. Life in the phalanstery was subject to strict military-like discipline.

18. and there was no Molinari or Bezobrazov to explain to the Foolsburgers that that was in fact true prosperity: The Belgian Gustave de Molinari (1819–1912) and the Russian V. P. Bezobrazov (1828–1889) were influential economists who were ready, in Saltykov's mind, to find persuasive signs of "well-being" and "progress" in any state of affairs.

The Epoch of Relief from Wars

This chapter deals mostly with two important questions: first, the question of the Foolsburg (i.e., Russian) legal system, which Mayor Benevolensky is so interested in, and, second, the conditions for prosperity, which comes to Foolsburg with Lieutenant Colonel Pustule, "the mayor with the stuffed head," who replaces Benevolensky. Interestingly, Pustule's total administrative inaction finally serves toward the real flourishing of Foolsburg.

1. In 1802 came the fall of Blaggardov. He fell, as the chronicler tells us, because of his disagreements with Novosiltsev and Stroganov in regard to a constitution: Blaggardov's fall is an allusion to the murder in 1801 of the emperor Paul I (1754–1801). N. N. Novosiltsev, P. A. Stroganov, Count V. P. Kochubei (together with the Polish prince A. E. Czartoryski—remember the "Polish intrigue"!), were members of the privy committee organized by Alexander I, who ascended the throne in 1801 after his father's assassination. They tried to develop "new principles" of governing the Russian Empire. Their project of making Russia a constitutional monarchy was further developed by M. M. Speransky, who is the prototype of the future Foolsburg mayor Benevolensky.

2. **Blaggardov belonged to the school of the so-called fledglings:** that is, associates, comrades, companions—the word "fledglings" in this sense was introduced by Pushkin in his poem *Poltava* (1828–1829), where it refers to Peter the Great's comrades in arms as "the fledglings of Peter's nest."

3. **he had at some point been a stoker in Gatchina, and . . . represented the Gatchina democratic principle:** Gatchina was the residence of the emperor Paul I near Petersburg. The Russian nobility was displeased with Paul, who stripped them of some of their privileges. After his father's murder, Alexander I immediately restored all these privileges and rights.

4. **First it was necessary to accustom people to polite behavior, and only then, once their morals were softened, could they be given supposedly "real" rights:** Catherine the Great often explained the impossibility of providing the people with rights by their "savage ways." The same arguments were used in the nineteenth century by the opponents of giving the people the so-called real rights publicly promised them by the emperor Alexander II.

5. **like Mark Antony in Egypt, led an extremely sybaritic life:** The Roman statesman and general Mark Antony, while governing the Roman eastern provinces, fell in love with Cleopatra, the queen of Egypt, and together with her gave himself to a life of luxury and pleasure.

6. **started sucking their paws:** According to Russian popular wisdom, bears, during winter hibernation, comfort themselves by sucking their paws. This belief gave rise to the metaphor of paw sucking as a way of satisfying one's hunger.

7. **The state councilor Feofilakt Irinarkhovich Benevolensky, a friend and classmate of Speransky in the seminary:** As has been already observed, the image of Benevolensky in many ways resembles the image of M. M. Speransky (1772–1839), one of the major figures of the beginning of the nineteenth century and an active member of the government committee for the new legal system.

8. **the question was what sort of lawmaker he would be—that is, would he resemble the thoughtfulness and administrative foresight of Lycurgus, or would he simply be firm as Draco?:** Lycurgus and Draco are semilegendary ancient Greek lawmakers. The former introduced strict laws and spoke against luxury and riches. The latter was famous for his severity, demanding capital punishment even for insignificant violations of the norms of public behavior. His name is at the origin of the phrase "draconian law."

9. **they are, in fact, not even laws, but, so to speak, the twilight of the laws:** In the story of Benevolensky's mayorship, Saltykov freely parodies some writings of Speransky. In one of his letters, Speransky wrote about the indefinite notion of God that is not grounded in anything in particular and calls it *"the twilight of faith."* Here Saltykov underlines the indefinite character of the laws that Benevolensky wanted to introduce in Foolsburg, thus making fun of actual Russian laws of the time.

10. **"A preacher," he said, "should have a contrite heart and, consequently, a head slightly inclined to one side":** "A contrite heart" is a phrase from Psalm 51:17. In one of his letters Speransky explained this phrase not as an inner but

as a physical experience. Saltykov mocks this explanation by having Benevolensky express this inner state physically.

11. **The fault lay with Bonaparte. This was the year 1811, and the relations of Russia and Napoleon became very strained:** Napoleon Bonaparte, then a general, later the French emperor, invaded Russia in June 1812.

12. **it seems that Napoleon himself spilled it out to Prince Kurakin at one of his** *petits levers:* A. B. Kurakin, Russian ambassador in Paris before the War of 1812, who thought he was a particular favorite of Napoleon. *Petits levers* were morning receptions in a king's bedroom for an intimate circle.

13. **and successfully proceeded to the back of beyond:** A saying in Russian, literally "to where Makar did not pasture his calves"—that is, to faraway places, usually Siberia. Like Benevolensky, M. M. Speransky was accused of secret connections with Napoleon. In 1812 he was removed from government service and exiled first to Nizhny Novgorod and later to Perm in the easternmost part of European Russia.

14. **"I was a commander, so I didn't spend, but increased":** Army commanders under Catherine the Great and in later years considered it the most natural and lawful thing to supplement their income by open and shameless stealing. In Saltykov's time corruption in the army achieved unheard-of dimensions during the Crimean War (1853–1856).

15. **under Prince Oleg:** Prince Oleg (died in 912) ruled Novgorod and its region from 879, then captured Kiev and

transferred his seat there in 882, having thus united the two major centers of the Eastern Slavs. In Russian chronicles Oleg is called *veshchy*, meaning "seeing the future" or "wise."

16. **local marshal of the nobility:** See note 16 on page 257.

17. **Meatfare Week:** The week before the beginning of the Great Lent, during which the faithful already abstain from eating meat.

18. **forgot nothing and learned nothing:** A proverbial phrase of Talleyrand's about the royalist emigrants upon their return to France after the downfall of Napoleon.

THE WORSHIP OF MAMMON AND REPENTANCE

This chapter shows how Foolsburgers were enslaved by the forcible introduction of stupefying ideologies. It also deals with the complex issue of ideological causes of the slowness of social development in Russia. Saltykov satirically portrays certain historical episodes of the reign of Alexander I: his relations with the Baltic-German religious mystic Baroness Krüdener (Barbara Juliane von Krüdener, 1764–1824), the flourishing of certain spiritual sects, the exile of a distinguished scientist, and others. The story of the conflict between the "paupers" and the "spirit of research" shows how obediently and easily Foolsburgers were enslaved and stupefied, as any glimpse of thinking among them was suppressed. The episode with the teacher Linkin, while concluding the story of Mayor Melancholin, prepares the way for the appearance of Sullen-Grumble, who declares reason his worst enemy.

1. **But we will hardly be mistaken . . . delay of social development:** The following story will describe how this happened in Foolsburg. The details of the story are drawn from the history of Russia in the first half of the nineteenth century.

2. **the chronicler tells mostly about the so-called mob, which even to this day is regarded as seemingly outside the limits of history:** Some Russian historians of Saltykov's time considered the lower classes, simple people, "the mob," as being merely a material from which princes and tsars, by their efforts, created the centralized Russian state.

3. **the enemy of mankind had been forever installed on the island of Saint Helena:** That is, Napoleon, who abdicated the French throne in 1815 and was exiled to the island of Saint Helena, where he died in 1821.

4. **the rights of the Bourbons:** The House of Bourbon became the royal house of France beginning in the sixteenth century. Later they also ruled Spain, and the present king of Spain belongs to this family. Their rule in France ended with the French Revolution of 1789.

5. **They immediately decided to build a tower, in such a way that its top would be sure to reach up to heaven:** For some reason the Foolsburgers are moved by the same ambition as the builders of the Tower of Babel (Genesis 11:1–9), which, as we know, ended with the confuson of tongues and the scattering of the builders.

6. **under Vladimir the Fair Sun:** Vladimir I, the Great (958–1015), called "the Fair Sun" in legends and epics, was prince of Novgorod and later of Kievan Rus; his embrace of Chris-

tianity thereby abolished pagan idols. **produced two idols: Perun and Volos:** Pre-Christian gods of the Eastern Slavic peoples. Perun was the god of agriculture; Volos, or Veles, the patron of cattle, trade, and wealth. Later in the story Yarilo, the pagan god of the sun, will be added to this pantheon.

7. **in verses from Averkiev's opera *Rogneda*:** The music to this now completely forgotten opera in five acts was written by Alexander Serov in the 1860s, with a libretto by the mediocre and also completely forgotten poet Dmitry Averkiev.

8. **"A moi le pompon" or "La Vénus aux carottes":** "Come to Me, Sweetie Pie" and "Venus with Carrots" were nineteenth-century French popular songs.

9. **and produced *La Belle Hélène*:** An opéra-bouffe (1864) in three acts by Jacques Offenbach. Mademoiselle Blanche Gandon, a French operetta singer of somewhat scandalous reputation, performed in Saint Petersburg more than once in the 1860s.

10. **the tenderness of Apuleius happily combined with the playfulness of Parny:** Lucius Apuleius (124–170? AD), a Latin prose writer, philosopher, and rhetorician, mostly known for his novel *The Golden Ass* (or *Metamorphoses*). Vicomte Evariste de Parny (1753–1814), French poet, author of elegies and prose poems, was best known for his somewhat libertine collection of love poetry.

11. **the famous beauty of the time Natalia Kirillovna de Pompadour:** Jeanne-Antoinette Poisson, the marquise de Pompadour (1721–1764), was mistress of the French king Louis XV. The name given here is an allusion to Maria An-

tonovna Naryshkina, the mistress of the tsar Alexander I. Saltykov calls her Natalia Kirillovna after the second wife of the tsar Alexei Mikhailovich, the mother of Peter I, whose maiden name was Naryshkina.

12. he once dressed as a swan and swam up to a bathing girl: This detail is borrowed from a Greek myth according to which Zeus seduced Leda, the wife of Spartan king Tyndareus, by taking on the likeness of a swan.

13. and began in a loud voice to recite *An Evening Sacrifice* by Mr. Boborykin: A novel of 1868 by the now-forgotten writer P. D. Boborykin (1836–1921), which Saltykov regarded as representing a tradition of "fleshly cynicism."

14. "It's sometimes nice to watch . . . when there's this exultation in nature": Melancholin likes to watch the exuberant behavior of the mating male wood grouse. This big, beautiful bird gets so absorbed in his mating ritual display that he becomes temporarily deaf (hence his Russian name *glukhar*, deaf), and can be caught with bare hands.

15. The amorous tryst . . . and so on: An imaginary travel memoir by the French writer Paul Tallemant titled *A Voyage to the Isle of Love*, published in 1663, gave rise to a whole culture of euphemistic names for various stages and displays of amorous behavior.

16. They were still ignorant of the truth that man does not live by kasha alone: Ironically altered words of Jesus Christ addressed to the devil, who challenged Him to turn stones into bread: "Man shall not live by bread alone, but by every word that proceedeth out of the mouth of God" (Matthew 4:4).

17. **So saying, she took the mask from her face ... as if covered with a veil:** This episode is based on a story told by A. N. Pypin (see note 7 on pages 250-1) about the encounter of Alexander I with Baroness Krüdener (see opening note to this section on page 275). She preached mystical ideas vaguely based on Christian teaching, claimed to know the future, and managed to acquire influence on the emperor and the life of his court. The "free city of Hamburg" is often mentioned by Saltykov as a place where one can find loose women and all sorts of amusement establishments.

18. **"I have been sent to proclaim to you the light of Tabor, which you seek unknowingly ... that foolish maiden":** The light of Mount Tabor is the light that Christ shone with at the moment of His transfiguration on Mount Tabor in Israel (Matthew 17:1–8, Mark 9:2–8, Luke 9:28–36). Baroness Krüdener urged Alexander to explore himself, showed him his sinful condition, the errors of his former life, and the pride that guided him in his projects. She finally called on him to mend his ways and turn to Christ for salvation. The foolish maiden appears in Christ's parable of the wise and foolish maidens (Matthew 25:1–4).

19. **Labzin:** A. F. Labzin (1766–1825), a figure in the movement called "Russian Enlightenment," was a Freemason, a mystic, and anti-Orthodox.

20. **On top of that ... cold and mysterious:** In Baroness Krüdener's novel *Valerie*, the heroine is a strikingly beautiful

woman of heavenly purity, so much so that her admirer's passion is incomprehensible to her.

21. **"No pain, no gain!":** A rhymed Polish saying in the original: *Bez pracy nie będe kołaczy!*, which became well-known in Moscow owing to the famous blessed fool and seer Koreisha, who resolved his lady correspondent's hesitation about marriage with this phrase. Koreisha was included in "The List of 26 False Seers and False Blessed Fools, both Men and Women" (Moscow, 1865). He is also portrayed satirically in Dostoevsky's *Demons*.

22. **At first they turned slowly, softly sobbing . . . then gradually began to turn and suddenly started whirling and guffawing:** This is a rather accurate description of the so-called zeals, séances of ecstatic behavior in the sect formed around E. Ph. Tatarinova, who for a while enjoyed the patronage of Alexander I. Tatarinova presided over these séances in the Mikhailovsky Palace in Petersburg. There exists a detailed description of them. At the end of these zeals, the participants began to have something like visions, and some of them were inspired to make incomprehensible utterances. It all concluded with the participants sharing a meal. According to some witnesses, distinguished persons were occasionally present, including the minister of spiritual affairs and education.

23. **put on chains . . . flagellation:** Wearing chains under one's clothes was a form of ascetic exercise. Flagellation or self-flagellation was also a form of ascetic practice exercised by some sects.

24. **began to see clearly:** A parody of Christ's healing of the man born blind in John 9.

25. **the impious and the Hagarenes:** That is, Muslims. Baroness Krüdener's visions are far from our notion of political correctness. Incidentally, she did write letters of this sort to the emperor Alexander I.

26. **Moral corruption reached such a point that the Foolsburgers ventured to probe the mystery of the structure of the universe:** The development of science was at the time regarded as a threat to faith in God. The accepted view was that the faith of the Russian people in God was the basis of their whole way of life. In the 1860s this led to the resistance to natural science and prevented the introduction of physics and biology into school curriculums.

27. **They burst into the lodgings of the teacher of calligraphy, Linkin:** According to some scholars, the prototype of Linkin was the academician A. F. Labzin, who was persecuted by the church and in 1821 was exiled to Simbirsk in Siberia.

28. **"my leg got blown off at Ochakov":** The Turkish fortress of Ochakov on the right bank of Dnieper Liman was taken by the Russians in 1737. This is one of the major episodes of the Russo-Turkish War of 1735–1739. Later on the fortress was several times taken and retaken. It finally became Russian in 1788. It is now in the territory of Ukraine.

29. **"And he just up and spits right in my eyes":** See note 24 on page 280.

30. **"And, taking a frog, I did some research":** The interest of young people of Saltykov's time in natural science was usually portrayed in Russian literature as the dissecting of frogs. Thus Bazarov in Turgenev's *Fathers and Sons* (1862) does experiments with frogs. Dissecting frogs remained a part of school studies of biology until quite recently, not only in Russia.

31. **Meanwhile Paramosha and Yashenka were at work in schools:** Here the prototype of Paramosha and Yashenka is not only the blessed fool Koreisha, but also the grammarian Magnitsky, Count D. A. Tolstoy, and other active figures in the area of education.

32. **Yashenka, for his part:** Yashenka's teaching is a mishmash of nebulous theories of the origin of souls that circulated in Russia in the nineteenth century. Paramosha's teaching is a parody of actual instructions for contemplation developed in Eastern Orthodox Christianity by monks of the fourteenth century and made very popular in Russia in the nineteenth century by the book *The Way of a Pilgrim*.

33. **She went around the houses telling how the devil once dragged her through the torments:** A warning to sinners. Aksinyushka knows what she is talking about. In nineteenth-century Russian demonology there was a belief that after death the souls of sinners were dragged through "torments."

34. **They began by reading the critical articles of Mr. N. Strakhov . . . a "ravishment":** Nikolai Nikolaevich Strakhov (1828–1896), Russian philosopher, publicist, and liter-

ary critic, whose ideas and writings were pervaded by a vague mysticism, which is why they could interest the Foolsburgers who were seeking "ravishments."

Repentance Confirmed. Conclusion

This chapter summarizes the whole development of Russian-Foolsburg history, as the history of the "touching compliance" between the all-powerful Foolsburg mayors and the "meek" Foolsburg "mob" of whom the chronicler talks in his "Address to the Reader from the Last Chronicler." On the one hand, the whole course of Foolsburg "history" is naturally crowned by Sullen-Grumble and his aim "to abolish the natural existence" of the Foolsburg townsfolk, who are stupefied to begin with, to cram living life into the framework of prison regulations; yet, on the other hand, this attempt to destroy natural existence leads to the sudden awakening of the Foolsburgers to the horror of their situation. It seems, however, that the last tragic pages of the Foolsburg martyrologue show that the author believed the end of Foolsburg history was imminent.

1. **"After me comes someone who will be still more terrible than I":** A parody of the words by John the Baptist about Christ: "He that cometh after me is mightier than I" (Matthew 3:11; Mark 1:7; Luke 3:16).

2. **hence, too, the far-from-merited name of "Satan," which popular rumor conferred upon Sullen-Grumble:** Elsewhere Saltykov gives his definition: "Satan is a grandi-

ose, a most despicable and narrow-minded scoundrel, who is unable to distinguish good from evil, truth from lie, general from particular, and who is concerned only with personal and most intimate interests. Therefore he is called the enemy of the human race, a spoiler, a slanderer."

3. **A portrait of Sullen-Grumble is preserved in the town archive to this day:** The name Sullen-Grumble, in Russian Ugryum-Burcheev, is reminiscent of Arakcheev. Alexei Andreevich Arakcheev (1769–1834) was a Russian statesman and military man, close to the emperors Paul I and Alexander I, at various points minister of the military, head of the chancellery and of military settlements, famous for being a great lover of drills and military parades. Saltykov endows Sullen-Grumble's portrait with some features of the emperor Nicholas I, reminding us once again of the general, all-embracing character of his satire. Sullen-Grumble realizes Fourier's dream of the phalanstery, in emulation of the military settlements created in real life by Arakcheev (see note 17 on page 270).

4. **Sullen-Grumble's very way of life . . . chewed up horse sinews:** In this description Sullen-Grumble resembles Prince Sviatoslav Igorevich, the prince of Novgorod and Kiev, who ruled from 961 until his death in 972, as he is described in the *Russian Primary Chronicle* and later by Karamzin in his *History of the Russian State*. This explains why Foolsburg is later renamed Steadfastia, "the town of the eternally illustrious memory of Grand Prince Sviatoslav Igorevich."

5. **a simple latrine scrubber:** "Latrine scrubber" here translates the Russian word *prokhvost*. The meaning of the word

originally came from the army use of the German word *Profoss*, applied to a prison guard or soldier responsible for scrubbing latrines and also for supervising flogging. The word later came to mean a scoundrel, a crook, a hustler, etc., which meaning it has retained in modern Russian. We have chosen to keep the original meaning of the word as more appropriate in the context.

6. **so-called nivellators in general:** The Russian word *nivellator* came from the French verb *niveler*, meaning to level or to make equal, referring in Saltykov's time to thinkers who wanted to reduce everything to the same (lowest) level.

7. **Sullen-Grumble belonged among the most fanatical nivellators of that school:** Sullen-Grumble's notion of duty did not go beyond everybody's equality in the face of flogging. His communism or deadening nivellating was, in fact, an attempt to set up a communal society in which every action was subject to strict regulation. See note 6 above.

8. See note 4 on page 284.

9. **In each residential unit time is allocated most strictly:** Sullen-Grumble's delirium, which follows, is a more or less accurate description of the military settlements organized by Arakcheev under Alexander I. They existed from 1816 to 1857 and were a system of organization of the army that combined military service with productive labor, mostly agricultural. It would be a mistake to see Saltykov's portrayal of it as a gross exaggeration or a parody. Several thousand peasants—old people, children, and adults of both sexes—were forced to become military settlers and

live a life subject to the strictest regulations, up to "the time of closing the window curtains, so that women could get dressed." Any discontent or protest was severely punished.

10. **"Maybe he's even a Freemason":** Freemasonry was imported to Russia from the West in the mid-eighteenth century and was regarded as a heresy by the Church and low-class people.

11. **The war with nature had begun:** Attempts to change the course of rivers were made in Russia in more recent times. Best known is Stalin's project of turning the north-flowing rivers of Siberia southwards for the sake of irrigating the dry southern areas. Naturally (and fortunately) the project remained unrealized.

12. **fern flowers:** In Russian popular belief, the fern flower has the mysterious quality of revealing hidden treasures and granting clairvoyance and power over unclean spirits.

13. **he said, thinking to fall into the Fotievo-Arakcheev tone that held sway at the time:** Archimandrite Fotiy (1792–1838) was a prominent church figure of conservative tendency, an ascetic and an ardent persecutor of Protestants and Masons. For Arakcheev, see note 3 on page 284.

14. **railroad concessions:** See note 9 on page 268.

15. **Iona's father, Semyon Trump:** According to the dictionary of V. Dal the word *kozyr* (which coincidentally means "trump" in English) signifies "a feisty, clever fellow, good at grasping or gripping."

16. **Orlov . . . Mamonov . . . Ermolov:** Prince Grigory Grigorievich Orlov (1734–1783), a favorite of Catherine the Great for many years, was a leader of the coup that overthrew her husband, Peter III, and installed her as empress. "Grishka" is a familiar form of his first name. (Ferdyshchenko refers to him absurdly as "Prince of the Roman Empire.") Count Alexander Matveyevich Dmitriev-Mamonov (1758–1803), a military man of distinguished family, was a lover of Catherine the Great's from 1886 to 1889. Alexei Donatovich Ermolov (1777–1861) was a Russian general, commander of troops in the Caucasus.

17. **two very famous philosophers of the time, Funich and Marasmitsky:** A comic distortion of the names Runich and Magnitsky. D. P. Runich (1778–1860) and M. L. Magnitsky (1778–1855) were two highly placed functionaries in the ministry of education under Alexander I, of obscurantist and mystical tendencies, who aimed at replacing scientific studies by religious education. They actually managed to do great harm to the educational system of the time.

SUPPORTING DOCUMENTS

1. **and offers bread and salt:** See note 10 on page 253.

2. **like Marius of old:** Gaius Marius (157–86 BC) was a Roman military commander and politician. He fought many wars, was repeatedly elected a consul, but ended up defeated in the internecine strife.

3. **with certain notions and rights supposedly natural for human beings, including even the structure of the uni-**

verse: A lot was written about natural human rights by Rousseau, Voltaire, Montesquieu, and other thinkers of the Enlightenment on the eve of the French Revolution. Their thought was greatly influential in Europe at the end of the eighteenth and the beginning of the nineteenth century. It also influenced the thinkers who paved the way for the Russian Revolution of 1917. The French "Encyclopedists," that is, members of the French Society of Letters who were authors of the *Encyclopedia* or *Explanatory Dictionary of Sciences, Arts, and Crafts* (1751–1780), were very interested in the problems of the origins and organization of the universe. The most prominent of them were Denis Diderot and Jean d'Alembert.

4. **To set up a special institute for educating mayors:** This suggestion was specially remarked upon by the censors of Saltykov's time. It was observed that the project of setting up an institute for mayors was an open mockery of the government, the satire referring not to the past but to the present state of affairs in Russia.

5. **the author, intending to pour sand on the written part:** Before the invention of blotting paper, sand was used to absorb the extra ink of writing. It was sprinkled on the freshly written paper.

6. **Pharaoh's Lean Kine:** The story of Pharaoh's cows is told in the Old Testament (Exodus 41).

7. **a short jacket of silver brocade with ostrich feathers in the back, gold armor plate in front, trousers also of brocade, and on the head a solid gold helmet crowned with**

feathers: According to his contemporaries, the emperor Alexander II liked to design uniforms and could even occupy himself with it during evening receptions. There existed different uniforms for various parts of the army, and also special uniforms for various civic orders. Those could be very whimsical or even absurd.

8. *That here, too, is a small drop of my honey:* A slightly altered line from Krylov's fable "The Eagle and the Bee," about an industrious bee who is content with its contribution to the common work of making a honeycomb. I. A. Krylov (1769–1844) is Russia's most well-known fabulist.